By Victoria Hislop

The Island
The Return
The Thread
The Last Dance
The Sunrise
Cartes Postales from Greece

Victoria Hislop

Photography by
Alexandros Kakolyris

headline
review

First published in 2016 by
HEADLINE REVIEW
An imprint of HEADLINE PUBLISHING GROUP

1

Cataloguing in Publication Data is available from the British Library

ISBN 978 1 4722 2320 3 (Hardback)
ISBN 978 1 4722 4047 7 (Trade Paperback)

Typeset in Bembo by Patrick Insole

Printed and bound in Germany by
GGP Media Gmbh, Pößneck

Headline's policy is to use papers that are natural, renewable and
recyclable products and made from wood grown in sustainable forests.
The logging and manufacturing processes are expected to conform
to the environmental regulations of the country of origin.

HEADLINE PUBLISHING GROUP
An Hachette UK Company
Carmelite House
50 Victoria Embankment
London EC4Y 0DZ

www.headline.co.uk
www.hachette.co.uk

CARTES POSTALES FROM GREECE

They arrived dog-eared, always torn, often almost illegible, as though carried across Europe in a back pocket. Once or twice the ink looked as if it had been washed away by rain, wine or even tears. Sometimes they were bleached by sunshine, and the faded postmarks showed that their journey had often taken many weeks.

The first of these postcards had appeared at the end of December, and after that they came with increasing regularity. Ellie Thomas began to look forward to their arrival. If she did not receive one for a week or more, she would sift twice through the mail, just in case. The content of her pigeonhole, one of twelve in the large communal hallway, was mostly bills (or reminders of unpaid bills) and junk mail for junk food. Much of it was addressed to previous tenants who had long since gone, and she assumed that the intended reader of these postcards, S. Ibbotson, was one of these.

Apart from the colourful images, always of Greece, she tossed the stray mail into the postbox on the corner of her street with the words 'Return to Sender' scrawled across the top. They were probably binned by the post office.

The postcards could not be returned to sender. The sender was unknown, always signed off simply with an 'A'. 'A' for 'anonymous'. And whoever S. Ibbotson was, nothing else had come for her (or possibly him) in the three years Ellie had been living in the gloomy Kensal Rise flat. It seemed a waste to throw them away.

On a large corkboard, for which she had no use except the occasional shopping list, and a scrap of paper with her National Insurance number, she began to pin the cards. As the weeks went by, they formed a colourful mosaic of mostly blue and white (skies, sea, boats and whitewashed buildings with blue shutters). Even the flag that appeared on some of them was in the same pure colours.

. . . Methoni, Mystras, Monemvasia, Nafpaktos, Nafplio, Olympia, Sparta . . .

There was a touch of alchemy in their names, and she allowed them to cast their spell. She longed to be in the places they depicted. They spun around in her mind, like any foreign words with musical sounds but unknown meanings: Kalamata, Kalavrita, Kosmas. On and on they went.

The tableau of images brightened up the basement flat, putting colour into her otherwise dreary home, something her Habitat throws had failed to achieve.

In neat, slightly 'arty' (if occasionally illegible) script, the writer conveyed little information but plenty of enthusiasm.

From Nafplio: *It has something special about it.*

From Kalamata: *It has such a warm atmosphere.*

From Olympia: *This picture gives you just a glimpse.*

Ellie began to let herself imagine she was 'S', to dream of the places that this 'A' seemed to be calling her to.

The sender often gave insights into a way of life she had never imagined.

It seems that people here don't understand solitude. Even while I was writing this postcard someone came up and asked me where I was from and what I was doing here. It was not easy to explain.

For the Greeks, the worst thing in the world is to be alone, so someone always comes to talk to me, to ask me or tell me something.

They invite me to their homes, to panegyris, even to baptisms. I have never encountered such hospitality. I am a total stranger, but they treat me like a long-lost friend.

Sometimes they might invite me to share their table in a café and, invariably, they have a story to tell. I listen and write it all down. You know how old people can be. Memory can make truth a bit soft around the edges. But never mind about that. I want to share these stories with you.

But they all ended sadly:

Without you this place is nothing. I wish you were here. A.

The sign-off was simple, sincere and sorrowful. 'S' would never know how much the anonymous writer wanted them to be there, together.

One day in April, three cards arrived all at once. Ellie found her old atlas and began to locate the places. She tore the page out and pinned it next to the cards on the corkboard, marking all the places and tracking the writer's journey. Arta, Preveza, Meteora. All of them magical and unfamiliar names.

This country that she had never visited was becoming part of her life. As the writer was keen to point out, the pictures could not convey the scents or the sounds of Greece. They merely afforded a snapshot, a glimpse. Nevertheless, she was falling in love with it.

Week by week, and with each *carte postale*, Ellie's desire to see Greece for herself increased. She longed for the luminous colours and sunshine the postcards seemed to promise. Throughout the winter, she had left for work before dawn and got home at seven, so the curtains had remained permanently closed. Even when spring arrived, it made no difference. The sun could not find a way in. It did not seem much of a life, certainly not what she had expected when she had moved here from Cardiff. The lights she had hoped for in London seemed far from bright. Only the cards were able to cheer her: Kalambaka, Karditsa, Katerini were added to the montage as soon as they arrived.

Her job selling ad space in a trade magazine had not thrilled her, even from the first day, but she had been persuaded by a recruitment agency that it was a way into publishing. The route must be a very indirect one, she had realised. Clients seemed susceptible to her sonorous Welsh voice, and she easily met the targets set her by the Head of Telesales. This left her a few hours a day when she could earn extra commission or, as she was now doing, while away the time on the internet, looking at images and information on Greece. Among the ranks of other people in their late twenties doing the same job, many of them were 'resting' actors or singers, wanting to be somewhere other than where they were. For most of those in the anonymous rows close by, the dream was to be on stage. For Ellie, it was to be somewhere much further away than the West End.

The postcards had become an obsession. The idealised images that she was gathering were becoming more and more important to her. With the summer came postcards from islands. They were impossibly beautiful images, with shimmering blue seas and skies: Andros, Ikaria. Were these places real? Had the pictures been airbrushed?

A few weeks passed, and no postcard arrived. Each morning throughout August, she checked her pigeonhole and, when she saw that none had arrived, she felt a stab of disappointment. Every fruitless search was a dashed hope, but she could not stop herself. For the bank-holiday weekend, she went to see her parents in Cardiff and spent the Saturday night visiting old haunts with old schoolfriends. They were all now married and beginning to have children. One of them, to whom she had been a bridesmaid, had asked her to be a godmother. She felt obliged to accept but, at the same time, was mildly disconcerted by her sense of separation from her peers.

Wales had been cold, but London looked greyer than ever as the train drew into Paddington. On the Underground back to Kensal Rise, her mind strayed to the postcards. Would there be one waiting? As soon as she was in the hallway, the vacant pigeonhole gave her the answer. She calculated that it was more than a month since the one from Ikaria.

Back inside the flat, she realised that the cards had begun to curl on the pinboard, though their colours remained as vibrant as ever. They tormented her a little. Was it finally time to see if the blue skies they depicted were real? To see if the light was as translucent as it appeared? Were postcards always an exaggeration? Or did they have an element of reality?

She checked her passport (last used two years ago for a hen weekend in Spain) and found a flight to Athens that cost less than the cheap boots she had just bought in Cardiff. She was not an adventurous traveller. In her entire life, she had been four times to Spain, twice to Portugal and a handful of times to France (on childhood camping holidays). It was coming to the end of the season, so it was not hard to find a reasonable hotel. She researched on a few sites and finally clicked on a name she recognised. Nafplio. A week's half-board in a nearby beach resort would cost one hundred and twenty pounds. At least she would see one of the places that A had visited, and perhaps some more, if she had time. The decision was utterly spontaneous, and yet she felt that the idea had been planted months before.

The following week flew by. When she told her smooth-talking boss that she would like to take ten days' holiday, he seemed unconcerned. 'Get in touch on your return,' he said. It was an ambiguous response and left her wondering if she had been fired.

Even as the printer clattered out her boarding pass, she was thinking that she would not miss the windowless room with its banks of telephones.

She couldn't wait to get away from the half-hearted warmth of an English summer that would soon seamlessly elide into autumn. The last postcard A had sent was of a beautiful harbour with pretty houses and boats. She could almost hear the water lapping against them. It looked peaceful and, most of all, inviting.

Ikaria: *It's from another age.*

It was high time to see this new country, and to see if what A said was true. Did people talk to strangers? Invite them to places? She had lived in London for three years and had never received an invitation from anyone she worked with, and certainly not from a stranger in a café. All these things she wanted to experience.

The night before her journey, she was almost sleepless with excitement. Then she slept through her alarm, and only the sound of some drunks in the street woke her. For them, it was the end of a long evening but, for Ellie, the beginning of a new day. She sprang out of bed and, without showering, pulled on yesterday's clothes. After a last-minute check of locks and lights, she let herself out of the flat.

Wheeling her case towards the outer door, she noticed something sticking out of her pigeonhole. Even though she was an hour later than she had intended, she felt compelled to retrieve it. The package had more than a dozen stamps stuck on it at different angles and was the size of a hardback. The name had been obliterated by the franking machine, but the address was legible enough. She recognised the writing straightaway and her heart beat a little faster.

There was no time to open it so she unzipped her handbag

and stuffed it inside. For the next two hours she thought of nothing but catching her plane. She had a twenty-minute walk to a night bus (ten minutes at jogging pace) that would drop her at the coach station for Stansted. The rush hour had not yet begun. Most of the people travelling were on their way to work at the airport.

The woman at the check-in was brusque.

'Only just in time,' she said. 'Your flight is about to close.'

Ellie grabbed her boarding pass back and ran. She was the last to get on the plane, and sank into her seat, hot, stressed, exhausted and already regretting that she was wearing her winter coat. It had been lying on her chair at home and, at four o'clock in the morning, she had not had time to think clearly about what she would need on her travels. It was too late now. She struggled out of the bright red duffel, rolled it up and stuffed it under her seat. The steward was already checking that seatbelts were safely fastened, and the plane was rolling away from its stand.

Even before take-off, Ellie was asleep. She woke three hours later with a stiff neck and a raging thirst. She had not had time to buy even a bottle of water and hoped that the trolley would come by soon. Glancing out of the window, she immediately realised this was unlikely. They were already in the final stages of descent. She caught a glimpse of sea and hills, rectangular fields, rows of trees, houses and some larger buildings, even the familiar Ikea logo. In Athens? Just as she was taking this in, the wheels hit the runway hard. A few people applauded the landing, which seemed strange to Ellie. She had always thought it was the pilot's *job* to get his passengers safely to their destination.

The moment the doors opened, a warm breeze entered the cabin and a new smell that she could not identify. Perhaps it was a mixture of pollution and thyme, but she found herself inhaling it with pleasure.

When she reached into her bag for her passport, the first thing she found was the package. The queue at border control was slow, so she had time to tear off a corner of the brown paper and peek inside. It was a notebook with a blue leather cover, and she could see that the edges of the pages were slightly yellowed. She put it back in her bag.

A coach from the airport took her to KTEL, the central bus station. It was busy and confusing, with the roar of engines and the shouts of the drivers announcing departures above the noise of passengers, who were coming and going by the thousand, dragging bags and cases. Ellie almost choked on the pungent smell of diesel.

Eventually, she found the right ticket booth for her destination, handed over fifteen euros and, with a minute to go, managed to buy a cold drink and some biscuits before boarding.

As she settled into a seat by the window, looking out at the teeming confusion of the bus station, she already knew that A was right about one thing. People here did not like silence. The woman next to her didn't speak a word of English but, in spite of this, they communicated for at least an hour, before the old lady dozed off. In that time, Ellie learned about her children, what they all did and where they lived, and had eaten two stuffed vine leaves and a piece of fresh orange cake (a second slice lay on top of her shoulder bag, wrapped in a napkin). She caught a glimpse of the parcel nestling beneath her cardigan. She had planned to look at the notebook on the journey, but the warmth of the sun coming through the window and the steady rumble of the bus lulled her to sleep.

It was only when the bus reached Nafplio nearly three hours later that she noticed she did not have her coat. It must still be on the plane. As she waited in the sunshine for her case to be offloaded from the belly of the bus, her annoyance with herself began to evaporate. With the heat on her back, she realised that heavy clothing would be an encumbrance here. She felt like a snake that had shed its skin.

There was a row of taxis at the bus station, and her guidebook suggested that she needed to take one of these to reach her hotel in Tolon. Before doing so, she was impatient to see a little of Nafplio. Wheeling her small suitcase behind her, she set out towards the old town, following signposts which were, helpfully, written in English.

She was soon in the main square, which she recognised immediately from the postcard. The sense of déjà vu made her smile.

Well used to being alone, Ellie did not feel self-conscious as she took a seat in the first café she came to. She was served quickly and her cappuccino arrived promptly, along with a glass of iced water and two small, warm walnut biscuits. For the second time in a few hours, she experienced the Greek hospitality that A had mentioned so many times.

As she sipped her coffee, she looked around her. It was a Friday, early evening. The square was thronging with people of every age, pushing buggies, riding bicycles, showing off on rollerblades, or just strolling, some arm in arm, older ones relying on sticks. The dozen or so cafés around the perimeter were all full. The mid-September evening was balmy.

The package lay on the table in front of her. Putting her finger into the slit she had made earlier, she made a tear right across the top and pulled out the notebook. Stuffing the brown paper into the side pocket of her handbag, she turned it over in her hands. Postcards were somehow public, on show to anyone that picked them up, but a notebook? Was it like reading someone's diary? Was it an invasion of privacy? It certainly felt like it as she nervously opened the cover. Flicking through, she saw that every page of the book was filled with the familiar black ink of A's meticulous but sometimes indecipherable handwriting.

With her forefinger, she absent-mindedly traced an S in the biscuit crumbs on her plate and gazed out across the square. The addressee was never going to have a chance to read any of this and so, with burning curiosity and only a little guilt, she turned to the first page.

After the first few words she stopped, realising that it would be better to wait until she reached the hotel. Clutching the notebook to her chest, she got up and walked to the taxi rank. 'Tolon,' she said, uncertainly. 'Hotel Marina.'

Later that evening, on the small balcony outside her bedroom, she began once again.

When I went to meet you that day at the little airport in Kalamata and you didn't appear, I waited for twenty-four hours in case I had made a mistake and you were coming on the next plane. Or perhaps you had missed it and couldn't get in touch. I suggested all sorts of reasons to myself. That night I slept on a seat behind the luggage trolleys. The cleaner swept the floor around my feet and even brought over a piece of spinach pie that his wife was about to throw out. She ran the kiosk and their son was the person at passport control – and, of course, it was a nephew at baggage security and then a cousin at the gate to check boarding passes. 'Small airports are a family business in Greece,' the cleaner told me with great pride.

Early morning on the following day, I had to leave the Arrivals area. Even the word seemed to mock me. It was mid-September and there would be no more charter flights coming in from the UK, and no possibility that you would suddenly appear, as I had allowed myself to fantasise. You didn't pick up when I phoned, but I knew that if something terrible had happened to you, then one of your friends would have called me.

I sat for a while on a bench outside the airport, not

knowing what to do or where to go. A few moments later my phone buzzed. There was a message. I was shaking so much as I reached into my pocket that my mobile fell to the ground. Through the spider's-web mess of the shattered screen, I could just about make out the words: 'She can't make it. Sorry.' I suppose you had dictated it to some friend. I stared at it in sickened disbelief for a few minutes and then rang the number. No reply. Several times I tried. Of course with the same result. 'Anger', 'fury', 'rage'. Those words don't get close to describing what I felt. They are just words. Puffs of air. Nothing.

There were no further messages. Just a 'Bon Voyage' from my brother later that day.

I could have gone straight back to Athens, but I couldn't face driving back – along the same road that I had just travelled with such anticipation and excitement. I was numb, almost incapable of getting the key in the ignition. I had no real idea where I was going. I didn't care. I have no idea how long I drove, but when I got to the sea I stopped. Right on the beach, where the road ran out, there was a sign saying 'Rooms'. This was where I would stay.

I did almost nothing in the days that followed except sit and gaze out at the Ionian. The waves were wild, endlessly rolling in and crashing on the sand, their mood reflecting the turmoil that I felt inside. It did not seem to subside. I could not eat or speak. Men are meant to be the stronger sex, but I have never felt so powerless. I think the sea would have dragged me in if I had got too close. Some days I would willingly have disappeared beneath the foam.

I could not stand the torment of looking at my phone, over and over and over again, and seeing the blank and broken screen. So I took it out of my pocket and threw it as far into the ocean as I could. It was liberating. The moment I saw the splash, I had to accept that I would not and could not hear from you. I was cut off from you now, and cut off from the world, too.

God knows what the nice couple who ran the place in Methoni thought of me, but they left me a plate of cold food each evening and took it away each morning. The wife put a bunch of fresh flowers in my room one morning and changed them when they wilted. All I could register was their kindness, but not much else. I did not feel hunger or thirst. Even temperature did not register with me. One day I stood under the shower until the water ran cold but realised I could feel nothing on my skin. My watch told me that an hour had passed. Despair had deprived me of all my senses. They were dark days. How I passed the time I don't know, but somehow the hours went by. I had no awareness of how many days or weeks it was since my wait at the airport but, one day, the owner of the pension greeted me as I was on my way out to the beach. 'Kalo mina,' he said cheerfully. 'Octomvris! It's a new month!' I had been there almost a fortnight.

The schedule that I had mapped out for us seemed ridiculous now: a tour of the Peloponnese, then a ferry to Kithera, and from there another ferry to Crete before we flew back to Athens and then to London. You said you had exactly two weeks' holiday to spare, and my meticulous planning would have made sure you were back in time. I had bought a ring while I was in Athens, a solitaire diamond from a shop called Zolotas. This is how much I had deceived myself. I had planned to propose to you against a blood-red sunset in the west of Crete. Even now, I sometimes find myself replaying a scene that never happened.

I hope one day that it will fade from my mind for ever.

That evening in Methoni (where I closed my shutters against the sunset), I had to make a decision: to return to London, or to travel alone. My research in Athens during the two weeks I was there had gone well. The curator at the Museum of Cycladic Art had been wonderful, opening up so many parts of the archive for me, so I had plenty of material to start writing my book. I could do this in a hotel room as easily as at home. The thought of London slightly chilled my blood, as I knew I would be looking for your face in every crowd. Another good reason for staying in Greece for a while would be to avoid the melancholy of a British autumn.

So I packed my bag and checked out. I was in no hurry now. I called my brother from a phone box in the village and asked him to pick up my post once a week and deal with any bills. I did not know how long I would be away. The advance from my book contract would last me a year, if I was careful. Before going into the general store to get chocolate, chewing gum, some water and a few other things I needed for the road, I paused at a rusty carousel where a few desultory postcards were displayed. The shopkeeper was probably not expecting many more tourists now, so he had not bothered to replenish his stock. I picked out one of the Venetian Castle (which, in all those days there, I had not even bothered to visit). Why did I do that? I didn't imagine that you cared about where I was, but I had a sudden desire to communicate with you. Perhaps it was simply to break through the silence that now existed between us. Or was it just to alleviate my loneliness? I couldn't be the person playing with a mobile and appearing to have friends and arrangements, but I could be the man busy writing a postcard and needing to find a stamp.

It would be a way to 'talk' to you without expecting any reply, a one-way conversation. The idea pleased me. Perhaps you might even regret that you had not come.

The man in the shop put several stamps on the card for me then packed up the other things I had bought.

'Kalo taksidi.'

'Thank you,' I replied. It was one of the few phrases I already knew. He was wishing me a good journey.

I rested the card on the roof of the car, scribbled a few lines to you and tossed it into the nearby postbox.

I was totally at liberty to go anywhere I pleased, but it is strange how discombobulating such freedom can be. I sat in the car for at least an hour, staring at the map, and it took all my will to put the car in gear and drive. I knew I was heading east because the sea was behind me, but I had no fixed destination and no idea where instinct or fate would take me. It was the beginning of my travels. This was all I knew.

In the following weeks and months, everywhere I stopped people talked to me. Most were warm and kind and, if they were not immediately so, then my attempts to speak Greek would often break the ice. Many of them told me stories. I listened and noted it down, each day learning surprising things about this country, and new things about myself. The voices of strangers poured into the void, filling the silence you'd left.

You will recognise some of the locations in the stories from the postcards. Who knows if the tales people told me are true or false? I suspect that some of them are complete fabrications, others are exaggerations – but perhaps some of them are real. You can decide.

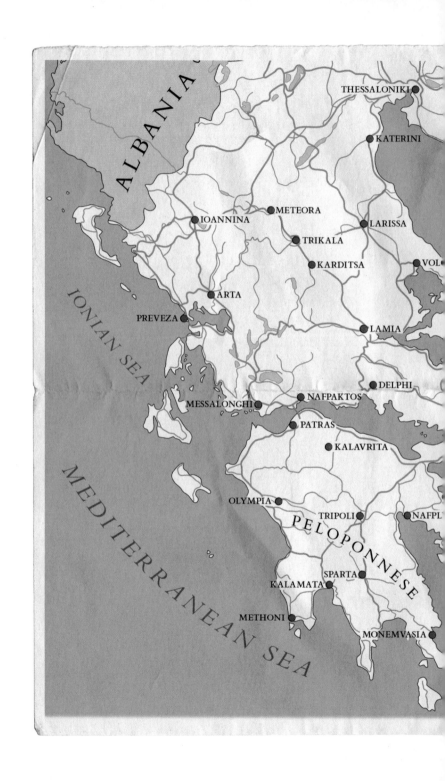

TURKEY

AEGEAN SEA

ATHENS *ANDROS*

IKARIA

CYCLADES

October 2015

The beauty of the Peloponnese, where my travels really began, did not soothe my pain. It only made me ache all the more. I felt scorned by its fullness, its lushness, the way that nature herself seemed bursting with life and health. The landscape was the very opposite of my mood, and nothing distracted me from the longing I felt. I had nurtured so many hopes about our future and it was impossible to stop myself returning to them. I learned over the following months that trying to forget can only make you remember all the more. In the evening, I drank to anaesthetise myself and to help me sleep, but soon I even began to dread going to bed. Sleep was like a deep, dark well where nightmares pulled me ever downwards. The owners of the guesthouse in Methoni had rushed into my room at four one morning. My screams had led them to believe that I was being murdered. You were in every dream. But they were bad dreams. Sad dreams. My subconscious was not going to let me forget you. At least, not yet.

It was not a mistake, though, to embark on this journey. Wherever I was, my unhappiness would have followed me. If I had returned to London, it would have been worse, since my friends would be looking at me with sympathetic death-in-the-family eyes but within a few weeks would be expecting me to have gone back to my usual self. Here, I could be with strangers and, if I moved around enough, people would never know what that 'usual self' looked like. I could reinvent myself completely with people who knew nothing of what had happened. Away from home, I could at least pretend to be a man in control.

People always want to direct a visitor to their favourite place, and my hosts in Methoni had been insistent about Nafplio. 'It's the most beautiful city in Greece, and the most romantic,' they told me.

I forced a smile as they pointed out its location on a map.

Whether or not Nafplio is the loveliest city in Greece, it captivated me. Its platia is the most glorious town square I have ever seen. Think of an enormous ballroom open to the sky. The marble paving stones are smooth and gleamingly clean and, even on a cool autumn evening, beautiful buildings on all four sides protect you from the slightest breeze. The walls of this 'room' are a montage of Greek history: a former mosque from the sixteenth century, a Venetian arsenal, graceful neoclassical buildings and some reasonable twentieth-century architecture. Situated on the sea, with three castles and a history that stretches right back to ancient times, Nafplio was the first capital of the modern state of Greece, from 1829 until 1834, and it feels like somewhere that matters.

I spent many hours there, watching the world go by.

I was glad of some conversation on one of my evenings in Nafplio, but the couple that spoke to me could not help commenting on the fact I was alone.

'Your wife . . .' asked the woman. 'Isn't she with you?'

So many assumptions were made in this question, but I did not bother to address them. Fortunately, her husband stepped in, sensing that his wife had been a little blunt.

'Ever since the Adamakos affair,' he said, 'people in Nafplio have been a little wary of men who sit all on their own.'

'The Adamakos affair?' I asked.

'I don't suppose it made the English news,' he said.

He was right, of course. Stories about Greece in the British press tend to be about the economy or, nowadays, the refugee crisis. They don't take much notice of anything else.

'Well, there was a man who frequently sat here alone,' he said.

'For twenty-five years!' said his wife, to emphasise the point.

'It was a big story here . . .'

'He didn't like people?' I suggested.

'There were certainly people he wasn't fond of,' said the wife cryptically.

'He was from the Mani,' the husband added darkly, leaning forward in case anyone overheard.

I had never been to the Mani, the remote area of land south of Nafplio, but I knew that in former times Maniots had a reputation for pursuing vendettas if their honour was disrespected. I had read something just that day about a dramatic event that took place in the early nineteenth century, close to the café where we sat. Ioannis Kapodistrias, the first head of the new state, had arrested members of an important but rebellious clan from the Mani. In revenge, two of their *relatives lay in wait for him as he was going to church. A first gunshot missed. Kapodistrias was then stabbed, and a second bullet hit him in the head. Violence bred violence. The assassins were executed shortly afterwards.*

'You know that the bullet is embedded in the church of St Spyridon, just round the corner?' he said, pointing to a stone staircase leading to the street above us.

'I saw it today,' I answered.

'Well, never disrespect anyone from the Mani,' he said. 'There are plenty of blood feuds that have lasted into modern times.'

Then he told me this story. By the end of it, I knew I would follow his advice.

The Boy In
The Silvery Suit

CARTE POSTALE

The immense square in Nafplio is the beating heart of the city. People flow in and out all day, to talk, to play, to watch, to drink, and at weekends there is hardly a spare seat in a café.

As if drawn by gravitational pull, couples of all ages file down the narrow, car-free Venetian streets, promenading two by two, like creatures from the ark. One old couple has taken a *volta* round the square each evening for five decades, always at the rate of a ticking clock. Even though the man relies on a stick these days, their pace has not changed.

Close behind are two handsome men, one younger than the other. In other cities, they might feel free to walk arm in arm. One has an extravagance of white hair like a Persian cat, the other is closely cropped like a vole. They are casually but expensively dressed, with pastel cashmere pullovers draped over their shoulders and knotted in front. They take a place at one of the newer café-bars. These are wealthy weekenders from Athens.

A heavily pregnant woman and her husband are making a slower circuit of the square. She is several days overdue

and hoping that the rhythm of her walk will stir the baby to begin his journey into the outside world. Each step is an effort, and even now she worries that she may not complete the tour.

A pair of men watch football in the café. One of them stands up with excitement each time anyone from his team gets close to the goal, almost knocking the table over, before calmly resuming the conversation with his friend. The latter is less bothered. Neither team is his.

A couple of small boys kick a ball, frantically running after it as it rolls away down the steep rake of the square. Two dogs chase each other, then chase their own tails, yapping and barking and spinning. One of them goes after the boys' football.

There are two women, over-scented, overdressed, hair freshly coiffed for this day. They are not twins or sisters but over the years they have grown alike, with the same bleached hair, and similar lines on their faces. The name they share, Dimitra, gives them a common saint's day and now, in late October, they are celebrating their *yiorti* and receive many greetings of '*Hronia Polla!* Many happy returns!' from friends they meet in the square.

Two girls, best friends in the fourth grade, are engrossed in imaginary games with their dolls. Both are dressed in candy-coloured sweatshirts and jeans, with trainers that flash as they run. Two boys, who go to the same school as the girls, ride their bikes round and round in circles, their wheels almost touching. They are squealing with delight, veering closer, closer, closer, until suddenly, in a tangle of metal and gashed shins, they collide. They are too proud to cry, but limp off home in opposite directions, wheeling their dented bicycles.

There is only one person in Platia Syntagmatos who sits alone. With his glass of clear *tsipouro* as company, he observes the scene with his heavily hooded eyes. Rolling a cigarette without looking down to see what he is doing, he smokes without pleasure and repeats the process again and again. An ashtray overflows in front of him, a sprinkling of grey across the table. No one bothers to empty it, though from time to time a waiter brings him another glass of fire water.

Akis Adamakos looks up towards the church of St Spyridon and inhales, pulling tar deep into his lungs. Every Saturday between four and six he sits in the café for two hours precisely. The time has dragged today.

This is a ritual he strictly observes. He relives the afternoon twenty-five years earlier when he arrived in a shiny grey wedding suit outside the church. He glances up and sees the stairs that lead up to St Spyridon, remembering his younger self, nervous, but ready to hand a bouquet to his bride.

The church and the narrow street in which it stands had been full of family and friends. Many had travelled a good distance, from the southern tip of the Mani, where the Adamakos family were from. The bride's relatives lived in or just outside Nafplio. The noise from the chatter and laughter of more than three hundred people was immense. People who had not seen each other for some time were reunited, and their faces were animated by the exchange of news and gossip. When the priest arrived, the volume dropped and the congregation became more reverential, but the conversation

never ceased to flow. Older family members perched on the few wooden seats, but most people milled about.

The guests were expecting a party that would go on until the early hours of the following day, so nobody so much as glanced at their watch.

Everyone was happy and relaxed, with the exception of two people: the groom and his *koumbaros*, the best man. They heard the tolling of the bell in the clock tower. It was now five, and the bride had been expected at four. Detaching themselves from the crowd, the two men walked a little way down the street, pausing at the top of the steps that led into the town square.

'Something might have happened.'

'Yes . . .'

'I'll find a telephone.'

Nikos, the *koumbaros*, made a call from a nearby *kafenion*. Listening to the phone ringing in the bride's home, he stood and gazed at the television that hung high up on the wall over the bar. He half expected to see news footage of a terrible accident, shreds of bridal gown, a wrecked car, but instead there was a black-and-white comedy on, starring Aliki, the nation's sweetheart.

Akis tried to continue in light-hearted conversation with a few friends but stopped when he saw his *koumbaros* returning.

People had begun to drift out of the church for fresh air, to see what was going on, to look around, to light a cigarette.

Nikos took Akis to one side.

'There's no answer,' he said close to Akis's ear. 'I think we should go. Right this minute.'

The congregation, mostly outside the church now, watched the receding figures as they walked purposefully to the end of the street and vanished round the corner. The volume of chatter dropped as news circulated, both inside and outside the church, that neither the groom nor, indeed, the bride were now there. The atmosphere became suddenly subdued.

It was a ten-kilometre journey out of Nafplio and up a narrow, winding road into the hills to reach the bride's village. Nikos was a fast driver even under normal circumstances, but today he drove recklessly to cover the distance. Neither of them said a word.

Everything in this village was concrete and newly built in the past twenty years, but the paint was stained and flaking. The bakery, general store, *kafenion*, school and oversized municipal building were uniformly off-white, and a row of trees had recently been planted in an attempt to soften the harsh lines of the street.

The bride's home came into view. It was the same colour. The creeper that grew over a pergola outside was dead and the olive tree next to the house was leafless. Outside, there was a car, borrowed and freshly polished, ready to bring the bride to church. It was blood red, the same colour as the roses that Akis still held in his hand, his fist locked around their stems.

A man of around sixty was standing outside. On his left was a young man, on his right a girl. They were the bride's father and her siblings. They were dressed up, the cheap fabric of the men's suits slightly shiny even on this cloudy day, the starched collars of new shirts cutting into their necks, narrow shoes pinching their feet. The men had no spare flesh on them, but the girl was puffy and overweight, something accentuated by her figure-hugging, acid-yellow dress, which was several sizes too small. Stains of sweat from under her arms were spreading down the sleeves and her eyes were swollen with tears. All three of them were colourless, drained of life.

Akis strode up to the father and looked him straight in the eye. They were the same height. Neither man spoke. Protectively, the son moved towards his father, and the daughter gripped his arm.

From the house came the muffled sound of a woman crying. The mother.

The father was visibly trembling and made a slight movement with his head, indicating the direction up the road and away from Nafplio. The road through the village continued northwards.

Nikos spoke.

'She's gone to Athens?' he asked sharply.

With a slight nod, the bride's father confirmed it. The children moved in closer still to protect their father. Even if they had wanted to speak, nothing would have emerged from their parched lips.

Akis felt the light touch of Nikos's hand on his arm and stepped back. Both of them suspected that Savina had not gone alone. Nikos had heard a rumour the previous week but had chosen not to mention it to his friend.

The father's eyes shone with fear, and Akis could see it. He looked at the older man with disdain. A father should be able to control a daughter.

He dropped the flowers at the feet of his never-to-be father-in-law, turned his back on the trio and calmly walked away, with Nikos at his side.

They got into the car and looked straight ahead as Nikos drove at speed out of the village. Both of them were silent. Five minutes into the journey, Nikos pulled over.

'We have to decide when,' said Nikos.

'*If*, not when,' said Akis quietly.

'There is no *if*, Akis. There is only when.'

The two men looked at each other. Both were from the Mani. Vendetta was in their blood.

'I can take my brothers back there tonight,' said Nikos. 'The father and son at least . . .'

'No,' said Akis thoughtfully. 'There is greater revenge than that.'

'Greater than shooting someone through the head?'

'Yes. Fear. Fear of when that bullet will come. This family will live in fear.'

Akis stared out of the window. He looked out over the landscape, saw the sea in the distance, wondered how far Savina had got, if she was in her pearly white *nifiko*, or whether she had ever even put it on. He struggled to control the jealousy that was raging inside him that his woman was now with someone else and that tonight she would be in the arms of another man.

He turned to his oldest friend and spoke slowly and with conviction.

'Savina will always be waiting for a call. Wherever she is, she will fear the ringing of the telephone. Her family will never have peace. Not one of them.'

'And you'll go to back to that church . . . and confront the crowd and face that humiliation? You'll turn the other cheek? Are you *insane*, Akis? Are you out of your *mind*?'

Akis did not answer. He understood revenge better than his friend.

They returned to the church, where everyone was now outside in the street.

The women moved slightly away, and the groom's friends gathered around him. Akis was happy to leave the explanation to his *koumbaros*.

The bride's family and friends were as shocked by the news as anyone, but fearful, too. They soon made their way out of town, except for those who lived in Nafplio, who

went to their homes and fastened shutters and doors.

All those who remained around Akis pleaded with him to take immediate action.

'No,' he said to them. 'Not yet.'

This evening, in the square, the clock has stopped. Perhaps the man in charge of winding it is sick. The hands point to one minute before five, and do not move. At this moment, all those years ago, Akis had still hoped. He had still been certain that his bride would come.

At this moment, he notices a boy of around eight years old running towards the two girls in pink, weaving around and between them as they play near the fountain. They don't

seem bothered by the way he interrupts their game, hardly appearing to notice him.

The boy is wearing a light grey wedding suit. His patent shoes make no sound on the marble slabs as he runs. Aside from Akis himself, he is the only person in the square who is unpaired, unpartnered.

Akis has been drinking more and more *tsipouro* as the years have passed, and perhaps he doesn't trust his eyes. What he sees is a vision of himself, innocent and carefree. He feels a lump in his throat and tells himself not to be sentimental.

The child, who is dressed like a man, looks at the man who cries like a child. He ducks away from the girls and skips up the stairs.

In the fading light, with the hands of the clock and the night air still, Akis leaves the usual clutch of coins on the metal table and follows him.

The child turns left at the top of the steps, towards the church.

By the time Akis gets there he sees no sign of the boy, but when he reaches the church the door is wide open.

It is twenty-five years since Akis has been inside. Passing the bullet-hole in the wall, he goes in. The door swings shut behind him. The church is solemn, its walls entirely covered with dark icons. He walks down the aisle, stands in front of the altar and looks up at the cross above his head. It rests on a golden skull with two bones crossed together, and the empty sockets seem to stare at him, holding his gaze so that he cannot look away.

Akis turns and sees the boy in the shadows at the back of the church. He is looking straight at him. The boy in

the silvery suit is challenging him. As the child opens the door again, his suit is sharply illuminated by the light from outside. And then he is gone.

By the time Akis gets out into the street, there is no sign of him.

He passes the square to get to his car, and as he does so he hears the clock strike five. It has started again.

Akis has kept a gun in the car for a quarter of a century. The time has come. It has been a long wait for them all.

*I asked the couple what happened next on that day. Apparently,
Akis drove back to the village outside Nafplio that very evening
and killed the father and brother, leaving the mother and sister
to live. He did not track Savina down, but her grief and guilt
must have been worse than death. She did not come back for
the funerals, even though Akis Adamakos had been arrested on
the day of the murders. Perhaps she feared that the best man,
Nikos, might finish the task.*

*The couple in Nafplio were not to know about my
situation, so they could not have appreciated the irony of telling
me the story of a jilted man.*

I am angry about what you did, but not enough to kill.

*Even if I had been brought up with the culture of revenge,
I wouldn't have had the energy to lift a gun, let alone to fire
one, sorrow weighed me down so heavily.*

*Perhaps murder would bring some kind of catharsis, but I
really don't think I will ever know.*

*Loss of his woman (or was it loss of face?) consumed Akis
Adamakos for a quarter of a century. Even then he did not kill
Savina. Presumably, he is languishing still in prison today,*

wondering where she is and with whom. I can imagine being consumed by similar thoughts until the end of my days, trying to picture you, where you are, who you are making love to.

The couple told me that there are still many marriages here that are semi-arranged between families who want to be linked together. Perhaps Savina's marriage to Akis was one of these. I still wonder about the bride's state of mind just before she climbed into that car and fled towards Athens – it must have been a powerful infatuation that made her do that. I wonder what it was that happened in your life and stopped you getting on that plane to meet me. I assume it was a lover. It strikes me now that you never had a gap between one man and another. You are not someone who could survive on your own. There would always be someone else.

I left Nafplio after a few days to explore other places in the Peloponnese. One afternoon, I passed a sign that read: 'Arcadia'. It's a word that conjures up a vision of utopia but until then I hadn't realised that our idea of a heaven on earth comes from an actual place. This region has been so idealised that I had never considered it could be a location on a map.

Suddenly I was there. In Arcadia itself.

Nearly three thousand years ago, the poet Hesiod wrote about life in Arcadia: 'The people there lived like gods without sorrow of heart, remote and free from toil and grief . . . when they died, it was as though they were overcome with sleep. They dwelt in ease and peace upon their lands with many good things, rich in flocks and loved by the gods.'

The Arcadian shepherds were blessed by nature itself, and this was not hard to imagine as I drove through Arcadia that day. I even saw a shepherd with his flock and imagined him as

Pan, the god of the mountains who, according to myth, lived there and had the legs and horns of a goat. He was renowned for his virility and prowess on the flute.

From one moment to the next, I felt I had passed from reality into the landscape of mythology, across a line between the real and the unreal to the best of all landscapes and lives, and sweet smells and honey, the sound of birdsong and the scent of flowers, a vision of pastoral harmony. It was a place so far from any city that people there were considered to be pure and noble.

I have never seen a landscape in Greece that was more deeply green – dense with leaves and flowering trees, with mountains and waterfalls. Its beauty was accentuated by the perfect sunny day. From time to time I caught sight of a slate-roofed cottage clinging to the side of a hill.

In a painting by Poussin that hangs in the Louvre (one day, perhaps, we would have gone there), shepherds are gathered round a tomb in Arcadia. The truth has dawned on them – death is always present, even in paradise. Maybe this was on my mind as well as I travelled through this idyllic landscape. My eyes were feasting on its beauty, but at the same time I had a feeling of unease. I know now that it's not possible for heaven to exist on earth, but writing this reminds me of how complacent I had been about us, and how my happiness had been an illusion.

I drove through a few villages with stone-built houses and stopped in one of them: Kosmas. Its square's general deadness sent a strange chill through me, so I decided to drive on. An hour or so later I arrived in Tripoli.

Still a little drunk on the beauty of Arcadia, I was relieved to find myself in a pleasant but more ordinary place. I noticed a bar tucked away in a sidestreet, between two abandoned industrial units. Every wall in the vicinity was covered with graffiti – bold, artistic, sometimes grotesque drawings, slogans and phrases. The place suited my angry, restless mood.

It was around six o'clock, and a girl was sullenly wiping the tables. She hardly bothered to look up when I entered. Perhaps she didn't even hear me come in, as there was music playing loudly. Her sleeveless T-shirt revealed shoulders and arms covered with tattoos; she had a nose ring, ears with a dozen piercings each and a half-shaved head. The hair that remained was purple, the colour of a fresh bruise, and I saw a criss-cross pattern of scars on her forearms.

After a while, she came across and took my order for a beer. I was her only customer, so we struck up a conversation. She had a really exquisite face but seemed angry at life itself and the very ground she walked on. More than anything, she was furious with her country, with Greece. Like millions of young people, Eva felt she had been let down.

Two years before, she had dropped out of university. 'There was no point,' she said. 'The majority of my generation are unemployed, so what does university do? Send me into the world with qualifications that nobody needs. It's all futile.'

I could feel Eva's intense frustration. It was obvious from the way she talked that she was intelligent and passionate. She was talented, too – the interior walls, as well as the exterior, were densely graffitied, and all her own work. The complex paintings were beautifully executed, and I complimented her.

'They aren't just random,' she said, with a note of challenge in her voice. 'They tell a story.'

I looked more closely. Following the curves of the strange, scarcely human figures and shapes, flowed black, spidery handwriting. She was right. The words and pictures together told a story.

By the time I had finished it, I knew I was not the only person who felt a strange contradiction in the Arcadian landscape between its potential to offer an ideal life and a harsher reality.

For Eva, this Arcadia, this place that could have been paradise, represented a nightmare vision of Greece itself.

ET IN ARCADIA EGO

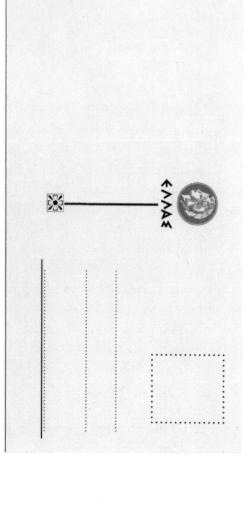

ΕΛΛΑΣ

ET IN ARCADIA EGO
'EVEN IN PARADISE, I AM THERE'

Athanasia, whose name meant 'immortality', had grown up in the dust and noise of Athens. She loved her city and had little curiosity to see what lay outside it. This Sunday morning, however, her destination was a village in Arcadia beyond Kosmas, even higher up in the mountains. It was her father's village, where she had been born twenty-eight years before.

Grigoris Malavas had died when she was two years old, and she had no recollection of him. While she was growing up, he was rarely mentioned. There were no photographs, no evidence of his existence, just herself. She was the only thing left behind. When her mother had died the previous year and she was sorting out her apartment, she had noticed that the wardrobe contained nothing black, and there was nothing among her papers, not even a marriage certificate, wedding photo or a letter with their joint names.

Athanasia had no memories of the village. Her mother had left after her father's forty-day memorial and there had never been a question of returning, even to mark the one- or three-year anniversaries of his death. 'His brother did what was necessary,' was all that her mother had said, many years later. And that was how she knew there was an uncle. Though whether he was still alive, she did not know.

And now that she was in her twenties, curious, independent and with unanswered questions (mostly unasked questions, in fact), she wanted to visit Arcadia, to see if everything that was written and said about it was true. To find out whether it really was the most beautiful place on earth.

As she followed the winding road ever higher up the mountainside, it seemed that it was. She stopped to admire the valley below, and the view of Mount Parnonas. She inhaled deeply and her lungs almost burned with the purity of the cool, clean air.

The landscape had inspired many paintings, but none had got close to the reality that she saw spread out below her.

Ten or fifteen minutes passed as she drank in its beauty. There were pine trees, plane trees and, in the distance, cedars. The whole force of life was there, an explosion of nature. The trees were dense with foliage, green, yellow and gold, heavy with nuts and berries, their boughs weighed down by cheerful, feasting birds.

Athanasia looked up and saw a waterfall cascading from a rockface to a riverbed hundreds of metres below. The powerful rush of water was the only sound. Beneath her feet lay some tiny, late-blooming wildflowers, delicate and star-shaped. She was careful where she trod.

Time was passing. It was early afternoon but the sun was already dipping below the mountain and, with reluctance, she got back into the car. A few bends in the road later, she had to slam hard on the brakes. More than a hundred goats blocked her way. At the front there was a man, hissing and shouting at one of his beasts which had taken a detour up the side of the cliff. Following behind was a woman with shoulders wider than a man's. She turned, and Athanasia felt the full power of her glare.

'You, wait!' said her stern look.

In her right hand was a rod with which she goaded the animals and in her left she held a small creature by the hind legs. It looked like a rabbit. When Athanasia wound down the window, she could see it struggling feebly. She realised it was not a rabbit but a kid, its fur still matted with afterbirth, blood still oozing from its mother, who waddled in front, her new offspring already forgotten. There was no sentimentality in nature.

Athanasia waited patiently for a lone, straggling goat to join the rest, and then drove on.

A few kilometres later a village came into view, curls of woodsmoke rising above the whitewashed buildings perched on the summit. Stone walls caught the golden light of the sun, and she imagined the glow of warm fires inside.

She parked under a vast plane tree in the main square. It was dominated by a massive church, whose lofty tower was the highest point in the village, and by force of habit she walked towards it, not to worship but to light a candle for her mother. Finding the door firmly locked, she crossed the square towards a row of cafés, each of which had a hundred chairs laid out on the cobbles. Their emptiness raised the question of why so many people seemed to be expected but none had come.

The huge expanse of the square and the dominance of the church emphasised the deserted state of the village, and the cool air which had so cleansed her lungs an hour before now sent a shiver down her spine.

In spite of the vast array of chairs in front of each one, there was only one café with an 'Open' sign.

She entered, but her presence was not acknowledged by the two men who sat playing *tavli*. Neither even looked up. The warmth of an iron stove filled the room and she took a seat close to it and reached out with her hands, surveying the strange selection of objects that decorated the room. Eventually, she heard a final *clack* of the counters and the shutting of a lid, and then a man's voice.

'*Ti theleis?* What do you want?'

Her mind had drifted. She was gazing at the chestnuts

that were sitting on top of the fire, warming and splitting in the heat.

'I would like a coffee please, *glyko*.'

He silently prepared her sweetened coffee. His only other customer left the café.

While she was waiting, Athanasia looked around her. The whole place seemed dusty. Random collections of miscellaneous objects crowded various cabinets and shelves. There was a 1950s radiogram, a camera, two hunting knives, some tattered magazines, a chipped coffee pot, a jar with some drachma coins and a framed black-and-white photo of three men. There was even an old revolver, rusty now, suspended from a hook. Every item had once had value or significance but now looked like meaningless junk. She found herself speculating about whether her father had frequented this very café, and whether any of these objects had been there during that time.

'What brings you here?'

'To Arcadia . . . ?' she asked.

Their conversation was curtailed by the arrival of another man, with twin boys of around five years old. Before he spoke, the father was served with a tumbler of clear liquid. He drained it in one gulp before slamming the glass down and helping himself to another. The bottle had been left on the bar.

Meanwhile, the boys, identically dressed in green nylon tracksuits, were in the corner, taunting a caged canary. One of them ran his father's car keys up and down the bars of the cage, delighted by the tune he was making and enjoying the terror of the tiny bird inside. The other hopped from one leg to the other, rhythmically pushing the stand so that the cage rocked from side to side. Their father ignored the cacophony. With his sons occupying themselves, he could enjoy his drink.

The broad, bearded owner put a coffee down in front of Athanasia. It was ten per cent liquid and ninety per cent the gritty sludge that lurks in every cup of Greek coffee. She drained the glass of water that he had placed beside it.

After a few moments he returned and pulled out the chair next to her, sitting astride it as though mounted on a horse. He was skinning roasted chestnuts and threw a few down on the table, scattering the debris. She noticed a grub crawl out and winced with disgust. It seemed impossible that it had survived the heat.

'Why are you here?'

It was more of a confrontation than an enquiry.

'My family – or my father, anyway – came from here.'

The man carried on peeling chestnuts and putting them in his mouth, displaying not the slightest interest in her answer.

'He died, so my mother left,' she said. 'I would like to visit his grave.'

'What's your family name, then?'

'Malavas.'

'I'm Malavas, too. Giannis. There are lots of us around here.'

He carried on peeling and eating.

'It doesn't mean we're close relations,' he said gruffly, tiny fragments of chestnut spraying from his mouth as he spoke.

'Where will I find the cemetery?'

CARTES POSTALES FROM GREECE

'Up the hill behind the square, keep walking, half a kilometre or so. Then you'll see it on your left.'

He lit a cigarette, stared at her until she felt uncomfortable, got up and strolled back to the bar.

'At least you know he'll be there,' he said. 'Once someone is buried in this village, that's where they stay. Space is not at a premium here.'

She put a euro on the table and left.

She was glad to get out into the fresh air, away from the noise of the two unruly boys and the smoke the bar owner seemed deliberately to have breathed into her face.

The village was dead, as before, but the landscape beyond it even more beautiful. The road to the cemetery was lined with old chestnut trees, their fallen fruit crunching beneath her feet. As she climbed, she looked out across the view. Into infinity stretched mountains and hills, in emerald and shades of gold, and the sky was cloudless.

It was a fifteen-minute walk up to the cemetery but, when she reached it, the iron gates were wide open as if to welcome her. For such a small village, the graveyard seemed immense. The tombs were all in white marble, many with grand statues above them. They all had photographs, poetry and tributes. It was not unlike the First Cemetery of Athens. Just before her mother had died, a legendary and popular singer had passed away, and Athanasia had gone there with her to lay a flower on his grave. She had been amazed by its grandeur, so to find similar memorials with elaborate stonework in this remote region was a real surprise.

The 'village' where the dead lived was considerably better kept than the one she had just walked from. It was neat, well ordered, weeded and swept. The older graves looked as if they were regularly cleaned – even those which housed people who had died more than fifty years before looked brand new. The standard faded silk or plastic flowers were nowhere to be seen. Every grave had fresh blooms, mostly carnations, roses and lilies, and she caught their sweet fragrance as she passed.

The sense of those who had passed away being cared for and cherished was striking, as was the realisation that the dead outnumbered the living.

Giannis Malavas was right. There were dozens of people with her family name and many with precisely her father's name, though none of the dates matched the one on which she thought he had died. Even if it had a photograph, she would not be able to recognise it. Her mother had not kept a single picture of her late husband.

Until dusk, she wandered up and down the avenues of graves. She was not sentimental about her father, a man she had never known, but many of the graves with photos, poetry and tributes to the deceased moved her. Half an hour into her tour of the cemetery, she was struck by the fact that every name was male. There were a few youths who had died tragically young, and several in middle age, but mostly they were septuagenarians or octogenarians, all of them men. Row after row after row.

As the light faded, she knew she must leave. She had not found what she wanted, but she had a question. Where were the women? As she walked through the quiet streets back to the square, it seemed more relevant than ever. The women were missing both from the village of the dead and of the living.

A few shops had opened now. She passed a butcher's, where a man was steadily chopping; a bakery, where two men were carrying trays of loaves; and a small grocery, where the male owner was serving a skinny youth.

It was well after seven when she turned the corner into the square. A battered car was parked there now. It was filthy, and she noticed a handwritten sign propped in its window: 'Taxi'. It took her a few moments to realise that her Micra was no longer there. She blinked. She knew with absolute certainty that it had been underneath the plane tree, and now it was gone.

Without hesitation, she went back into the café to ask the owner if he had seen anything. There were several other men in there now, mostly sitting at separate tables, and she felt their eyes on her as she entered. They were all about the age her father would have been now.

She stood at the bar, waiting agitatedly for Giannis Malavas to appear. He seemed to have gone out, though all the customers had drinks in front of them.

Finally, he emerged from the back of the café, but there was not the merest hint of recognition on his part, even though she had been there such a short time before.

'My car has gone . . .' she blurted out, expecting at least a little concern. 'Is there a police station in the village?'

The barman nodded.

'Policeman's over there,' he said.

It was the same man she had seen earlier, with the twin boys. He was still drinking.

'But he is off duty.'

His total indifference was alarming her.

Perhaps she could get a friend to drive out from Athens to pick her up? Or maybe there would sooner or later be a bus to get her out of here? She was overwhelmed by the desire to leave.

'Do you have a phone I could use?'

'We've got our old payphone,' he said, pointing to the corner. 'But it doesn't take euros.'

The euro had come in just a couple of years before, but he had not bothered to adapt it.

'So how . . . ?'

He shrugged his shoulders.

'Can't really help you,' he said, turning his back on her.

'A taxi?' she asked, beginning to feel desperate now.

'Not at this hour,' said a man in the corner, whom she had not noticed before.

Athanasia looked around at their impassive faces. The hostility was palpable, the air dense with smoke and silence.

This is the population of paradise? she asked herself. She recalled the face of the only woman she had seen that day, realising that the shepherdess had been obliged to become like a man to survive. Perhaps all the others had left long ago. Just like her mother.

Athanasia knew there was no choice. She had to get out as soon as she could.

As the moon was rising, she began to run. Arcadia was no place for a woman.

I could see how Eva's story had evolved, and I greatly sympathised with its message. I wonder what will happen to her generation, who live day to day with the knowledge that so much is denied them.

It's quite likely that Eva and her friends will wake up in a few decades' time, having missed the chance to fulfil their potential and having lost out on half a lifetime of opportunities. This sense of alienation is very, very strong in Greece. I could feel it in every town and city. Graffiti is the obvious expression of it, but disillusioned faces are the real human sign of it. There are millions of young people who cannot see a future in their own country. They feel as if it has turned against them. If they can, like Athanasia, they run. Perhaps Eva will do that, too, if she has the will.

Around ten o'clock, the bar began to fill with a few other disenfranchised twenty- and thirty-somethings (maybe forty-somethings, too). All of them were well educated, opinionated, happy to practise their English, and several of them were gay (both men and women). Debate ranged from corruption to Cavafy, from capitalism to the crisis. We talked about gender and power and the dominance of the male ego in Greek society. Women are strong in Greece, but quite often members of the older generation still appear subservient to their husbands. Nobody disagreed. All of them had mothers who did all the shopping, cooking and cleaning, even if they had full-time jobs.

Eva was busy keeping everyone supplied with drinks, but she joined the conversation every so often. The story she had told reflected her own experience, and I could sense that her anger was explosive and specifically directed towards the destruction that men have wreaked on her country. She laid the blame on corrupt male politicians who have led Greece for many decades. Given that women have not played a significant role in Greek politics up until now, there was not even a murmur of dissent.

'The gods gave the Greeks this idyll,' she said, putting down a tray of shot glasses, 'but look what they have done with it . . .'

Men and women all agreed. It's a mess.

'Stin iyeia mas! Cheers!'

Twenty of us clinked glasses.

We lived for the moment that night. It was pointless to do otherwise.

The majority in the bar were unemployed but somehow still had money for alcohol, cigarettes and strong weed. One of them was a DJ, and at midnight started to play. The music was hypnotic and I soon lost myself in it.

I have no idea what time we spilled out into the street. I dimly remember noticing that day was breaking and being aware that I could not drive. When they realised that I had nowhere to stay, all of them, without hesitation, offered me a sofa. I followed two bearded brothers who rented a small flat opposite the bar, and slept like a dead man until two in the afternoon. My hosts were still sleeping when I woke, so I left them a note and my email address in case I could ever return their hospitality in London.

Before leaving town, I returned to the café, hoping that I might be able to get some coffee. Eva was there, as unsmiling as before. Her mood was the same as on the previous day, and her fury began to stir all kinds of darkness in me. Fascinating as I found her, there was an anger in her spirit that I found disturbing. She made me a strong, bitter coffee, I thanked her for a great evening and, as I left, I noticed she was furiously scribbling on a patch of wall, one of the few that still remained blank. Perhaps one day I will go back and read another of her stories. Part of me hopes that she will not still be there.

I headed south again. I wanted to visit Kalamata. I had not been in the right frame of mind after my 'stay' at the airport, but a few weeks on I was ready. There is an archaeological museum there that I wanted to see.

It's best not to read too much about Kalamata: you would probably think twice about visiting. Books mention the port and the pimps and the prostitutes, and they refer to the exports of olives and raisins. The town may not be a place that is especially alluring for tourists, but it has a charm that people rushing through are likely to miss.

A more complimentary description suggests that its name is derived from kalamatia, meaning 'lovely eyes'. It could also be a reference to good luck, referring to the 'mati' – the eye that wards off evil. I admit that simply being there for some reason lifted my spirits.

Kalamata has a dilapidated port, a main square about a kilometre from the sea with dozens of thriving cafés, an old quarter and even a castle. Nothing is exactly 'picture-postcard' pretty, but its authenticity makes up for this, and in mid-October there was a final burst of warmth before winter came.

I was almost happy there, visiting the archaeological and military museums, sitting in cafés, exploring the town, even strolling through the quirky train museum, which is like a retirement home for disused railway carriages. Who can say why one likes one place above another, but the people here were even friendlier than in other parts of Greece, and I have fond memories of their smiles and a sense that they were aware of their good fortune.

I went to buy some tobacco (yes, I have given in) at a kiosk and noticed a busker setting down his bouzouki case opposite.

'Panagia mou! In the name of the Virgin!' said the man behind the counter in the periptero, slamming my change down on the plastic counter in front of him. 'Not him again . . .'

'Not much good?' I enquired.

'After Antoni, nobody is any good,' he said regretfully.

'Antoni?'

By now, the musician was belting out a song. People walked by as though he did not even exist, and nobody threw even ten cents into his open case.

Although it was hard to hear above the noise, the kiosk owner leaned towards me and, through the small window that separated us, began to tell me about a man called Antoni.

'He was the greatest musician who ever visited this town,'

he said. 'It's a few years back now, but some of us still talk about him.'

I was immediately spellbound.

'Mia fora kai enan kairo . . .' he began. 'Once upon a time . . .' and it was hard to know how much he was exaggerating. Whether or not every element was true, there was definitely a musician who once came to Kalamata and left a lasting impression.

When he got to the end of the story, the busker was still singing.

'Nowadays I just want to block my ears,' he said.

AIR ON A G STRING

CARTE POSTALE

Kalamata Harbour

'AIR ON A G STRING'

One autumn day the stationmaster, who noted the arrival and departure of every stranger, saw a man get off the train from Corinth with a battered violin case. He was very distinctive, with a radiant smile and sparkling eyes.

On feast days in Kalamata, there were always groups of itinerant *bouzouki* and *klarino* players, but this musician was not like them. He was dressed much more smartly, and when he began to play the streets of the town were filled with a new kind of music.

Even the children stopped their games and gathered to listen. They were bolder than the adults, lacking in inhibition about approaching him. When he stopped his playing, one of the children reached up to touch the violin.

It was not a clumsy gesture. He wanted to see it, to feel whether it was hot or cold, rough or smooth. The violinist understood.

He bent down to show the child, who plucked at one of the strings and ran his fingers over an elaborate carving on the tailpiece. It was a face.

'It looks like you!' the child exclaimed. 'Is it you?'

The child looked at the violin and then at the man and then back again at the violin.

'Yes, it's you! Look!' he shrieked, summoning his friends. 'It's him! It's him!'

The boy's friends crowded round.

It was true that the little figure did resemble him.

The child was fascinated by the violin, instinctively appreciating its beauty.

'Like a tiger,' he said, admiring the violin's back, made out of a single piece of striped maple.

His friends had all disappeared and were now chasing a ball around the square. Meanwhile, the little boy was becoming more and more engrossed in the detail of the violin, examining its ornate pegs with tiny pearls on their ends, the fineness of the bridge, the purfling that ran around its curves. Perhaps only a child's sharp eyes could appreciate such minutiae.

All the time, the violinist kept a light hold on the instrument but allowed the child to twist it this way and that as he studied every part of its surface. A beam of light shone into the instrument and illuminated the writing inside, just visible through the curved, f-shaped hole cut into the wood.

'*An-to-ni . . .*'

He was a bright kid and had already learned the Roman alphabet, so was able to make out the letters inside.

'*Antoni! Antoni!*' he cried out with delight. 'My name is Antoni, too! We have the same name!'

He assumed that someone had inscribed the man's name inside.

The child wanted another look.

'Antoni S-t-r-a . . .'

He gave up on the rest. It was a long word and hard to read in the shadows of the violin's interior.

The violinist smiled and put his instrument up on his shoulder once again, and then continued playing. The tone of his music was as sweet as honey, as mellow as old wine. There was never a discordant twang, a note out of place or out of time.

With children near, he chose bright, easy melodies. The boys abandoned their ball, drawn back towards him.

They started to chase each other round and round the musician until they were giddy, hopping up and down to the rhythm of his tunes. Girls linked hands and skipped around in circles. The music was full of joy and movement and the children could not stand still to listen.

'Antoni, Antoni!' they shouted, until the whole town knew his name.

Aris, the owner of the nearest taverna, had heard the exchange.

'Hey, Antoni, come and eat.'

His place was unusually busy today and, with all the competition around, he surmised that something new was bringing customers to his tables. There could be only one reason. He wanted to stay friendly with this man.

'Antoni' had been delivering his concert for more than three hours, and yet his fingers had not tired. Now he scooped the coins that had been dropped into his open case in his pocket and released the tension on the bow with a few twists of its silver screw. Then he carefully repacked the instrument, propped the case against a chair, sat down and waited for his lunch. The square seemed silent without his music.

Aris reappeared with several dishes on a tray and put them down in front of the violinist.

'*Stifado, horta, fasolakia,*' he listed. 'Stew, greens and beans.' He had already brought a half-kilo of red wine in a copper jug and, within moments, it was gulped down.

The musician was soon shovelling the food direct from dish to mouth. There was no question of making conversation, so Aris left him to it.

When all the dishes were empty and every last drop of sauce wiped up with hunks of soft, doughy bread, the violinist picked up his violin and walked away towards the other side of the square. He disappeared in the direction of the sea, where there would be more cafés and a new audience.

'Come back later,' called the taverna owner, knowing that, even with his 'gift' of a meal, he was still way up on his normal day's takings.

Magda was one of the very few unmarried women of her age in the town. Her parents had both died and she lived alone above the family shop, which sold knitting wool, ribbon and thread. She had once been engaged, but the wedding had not taken place after it became clear that she could not have children. Now she was known as the *yerontokori*, the spinster. The great irony was that she was, without competition, the most beautiful woman in Kalamata and, with her abundance of glossy hair, extravagant lips and ample breasts, by far the most desired.

That evening, as she often did, Magda took a walk from the shop, which was in the old part of town, via the main square to the sea. She was greeted by wolf whistles and catcalls. They were not hostile. The majority of the men who sat in the cafés here were known to her, and the sounds they made were appreciative.

She was resigned to their attention, aware that her breasts were difficult to conceal, always pushing against the front of her blouse, giving her buttons an impossible task.

'Magda! How are things?'

They all knew her name.

'Nice day?!'

'Having a good evening?'

Their greetings were cheerful, jovial. These were the salutations of old friends and acquaintances. Most had been in her class at the *gymnasio*, and a few had had their first stolen kiss with her twenty years before.

She smiled and waved in response.

The air was warm for the time of year and the *neradzia*, the bitter-orange trees, that lined the street, were heavy with bright fruit.

Magda approached the port from the road that ran along by the sea, where there was a row of lively cafés.

She always went to the one owned by her cousin Andreas and she sat outside and lit a cigarette. The water was still and the concrete expanse of the port was deserted, except for a handful of people loitering in the distance, waiting to bring in and reload a boat. The warehouses were full of crates of dried fruit, ready to be shipped, and huge drums of olive oil.

Against a sky that was slowly turning pink, a man on a bicycle pedalled by.

Suddenly, something broke the silence. Its source was not far away. It was a single, sustained note, and Magda turned her head in its direction.

She saw a handsome, middle-aged man with a violin. He drew his bow steadily across the strings, then played a second note. He was looking at her, perhaps drawing inspiration, perhaps not even seeing her, but she felt the music was being played for her.

He stood alone. She, as usual, sat by herself. Married women regarded her with suspicion and few ever invited her to join them.

What were these notes? She was familiar with the sounds of the *bouzouki* and *baglama* and could dance the steps of the Kalamatianos better than anyone. Music usually went with movement, but this melody stilled her. The exquisite sounds that she heard from the violin captivated her.

She was immediately under the spell of the music and closed her eyes, listening to each note and even appreciating the spaces between them.

First, the hairs on her arms rose like a cat's in a fight. Then she felt an unfamiliar pricking sensation at the back of her eyes, a tightening of the muscles in her throat, a flush around her neck and the unmistakable sensation of tears rolling down her cheeks. She reached across the table to take a paper napkin from the holder and dabbed at her face, but still the tears fell.

Like most other people of the town, she had never heard such music before. She watched as both men and women tossed coins into the violin case before walking away. A few cents here, a euro there, and soon they added up to the price of a meal. They were not just paying for his music but for the effect it had on them. Before the violinist had arrived, the only sound had been the hum of chatter. Now the stillness of the sea seemed to magnify the music and, even when the violin 'whispered', its voice could be heard across the space. When it rose to a crescendo, the notes burst through conversation like an explosion.

Magda was unsure if she liked the involuntary response she was experiencing, but there was nothing she could do. The tears continued and soon a small mountain of screwed-up napkins lay abandoned on the table. She noticed that she was not the only one to have been affected by the violinist's music.

He played on and on but, towards the end of one piece, his bright eyes danced around, reacting to, looking for, feeling his way towards something that would tell him what to play next.

The Venetian mansions near the sea and the crisp November evening had made him think of Vivaldi, and of 'Autumn' from the *Four Seasons*, and his bow glided into it without a pause.

More people were coming out, now that the sun had set. There were a few couples strolling hand in hand, some elderly men who had eaten dinner and were emerging for companionship, and some younger men looking for love. In late autumn and winter, both men and women here worked hard to harvest the huge olive groves outside town, and in the evening hundreds of them congregated for a well-earned drink in one of the cafés.

The music Antoni played was slower now.

Another boat came in, but the sound of an anchor being dropped did not stop the music. Magda's eyes did not leave the musician.

Once the boat was fastened, a few sailors and dock-workers drifted in her direction, but they could not catch her eye. She kept her gaze on the violinist.

His eyes were firmly closed as he played, aware of his surroundings and feeling the mood of his audience, selecting and then selecting again the appropriate piece from the enormous repertoire that filled his head, as if it were a Rolodex. Bach, Mozart, Telemann, Corelli, plenty

of Vivaldi (he had felt the surge of pleasure in the crowd's response). He played compulsively, as if he could not stop.

'Where's he from?' Magda asked her cousin.

'I don't know,' he replied. 'But someone heard one of the children calling him Antoni.'

By now it was past ten. All the cafés were full. More people were coming, and nobody was leaving. There was not an empty seat. In a town where nothing was free, a recital like this had never happened before. Sometimes, the violin emitted such volume and purity that it sounded as if various passages of music were chorded – or as if another 'ghost' violin were being played somewhere close.

At around eleven thirty, the last note died away. There was rapturous applause and the musician laid the violin in its case and loosened the tension in his bow. The only spare chair on the seafront was at Magda's table. Even after he sat down opposite her the clapping continued, and he smiled warmly to acknowledge the appreciation.

'They loved you,' said Magda. In truth, she was referring to herself.

'They love *this*,' he replied, tapping the outside of his case. '*This* is what they have been listening to.'

He spoke with an accent that suggested he was from another part of Greece, near the mountains in the north.

'But you were playing it,' said Magda.

'It was the voice of Antoni that you were listening to,' he said.

Andreas approached to see if there was something he could offer the violinist. Like the taverna owner earlier that day, he felt he owed this man for that evening's record-breaking takings.

'Mr Antoni,' he said. 'What can I offer you?'

'I could do with a cognac,' the violinist replied.

'Something for you, too, Magda?'

Andreas was feeling generous that night.

'The same,' she said.

They sat for a while in a comfortable silence. Both of them were used to being alone. Nobody was waiting for them at home.

'How did you learn to play like that?' asked Magda.

'I think the violin taught me,' he replied, smiling. 'With such an instrument the music is there already. It's as if it is waiting for someone to release the sound inside.'

Magda tilted her head to one side, her thick hair tumbling over her shoulders.

'So if I picked it up, I would be able to play like you?'

'It might take a while, but let's see . . .'

He bent down to open the case, lifted the violin from

its red velvet bed and then drew the bow across the strings, adjusting the pegs fractionally to tune it. Magda fixed her eyes on the carving on the scroll.

He gently moved her hair to one side and propped the instrument under her chin, held her left hand in position to support it, then took the fingers of her right hand and showed her how to spread them along the end of the bow to balance it as she played.

Then he placed the bow on the bottom string and gently pulled down on her elbow so that she could feel it glide lightly across the steel. People around them were watching.

The note rang out.

It was an open G, the lowest note on the violin, rich and deep.

Then he carefully placed her forefinger on the E string and F sharp rang out. It was the same note with which he had begun tonight, when he played Bach's 'Air on a G String'. The sound was pure and penetrated the lively chatter that had now resumed along the street, continuing to ring in the air for a few moments after.

When the note finally died away, Magda took the violin from her shoulder and placed it in her lap. She looked down at it as if it were a baby, a precious creature she did not quite know what to do with. Then she allowed her fingers to trace the shape of the small wooden body. Like the child earlier that day, she was intrigued to see that through the f-shaped hole she could glimpse some writing.

'What does it say?' she asked.

'Antonius Stradivarius,' he said.

'So that's your name?'

'No,' he laughed. 'It's the name of the man who made this. The name of the man you hear when this is played.'

'And he put his name inside every violin he made?'

'Every single one,' confirmed the violinist. 'And each one is unique, but each of them has Antonius's voice. When people read the label and think that Antoni is my name, I don't disagree. In some ways they are right: the violin and I are one and the same. I am speaking with his voice.'

Magda gazed at the musician as he talked.

'It's the most precious thing I own. It is the *only* thing I own, apart from the clothes I am wearing. Without it, I don't eat.'

Magda handed the precious instrument back to its owner, catching a glimpse of its rounded back.

'How many years . . . ?'

'It seems like my whole life.'

People up and down the row of cafés were talking about the violinist now.

Normally, people did not talk to buskers here, and it was equally unusual to see Magda talking with a stranger. Her voluptuous looks sometimes attracted unwelcome attention from visitors to the town, so she tended to be a little aloof.

'Sometimes I feel possessed by this violin, as if it is playing me. And even when I am not playing, I have to protect it because of its value. It's on my mind twenty-four hours a day.'

Andreas approached them with another tray of drinks.

'From the table over there.' He indicated with his head. 'And there are plenty more who want to send something over.'

Magda smiled.

'It must be nice to be so appreciated,' she said.

'It is . . . I just wish I could have a few hours to forget it. A night without its voice.'

They picked up their glasses and clinked them together. '*Stin iyeia sas.* To your health.'

'Will you play that tune again . . . the one you were playing before. The first one?' she asked.

'Just for you,' answered the violinist, finishing his drink.

The exquisite notes of the Bach 'Air' rang out once again, sedate, unhurried, powerful.

The people of Kalamata listened. Nobody stirred until the music ended. As people got up to go home, they noticed Magda with the violinist, their heads close in conversation.

Eventually, when most of the tables were empty, Andreas emerged from the café with an industrial-sized tin of olives. The original contents were gone, but the tin was full to the top with coins, and he struggled to carry it even with two hands. The money had been left by customers for 'Antoni'.

But the violinist was nowhere to be seen.

Magda had vanished, too. The table at which they had been sitting was empty.

The next day, Andreas saw Magda in the street and, as she approached him, he heard her humming. It was a familiar tune. The distinctive notes lingered in his mind from the previous night.

'Good morning, Magda,' he said.

She nodded, smiling at him.

'It was a lovely tune, that one . . .' he said.

'"Air on a G String",' Magda said knowledgeably. 'Bach.'

'What a virtuoso, that man . . .' said Andreas. 'And people left so much money for him! More than three hundred euros. I need to give it to him.'

'He's gone,' said Magda.

'Are you sure?'

She nodded.

'He won't be coming back?'

She shook her head.

'No,' she said.

Andreas noticed her fiddling with something on her wrist. As it was a warm day, she had pulled the sleeves of her cardigan up to her elbows and he saw coiled around her arm a length of what looked like silver wire.

'We exchanged gifts,' she said, responding to his quizzical look. 'It's a violin string. The G.'

'And what did you give him?' asked her cousin.

She smiled enigmatically and walked on, resuming her tune. The notes of the famous Bach melody rose once again in the air.

It seems that for one night only there was a connection between two people that made them both happy. I don't believe that 'Antoni' made love to a woman in every town, but when there was someone whose response and openness to music was similar to Magda's, perhaps it happened. I am certain that Magda was not the only one on his route to be seduced by his Stradivarius.

I imagine that Magda will always keep the violin string. A metal G is indestructible, so there is no reason why she would not have this wrapped round her wrist for the rest of her life as a reminder of that night of happiness. She was joyful for the experience itself, rather than regretful for its transience. If only love could always be as free of pain. As I write this, love seems to be a force that has made me both sad and mad.

Just for a while, I long to be like Antoni, travelling without a heavy heart, or cheerful like Magda and happy to stay in the same place. I will keep striving for one or the other, but it shocks me how difficult I am finding it to turn off the tap of my sorrow and regret.

For months I avoided listening to music. It had triggered

too much emotion in me. Not that you and I had any special connection through music but, for me, music (especially the violin) has a direct link to the heart. I have even left a café once or twice because they were playing something sentimental and I could feel myself beginning to lose control of my feelings. I downloaded some Bach sonatas the night after I was told the story of Antoni and Magda, and they now keep me company in the car. They include 'Air on a G String', of course. Little by little, I will bring some other music into my life, like a convalescing man gradually reintroducing some richer foods into his diet. I will have to be ready, though.

My week or so in gentle, unpretentious Kalamata came to an end. I travelled north again, two hundred kilometres up the coast to Patras. It was a beautiful journey, and a perfect autumn day. I stopped at Olympia on the way and stood on the running track. Like every tourist, I imagined the roaring of the crowd.

On a map of Greece, there are dozens of places marked as ancient sites, many of them temples and palaces which are thousands of years old but now merely skeletons of the originals. Some are recognisable structures, such as the Parthenon, but many are merely rows of stones on the ground, the only traces that survive of a wall or a temple. For some people, these remains are the primary reason to visit this country.

Something I have noticed on my travels is that the next generation of ruins is already in the making. They are not marked on the map, and they don't appear in guidebooks, but Greece is full of them. Empty, derelict buildings are to be found in every town and village. Some look as if they were built a few hundred years ago but others seem only a few decades old. Often they have been abandoned because inheritance arrangements left them divided an impossible number of ways and no single individual will take responsibility. But this is not always the case. Most buildings are created with optimism and an eye to the future, so the presence of a plethora of buildings with dark and often glassless windows always intrigues me. Behind each one of these strange, eerie places must be an explanation for its state of ruin.

This story was told to me by an old couple sitting at the adjacent table in a Patras taverna. Not far away was a huge eyesore of an empty hotel and, although the couple had not lived in the town for long, they were keen to tell me what they had heard.

NEVER ON A TUESDAY

POST CARD
CARTE POSTALE

NEVER ON A TUESDAY

There are some Greeks who do not plan anything of the least importance on a Tuesday. This was the day of the week on which the great city of Constantinople, the most significant place in Christendom, fell to the Turks. It may have been more than five hundred years ago, but the 1453 catastrophe still casts a shadow. It is an event that some people think of every day, and on Tuesdays the 'memory' is especially stirred.

Constantinople, still referred to by many as *i poly*, 'the city', had been under siege by the Ottoman forces for forty days. As the Greeks tried to repel the attackers outside their walls, they witnessed a series of terrible portents: a lunar eclipse, an icon of the Virgin slipping from its platform as she was processed round the city, and a violent thunderstorm. As the Turks finally broke into the city, on Tuesday, 29 May, men, women and children were butchered, but some felt that the greatest atrocity of all was the desecration of the basilica of Agia Sofia and the massacre of the priests and congregation who were worshipping inside. Even now, many Greeks cannot bring themselves to say the name that the Turks gave it: 'Istanbul', and on airport Departures and Arrivals boards the old name is still used.

There are others, of course, who treat Tuesday as any other day and do not believe in such 'superstitious nonsense'. This was the position taken by the Papazoglou family.

On 29 May 1979, two hotels opened under their ownership. People were aghast. It was a Tuesday and the very anniversary itself.

'How could they even *think* of it?' muttered the old men in the city's *kafenions*. 'They could have waited just a day . . .'

Over their pastries in the *zacharoplasteion*, the old ladies said the same. 'Think of it! A Constantinople family, of all things!'

Apostolos Papazoglou had been among those who fled Istanbul in 1955, during a pogrom against the city's remaining Greek population. The violence against his community meant that Papazoglou had no choice but to leave his home and a popular guesthouse. He and his young wife, Melina, arrived in Greece with nothing but their two small sons and a handful of keepsakes that they had managed to carry.

Papazoglou had a family to feed and immediately began looking for opportunities. He found his way to Patras, where he and his family could see the sea from where they lived, just as they had back in Constantinople. He worked long days in a *kafenion* and, for a few hours each night, as a porter at the docks, earning enough to feed his family and even to build up some savings.

During the military dictatorship in the late 1960s, tourist hotels were opened as a way to boost the economy. When the junta ended, and freedom for tourism increased, there was exponential growth in the industry. Papazoglou took his chance.

Foreigners were flocking in to enjoy the climate and the light, and everything that the Mediterranean had to offer. Even the inflated currency had its charm, and people enjoyed paying thousands of drachmas for a beer, especially when they worked out it cost just a few pence. They felt like millionaires.

Apostolos observed with interest as a very plain-looking hotel, the Xenia, began to thrive. It was close to the beach but offered the bare minimum in the way of comfort. Whenever he strolled past, he saw the German guests lined up on cheap sun-loungers, enjoying little more than what nature handed out for free. They were satisfied with sun, sea and sand, cold local beer and cheap meals. For a northern European who had never before tasted taramasalata, the zing of cod's roe was a life-changing moment, as was the moment when they first bit into fresh watermelon.

Apostolos took out a loan on a small strip of land nearby. He built a similar hotel, very plain, no frills. The beds were narrow, the rooms were small and the curtains did not meet. Sometimes the hot-water system did not work, but in the heat of summer few complained. It was part of Greece's charm.

By the end of the first summer, he had already made plans for a second hotel. And for five years, he built an additional one each winter. Every season, they were full to capacity, from Easter until the end of October.

Papazoglou continued to keep up with demands from the tourist operators, who were now looking for greater comfort and higher-specification accommodation. In the space of two decades, the number of guests multiplied twenty-fold, as did his profits and financial forecasts. He had invested in undeveloped land on coastal strips before many others had noticed its potential. Most had been thinking only of urban or industrial development.

His luxury-hotel empire spread around the coastal resorts of Greece, and to the islands.

His two sons, Manos and Stephanos, were now in their twenties. For a decade they had spent their summers playing in various beach resorts that were part of the luxury brand their father had created, living on room service and Coca-Cola, and had never in their lives made a bed. They had no memory of sleeping head to toe on a divan in their parents' one-bedroom Patras apartment. These days, they constantly bickered with each other.

Their mother had always made them feel like gods. They were praised even when they did badly at school, and grew up thinking they were beyond the reach of rules. It was not their fault for being spoiled. They were simply victims of an over-indulgent mother, and an older father who was too preoccupied with making money to notice them.

As Papazoglou's seventy-fifth birthday approached, he was puzzling over what would happen next to his business. He wanted to retire, but he did not want to see his hotel group divided. Nor did he want to leave it automatically to Manos, as everyone expected. He was the elder of the two, but that did not make him more deserving. Papazoglou secretly believed that Stephanos had the greater charm and was better suited to the role.

'Why don't you set them a test?' suggested Melina Papazoglou. 'Find out who will do a better job, and decide who becomes head of the business that way.'

Old Papazoglou agreed.

On his birthday, 13 October, he took an old drachma coin out of his desk drawer and joined his family to celebrate in a smart restaurant in town. As a rich chocolate gateau was being served, he silenced the argument Manos and Stephanos were having about football with an announcement. He had two sites in Patras that he had never developed. One was close to its busy port and the other was outside town on a stretch of sand. The coin would decide who took which plot; whichever of them developed a more successful hotel would take over their father's entire empire.

As Papazoglou tossed his drachma in the air, the waiters eavesdropping on their conversation muttered quietly. No such decisions should be made on the thirteenth of any month, they said. The number was unlucky the world over, but even more so in Greece. The digits of 1453 added up to thirteen. Choosing tonight for the coin toss was not merely ignorance. 'It's pure stupidity,' said the maître d', under his breath.

The coin decided that the elder son, Manos (heads), should have the site close to the port, and Stephanos (tails) would have the beach plot.

'Both of these have great potential, so let's see what you can do,' said Papazoglou. 'In two years' time, I'll look at your balance sheets. Whoever is ahead, even by ten drachmas, will take over.'

Both boys had left school at the age of sixteen and done no further studying. What was the point in pushing themselves to the limit at university when they had a rich father and knew what business they were destined for? With the poor grades they had achieved, few universities would have admitted them in any case.

Each had assumed that half the business would eventually slide into their hands. They were shocked by the test their father had decided to set them. It was daunting, and it put them in a vicious, all-or-nothing competition with each other.

Manos, being older, felt he had one up on his brother. He was the one with his late grandfather's name, so he was inevitably his grandmother's favourite and had been even more spoiled for that reason. It annoyed him that Stephanos always had prettier girlfriends, but he was scornful of their low level of intelligence. Manos constantly fought with his weight (he had inherited his father's short stature) but at the same time prided himself on being a gourmet and a lover of fine wines.

Stephanos was indisputably better-looking. He had inherited his mother's perfectly proportioned features and had a physique to match. Sport was his passion and he played football and water polo for the town. As Manos jealously observed, there was always an adoring woman clinging to his arm.

Manos decided that tourists were not going to be his main clientele. He wanted to make money twelve months of the year, and in order to do this he focused on businesspeople, commercial travellers and even the men who worked in the docks. These were all people with cash to spend, and Manos decided to attract them with something more sophisticated than they were used to in this workaday town.

On his site, there was already a vast, empty office block. It was like a huge box, with holes cut for windows. There were no other architectural features. He was faced with a choice, either to demolish it, which was a huge and costly process, or to convert this existing building into a hotel. The latter was by far the best option: faster and cheaper.

With a ruler, a set square and a large, blank sheet of paper, it took him twenty minutes to draw up his vision. It was a mediaeval castle. As a child, he had been taken on a visit to the old castle at Nafplio, and this was his inspiration. It was solid and square, and had turrets and crenellations. Hotel Pyrgos would be his own personal fortress.

While the outside was being adapted and balconies added, he started on the interior. Old office spaces were divided and subdivided with thin partition walls and bathrooms were installed. The most important spaces were on the ground floor. This was where his profit would be made.

A focal point of the reception rooms would be the murals, pseudo-classical but with an erotic undertone. As well as ensuring that the hotel had the best 'fine dining' in Patras, there was to be a series of small bar areas for music and dancing, and one for a 'private' club, where gambling would take place.

Manos commissioned copies of Botticelli paintings (more pastiche than facsimile) for the gambling room, and he asked for the figures to be even more scantily clad than

in the originals. The hostesses would be similarly dressed (or undressed, as he joked to his friends).

The exterior of the hotel was solid-looking and the ground-floor rooms were luxurious, with no expense spared. Manos was satisfied that he had got his market just right and also that he was winning in the race against time.

As a very keen swimmer, it seemed appropriate that Stephanos should build a beach hotel. He was starting from scratch and needed to get to work as soon as possible. He had just over six months, until the beginning of summer, to construct a building and get it fitted out in time for the start of the tourist season.

Using the model that had first inspired his father, a very plain, unadorned style, with simple rooms all overlooking the sea, his beachside hotel, the Thalassa, would soon be ready to open. The building went up in record time. The foundations were shallow and the walls made of little more than a single sheet of plyboard, but everyone who came to stay would spend most of their day on the beach and their evening in a local bar. He had spent the minimum on construction, and this would be to his advantage on the balance sheet.

As soon as he knew his brother was planning the opening of the Pyrgos for 29 May, Stephanos aimed for the same date. Two rival launch parties took place on that night. Apostolos Papazolglou went to the Pyrgos first, and his wife to the Thalassa. Then they swapped locations.

The first summer seemed to go well for both sons. In terms of profit margin, their father was impressed and surprised by what they had both achieved and, to his sons' relief, did not look any deeper into their businesses.

Manos always hid from his father the truth of what was taking place behind the scenes. He almost hid it from himself. But a few months after the opening, he had a 'visit'. Giorgos Kourtis had been an occasional customer and seemed to enjoy what he found. He had even slipped into the private room once or twice to do some gambling and had spent the evening there with one of the girls. However, it soon became clear what his real interest was. Kourtis owned a rival hotel in the centre of town, and Manos heard that he was losing some of his business to the Pyrgos. He was also a man with powerful connections.

One night, perhaps five months after opening, the hotel's electricity failed. It was manageable at first. Candles were fetched, and Manos persuaded his clientele that it was 'romantic'. When the electricians were called, it seemed that there was no fault in the system. Manos had simply been cut off. And there was nothing he could do to get reconnected, apart from pay five million drachmas. The same then happened to the water, with the same fee to reconnect. The prices were extortionate. It was, as he came to realise, extortion.

After that, there was the visit from the police. They were heavy-handed and destructive in their search for evidence of gambling, which, of course, they found. They knew exactly where to look. And they returned regularly. Manos soon realised that only a hefty bribe into the right hands could prevent these visits. There was no choice if he wanted to survive.

To his dismay, Manos's figures soon showed that his outgoings far exceeded his incomings. The random power cuts were atmospheric enough in the summer, but in the winter they left the rooms unheated. Occupancy dwindled during the colder months. And when the winds blew in across the Ionian, the temperatures inside could drop to less than ten degrees. The walls began to drip with condensation, and Botticelli's muses began to flake away. Guest numbers fell drastically. As the new summer season began, the hotel, which like a true castle was meant to last for ever, began to deteriorate.

Manos attempted to avert financial disaster. The most important thing for him was the balance sheet that he would have to present to his father in October. It was now only four months away. He had taken out several different loans in order to keep paying out for the extortions and the bribes. He knew that Kourtis was masterminding all these troubles, and that if he did not cooperate he could kiss the hotel and his future goodbye. Already, he was buried under so much debt that he could not sleep at night, and in the day the stress induced regular attacks of asthma. His weight had increased to such an extent that he could scarcely get to the second floor of the hotel where his office was based, and he could not afford the cost to fix the lift. His girlfriend of six months (a record) made her excuses and left him. Initially attracted by his status as owner of the grandest hotel in town, she had realised the price was too high.

Manos's desperation was made worse by news that business at the Thalassa was booming. Stephanos only had to be open for six months of the year to make his profits. Guests were given very little, but they gave a lot in return, drinking cold beer and fizzy drinks all day at the beach bar and paying inflated prices to water-ski.

One warm June night, so sultry that every guest in the Thalassa had their windows thrown open wide, the earth began to rumble. It was around four in the morning, when dreams are deep and the sun is not yet up. The sleepers heard nothing at first, but they felt the force of the earthquake; it shook them from their beds. On the Richter scale it was not a significant quake (a mere 4.3), but the floors shifted several millimetres each way, back and forth, back and forth. There were no fire escapes and no instructions for what to do or where to go. In any case, there was no time.

The building crumbled to powder, the fifth floor tumbling into the fourth floor, which tumbled into the third floor, leaving a jumbled heap of concrete, metal railings, beds and bodies. Some of the outer walls remained, but most floors disintegrated. It took no longer than a few minutes for the hotel to teeter and fall.

Stephanos himself did not live in the hotel, but he was woken by the earthquake and sprinted down the road to see the Thalassa already in ruins. Like a hit-and-run driver, his instinct was to flee as fast as he could in the other direction. There were over two hundred guests staying. Thirty of them were killed. When the forensic team investigated the wreckage of the building, it was clear that it had been built without any regard for the safety of its guests. The bereaved families, along with the one hundred or so who were wounded, took Stephanos to court for negligence. Everything in the construction of the Thalassa was substandard. Only one other hotel in the area, the Pyrgos, had been affected by the earthquake. It suffered a single cracked window.

A broken window was the least of Manos's problems. He was finally facing the fact that his debts were unpayable. The interest on the interest on the interest was more than he could pay in one lifetime, even if the hotel remained full. On the same day that Stephanos was charged, Manos's final guest departed and the last remaining member of staff left, unpaid for six months.

Manos walked into the bar and took a bottle off the shelf. It was the only decent whisky left and, unscrewing the cap, he took long gulps straight from it. Still holding the half-empty Johnnie Walker bottle, he walked unsteadily down the corridor, his footsteps echoing on the stone floor.

Someone was hammering on the main reception door. On tiptoe to muffle the sound, Manos stealthily made his way to a small office from which he could glimpse who was outside. It was a local police officer, the same one who had been coming regularly in the past months. He stood there, arms folded, and Manos noticed him checking the time. The watch that Apostolos Papazoglou had given his son for his twenty-fifth birthday was on the man's wrist. Last time Orestes Sakaridis visited, when Manos was already out of funds, he had accepted the watch in lieu of money. Manos was incensed to see him yet again. He had nothing left to give, and nothing to lose. He unbolted the door and threw it open.

Sakaridis could see the anger in Manos Papazoglou's eyes.

'What the fuck do you want?'

'I think you know the answer,' said the police officer, smirking. 'The usual.'

Manos lurched drunkenly towards Sakaradis, swinging the bottle towards his face.

The police officer avoided the blow and grabbed Manos's shoulders to contain him, but Manos wrenched one arm free and rammed his elbow hard into the man's stomach. His entire weight was behind the punch.

The officer was badly winded and fell clumsily on to his back, the side of his head striking the marble step. He lay very, very still.

Manos, panting hard, took several moments to regain his breath.

The street in front of the hotel was as deserted as the Pyrgos itself and, without touching the inert body, he turned on his heels and walked calmly towards his car. It was parked close by in the street. He took off, his foot hard down on the accelerator, along the coast road, no thought in his head except that he must get away.

He passed through several red lights, almost losing control on a bend and narrowly missing a police car. With lights flashing, siren screaming, it gave chase and forced him to pull over to the side of the road.

The two policemen immediately smelled the alcohol on his breath and made him get into the back of their car. As they drove along, they picked up on the radio that the body of their colleague had been found on the steps of the Pyrgos.

Apostolos Papazoglou's seventy-seventh birthday was not as he had imagined. It was to have been the day of his retirement, when his hotel empire would be given over to one of his sons. Instead, he had a different choice to make. His sons were both facing trial, and proceedings were to begin on the same day in Athens. Which one would he attend? His wife suggested tossing a coin.

The people of Patras had not forgotten the date of the hotel openings. When the verdict of manslaughter was given in both cases (seven months later, on 29 May), they nodded their heads knowingly. The bill for compensating injured guests and bereaved families could not be covered by the sale of the entire hotel empire. Apostolos Papazoglou was obliged to declare himself bankrupt.

For many years, the crumbling remains of the two hotels stood like ghostly reminders of the sack of Constantinople. The power of superstition and religious belief tightened its hold.

Whenever they passed by, the old people tut-tutted. 'They should have known better,' they said. 'That day must never be forgotten!'

I kept thinking of the day I first met you. It was a Tuesday.

Patras has much lovelier things than these desolate buildings. There is a very spacious square (with a nineteenth-century theatre designed by Ernst Ziller), elegant, pedestrian streets with good shops, and the hustle and bustle of a port, with boats to some islands.

When I arrived there, I had been in Greece for nearly two months, including the fortnight I had spent in Athens researching, and was beginning to learn a bit more Greek. I had got beyond just being able to exchange greetings and order food and could now even read newspaper headlines, though there never seemed to be any good news. The economy was as bad as ever and I knew I was very fortunate being able to travel so freely. As the sun began to lose its strength on those late-October evenings, I could see that life was becoming harder for most people in Greece. Sometimes the general dilapidation depressed me and the decaying state of so many buildings seemed to reflect the weakening fabric of the country. If I made the mistake of trying to interpret the graphs and diagrams on the front page of a newspaper, I could not see how this country could ever dig itself out of debt, let alone start to rebuild.

For the first time, I had the experience of someone coming up to me asking for money and realising that they were not a newly arrived immigrant (though that happened, too) but an elderly Greek whose pension had been slashed to below subsistence level, or someone with a family and no money to feed them with. Such a moment always jolted me out of my self-pity. I could eat and drink any time I wanted, but this was not the case for many people. The frequency with which I saw a Greek person going through a bin was increasing. How could I wallow in my own situation? There were moments when I despised myself, knowing that other people had much bigger problems than mine. My affliction was an emotional one, but I could at least survive.

Something that never seems to be affected by the economic crisis is the Greek Orthodox Church. I saw whole rows of shut-up shops but never a closed-up church. Large, medium, small, they are open, gleaming with treasure, and never without priests and the pious. There is a vast one in Patras. It was consecrated in 1974, and I found its exterior so off-puttingly vulgar that at first I did not bother to visit. Then a local person told me that the inside was well worth seeing.

Beforehand, I went into a nearby shop to see if I could find a guidebook. It was a huge shop selling icons of every saint you can imagine, and the woman who ran it was friendly and cheerful, asking my name and then insisting I buy an icon of Agios Antonis.

Everything about her was exaggerated. She was like a Disney cartoon character, with big red lips, a tiny waist and enormous hips, and she told me the story of the church.

Apparently, when the apostle Andrew arrived in the town two thousand years ago to tell everyone about Christ's resurrection, he learned that the Roman governor's wife was sick. He healed her and, as a result, she became a convert to Christianity and tried to persuade her husband to turn his back on the Roman gods. She told him that they were false.

The governor was furious that his wife was preaching this new and dangerous religion to him and had Andrew tortured, before executing him on an x-shaped cross. The apostle's remains disappeared but, years later, some parts were brought back to the city, along with relics of the cross on which he died.

The shopkeeper described the church with such joy and enthusiasm that I left the shop with high expectations of what I would find inside. Just as I shut the door behind me, she rushed out on to the pavement. I had forgotten to pick up my icon. 'And I must tell you one other thing!' she said breathlessly. 'Saint Andrew still performs miracles! The power of his church changed my father's life. It made him a new man. 'Itan thavma! A miracle! A miracle!'

LEAD US NOT INTO TEMPTATION

CARTE POSTALE

Exterior of the church of Agios Andreas, Patras

'LEAD US NOT INTO TEMPTATION'

'ME EISENENKES EMAS EIS PEIRASMON'

Some people still preferred the nearby Byzantine church that had housed a relic of the saint's finger. This tiny building was now in the shadow of the brand-new church, about which some of the elderly ladies were far from enthusiastic.

The basilica was huge and white, like a giant cake, and its dimensions alone were impressive. It was one of the biggest churches in Greece and bore no comparison with the intimate space of the older, darker building that had originally been built to honour Saint Andrew.

When it was first consecrated, older people saw only the drawbacks. Even before they got to the entrance they complained; it took them an age to get from the street and across the marble forecourt. Once inside, the journey from the candle box and then to the icon seemed to take another five minutes. It was very time-consuming, but they felt obliged to do their duty to the new church.

For most, the moment of opening the door and going inside was one of surprise and wonderment. Visitors, who came from all over Greece and further afield, were amazed. The interior was breathtaking.

The architect had wanted his cathedral to embody 'the Light of the World' in every sense. Sunshine flooded in from every side of the building, from windows cut into the huge dome above, and on the lower levels, too, and through the glass in the doors. On every wall, the gold leaf of the mosaics reflected the light and brightened the church. In the centre hung a mighty candelabra on which more than five hundred bulbs burned, sending out a dazzling brightness.

As well as light, he wanted to convey the life of the world and the glory of creation. His ambition, faith and budget for the church had no limitations. Dazzling images of birds and beasts adorned every gleaming wall, fronds and flowers embellished pillars and arches, and images of the saint's life decorated myriad surfaces with colour and movement. The very city that had martyred Saint Andrew now welcomed him back with open arms and glorified him. The whole building seemed to cry out: 'Forgive us!'

They had created magnificent silver reliquaries for his crumbling bones, which drew thousands of pilgrims to pay their respects and to prostrate themselves before the pieces of this man who had been in the presence of Jesus Christ. They came into contact with something that perhaps He had touched, too.

Someone for whom life had changed for the worse when the basilica opened was Maria Leontidis. For years now, she had cleaned the tiny Byzantine church next door, knowing that the low light would reveal neither dust nor cobweb. In the summer, she spent much of the day on the little bench outside the church, enjoying a cigarette and a frappé. In the winter, when she had flicked her feather duster once or twice round the reliquary, she warmed herself in the nearby *zacharoplasteion*, returning to lock up again once people had finished coming for the day.

She was invited to clean the new church when it opened that summer. At the age of sixty, she did not feel ready to stop working and it was a matter of pride to accept the new job.

In the cool space of the basilica, a pleasant breeze kept the flames of the candles flickering and the congregation comfortable, but she found herself overheating, the heat rising and boiling over like coffee in a *briki*.

When she began the 'new' job, it was not long after her brother's funeral. They had never been close but, nevertheless, she was observing the protocol of wearing black for forty days. Although it was hot, all the women in the family felt obliged to honour the tradition.

'It will take me a month just to polish all the candlesticks,' she said tearfully to her granddaughter, Pelagia, that evening. 'And it took me all day to sweep the floor, and by the time I'd gone round once, it needed doing all over again.'

Maria already looked back with nostalgia to the old days of cleaning the small church, when she could tidy the whole place in an hour. Now it took that amount of time just to empty out the dead candles. There were three thousand chairs, and every single one of them caught the dust in its nooks and crannies.

For a few weeks she managed, but soon the strain began to show. Her legs were as veined as the marble pillars in the new church, and her face as crimson as the strip of fresh carpet that led up the steps towards the altar. Her aches and pains intensified: knees, wrists, ankles, elbows. Every joint in her body ached. This new church was killing her.

One day when she woke up, her back was so stiff she could not get out of bed. She called Pelagia, crying with pain and anxiety. If the church was unattended for a day or two, she would never get on top of the dirt again. Already she pictured the white marble steps blackened with footprints, thousands of little candle stumps sticking out of the sand in their trays and the glass that protected icons and relics opaque with lip stains.

'Don't worry, *Yia-yia*,' said Pelagia. 'You need some time off. I'll go and clean for you.'

Pelagia hastened to the church. She knew that there were plenty of women who would be happy to take over her grandmother's job and she did not want her absence to give them the opportunity.

The Leontidis family lived on the other side of the city. For Maria, the church was a long bus ride away, but Pelagia, despite the eight-hour shift she had done in a bar the night before, walked and arrived much earlier than her *yia-yia* would have done.

She saw the priest leaving as she crossed the square. It was nine o'clock, and he had just unlocked.

Pelagia found the huge church empty. Her grandmother had described to her where all the cleaning materials were kept, so she was hard at work within minutes. She started by methodically polishing the tarnished silver. Young and energetic, it took her less than a quarter of the time her *yia-yia* would have required. By ten o'clock, the gleam of the silver matched the glint of the gold leaf. Pelagia even had time to stand back to admire the paintings and mosaics.

When the priest returned from his visit to a nearby *kafenion*, he blinked. A shaft of sunlight was coming through one of the upper windows in the dome and was falling directly on to a huge silver candlestick. It threw back a dazzling beam of almost supernatural brightness and, for a moment, he believed it was a divine sign rather than a perfect alignment of sunshine and polished metal.

A second later the sun had moved, and the moment passed. The priest went into his office behind the sanctuary and busied himself with the church's paperwork. There was always plenty.

At around ten thirty, one or two people began to drift through the doors, cross themselves and light a candle, before walking down towards the reliquary. These were people who were in the habit of coming every day, mostly widows, but a few recently widowed men, too. It was part of the ritual of their day. For the men, it was what they did before going to the *kafenion*, for the women it was a prelude to cooking the midday meal, a routine that could not be broken. Some left quickly; a few others sat in the body of the church, men on the left and women on the right, before leaving.

They were used to seeing Kyria Leontidis there, dressed in mourning, so the woman in black cleaning at the front of the church did not at first attract their attention.

Pelagia was sweeping the floor with a soft broom, meticulously chasing dust even from the most obscure corners. She moved into view in front of the altar, her broom swishing to and fro. Most of the small group who had been in the church had now left. Just one man, Spiros Kouris, remained.

He stared straight ahead. He did not have especially good eyesight, but what he was looking at astonished him. It was not the image of sacred beauty and purity as portrayed in the spectacular representation of the Virgin Mary in the dome above. This was very different. Framed in silhouette against the fretwork screen was a woman who looked more like a goddess than the mother of God. Her black Lycra top and trousers hugged her figure tightly. Her mane of glossy, dark hair caught the light. It reached her waist and seemed to move independently as her body rocked from side to side as she swept. She was unconscious of her perfection, and totally unaware of being observed.

Spiros sat in the church longer that day than was his usual habit. And the following day he came earlier. And stayed even longer. When a friend asked him why he was so late turning up for a game of cards at the *kafenion*, he was vague about the reason. When asked by his wife why he was later than normal getting home, he said that the queue for vegetables had been unusually long.

Spiros Kouris began to notice another man, twenty-five or so years old, also staying longer than usual in the church. He knew that Socrates Papalambros's mother had died recently, as he had seen her photograph on a death notice pinned outside.

The younger man stood in the corner of the church, scribbling on small squares of paper before scrunching them up, one after the other, and stuffing them into his now-bulging pockets. Kouris knew that they were requests to the priest, but clearly Socrates was unsure of what to ask or how to ask for it.

Socrates was contemplating a picture of Saint Andrew, who had been tied for three days to the cross. Three days of suffering seemed very little compared with his own, he thought. He withdrew to a seat at the back of the church and sat, looking ahead.

Meanwhile, Pelagia innocently dusted and polished.

Word got around. Little by little, nearby *kafenions* started to empty and the church began to fill. How wonderful that people appreciated its beauty and its art, thought the priest. Some days, almost every seat on the left-hand side of the church was taken.

One after another, they queued to kiss the icon. Many of them had been eating *souvlaki* and imprints of their greasy lips were left behind. They sat as if to pray, and, with a flowing river of Byzantine chant in the background, they stared without shame at the female figure in front of them, just as they would look upon an icon. She moved around,

still unaware of their gaze; often her cleaning rhythm almost became a dance. Her ears were plugged into playlists made by her DJ boyfriend and, whether she was vacuuming, polishing or dusting, she threw herself into the task with every gram of energy she had. Sweat sometimes ran down her arms, and the back of her T-shirt became transparent, her temples damp.

Spiros Kouris began to dress much more carefully, rotating the four suits in his wardrobe and putting on a tie, and made regular visits to the barber to have his greying hair and moustache trimmed. He had not taken such pride in his appearance for many years. His wife was happy to see it. Like all the other men in the church, he imagined that his connection with Pelagia was real, just as real as the relationship they experienced with the Virgin herself. The fact that every man in the church felt the same did not affect him. He sat there for several hours, until Pelagia's cleaning duties were over, and then went to buy groceries, before taking them home with a spring in his step.

The money the priest counted for candles rose exponentially and, though he kept reordering, deliveries could not arrive quickly enough. He was also kept busy with a flow of requests written on small pieces of paper asking for special intercession. Many of them simply said: 'Lead us not into temptation.' Very few were more specific.

The only person who did not seem to notice Pelagia was the priest. He had not even realised that there was a new cleaning lady. All he saw was that the church looked as pristine as it had on the day it first opened its doors.

Early one morning, he was kneeling in private prayer, his eyes shut against the world so that he could concentrate.

Then he caught a whiff of something. It was not incense or candles. It was something sweeter, though he could not identify it. When he opened his eyes, he found himself staring straight into a woman's bosom, round and firm. Pelagia, at last no longer wearing black for her late great-uncle, was close by, polishing the glass that protected an icon. He hastily got up, almost tripping over his habit, and left the church. He needed some fresh air.

'God moves in mysterious ways,' he said to himself. 'No wonder the church is so full.'

The 'disappearance' of the menfolk had upset their wives. One woman had taken on a private investigator to track her husband and had been incredulous when he had reported back, simply, that he was in church.

Several *kafenion* owners also now complained. 'Get rid of that girl,' they said to the priest. 'She is destroying our business.'

The priest considered the situation carefully. Pelagia was not to blame. This woman was a divine creature, a manifestation of God's omnipotence, her innocence no crime; her beauty no fault of her own, no act of malice. He had an immaculate church, a big congregation and the coffers were full. It would be wrong to fire her.

One morning, the church was so full that a few men had even been obliged to sit on the right-hand side. They waited for the young woman to appear. And then they waited some more.

Eventually, they heard a buzzing sound. A few of them leaned forward. An industrial-sized vacuum cleaner appeared, followed by a woman, her head held high. She was like a farmer pushing an old-fashioned plough. It was not Pelagia. If the vacuum cleaner had not been so noisy, the murmurs of disappointment that rippled across the church might have been audible.

Maria Leontidis had rested. She was a bit plumper now after her convalescence, and the warmth of the spring sunshine had made her aching bones feel young again.

As the men were all leaving en masse, the priest walked into the church. He immediately understood the reason. The huge profits from candle sales had allowed him to buy better cleaning equipment for the church. Maria had returned in triumph.

The *kafenions* were full again that day, and wives welcomed their husbands home for lunch. Spiros Kouris walked slowly home. His wife smiled at him fondly when he came in. He reminded her of the man she had married.

I doubt that old Spiros ever really imagined that Pelagia would notice him, but female beauty can have a strong effect on a man, as I know myself, all too well.

It's so easy to fall into the trap of worshipping it. We are all attracted to certain aesthetic ideals, even if we tell ourselves not to be, and I know that your looks were what made me notice you that first night in the cinema bar. Instant attraction takes us unawares, unprepared. Perhaps it is a curse to be so good-looking that people are immediately drawn to you, maybe it's a burden to be judged initially by what you look like rather than on your personality. Wherever you are now, perhaps someone else has walked into a room and felt as if their heart has somersaulted inside their chest. I don't suppose I was the first, or last, man on whom your smile had that effect.

I stayed in Patras for nearly three weeks, enjoying its scale and the anonymity it gave me. I went to different cafés and tavernas every day and did not have to explain anything about myself to anyone. That first visit to the church was not the last. I often went there just to sit, to enjoy its extravagant decoration and to think. Maria Leontidis was often there, noisily vacuuming. It made me smile.

Whether or not Saint Andrew really did perform the miracle of healing the governor's wife, the new basilica dedicated to him has some kind of power. I felt it myself. The light and the beauty gave me some moments of pure joy.

I was still thinking about my infatuation with you, and whether you felt even a fraction of what I did, as I drove up into the mountains towards Kalavrita, a beautiful but melancholy place whose people suffered extreme brutality under the German occupation. The monument to the innocent victims of the massacre that took place there on 13 December 1943 was one of the most powerful I have visited. The various memorials in the town (including a museum dedicated to the events leading up to the killings) will never allow anyone to forget the murder of nearly five hundred men and boys, and the torching of every home. Spelled out on the hillside above this town was the word Eirini – Peace. The town will always remember what happened there, but I came away with the understanding that healing begins with forgiveness. I am not comparing what you did to me with the suffering of the people of this place, but the same principle applies, and I know I am not there yet. Despite the heavy atmosphere, I stayed in Kalavrita for a few days before going on a narrow-gauge railway line that took me down a spectacular gorge to the sea. There was something very innocent, very charming, about arriving at an old-fashioned train station, and I stayed there by the little harbour at Diakofto for more than a week, before returning to Kalavrita to pick up the car. My journey from there took me down a precipitous mountain road, past gushing waterfalls and through small villages.

I eventually crossed the strip of water that divides the Peloponnese from Central Greece via the graceful suspension bridge at Rio. I was heading in the direction of Messalonghi, a place famous for its association with Byron (a byword for seduction).

Everywhere I travelled in Greece I noticed streets and squares named Vyronas: Byron. I hear that there is even a whole area of Athens that bears his name. It's tantamount to hero worship. The city of Messalonghi bears Greece's closest connection with the English lord. I didn't like it at first, but after a few days began to appreciate that it is a place dense with history.

Messalonghi is so low-lying as to be almost below the water. It is not picturesque in any sense, but the setting is dramatic, with towering mountains rising immediately behind, and it occupies a strategically important position on the map.

The way he is memorialised throughout the country, one could get the impression that Byron single-handedly kicked the Turks out of Greece. The fact is that he did not once raise a sword in the war of independence, but he was the inspiration to other nations to aid the Greeks in their aim to free themselves from almost four hundred years of occupation.

I wanted to try to understand how the most famous Englishman in Greece is seen by the Greeks themselves. He was charismatic and roguish, but deeply damaged by the events of his childhood and the physical disability with which he struggled throughout his short life. I met several Greeks who disapproved on moral grounds of his treatment of women, of an incestuous relationship he'd had and of his homosexuality. He is still remembered as a hero, though many people are not quite sure why.

I went into the local museum in Messalonghi, housed in an old mansion where the walls literally drip with the damp and humidity that permeates this town.

Oil paintings would be destroyed by this atmosphere, so only copies hang there. One is a famous portait of the poet in which he wears the extravagant military dress he had commissioned for himself.

There is also a copy of a painting by Delacroix, 'Greece on the Ruins of Messalonghi'. It was the first time I have ever seen a faded copy of an original and yet still been moved by it. A ravaged and decolletée woman in Greek traditional costume stands on the remains of a building, the hand of a dead man protruding from the rubble. A turbanned invader plants a flag in the background, and there is no doubt that the violation of this beautiful figure is a crime. This picture tells you about the bigger story of Messalonghi: in 1826, two years after Byron's death, the town was under siege for a third time, and the population made an attempt to break out. Thousands were killed in what is known as the 'Exodus'. The town will always be in mourning for its past.

From the museum, I strolled to the memorial garden commemorating the Exodus. Here there is a graceful, perhaps idealised, statue of Byron. In the sharp winter light, his expression made me think of a dejected child. While I was standing there gazing at it, a municipal worker who was clearing some fallen palm-tree branches stopped to talk.

'People don't know about this act of bravery by ordinary folk against the Turks,' he said. 'They think Byron expelled them . . . Byron! He died long before we got rid of them!'

I knew that Byron hadn't died fighting and thought that he had been struck down with malaria (easy to believe, having been savaged by mosquitoes myself every night of my stay). The man leaning on his broom, however, was eager to tell me a different version of Lord Byron's 'death story', a tale that he regarded as the true one.

'Being handsome, clever and rich doesn't always do you any good,' he said afterwards, going back to his sweeping.

EYEWITNESS
1824

CARTE POSTALE

Rio-Antirrio Bridge

Messalonghi had always been something of a backwater. For some months of the year, it was almost *under*water. A fishing town only just above sea level, Messalonghi had marshy meadowland all around it and streets that turned into swamps in the rainy season. It sometimes seemed that the whole town would be swallowed by the sea and would sink beneath the sludge. One day it might get cut off from the world and cease to exist altogether, with the millions of mosquitoes being the only inhabitants – along with a few fishermen living in houses on stilts in the lagoon.

In recent months, Messalonghi had been packed with hungry brigades of Suliotes, unpredictable and underpaid soldiers from Epirus. Some said that they presented an even greater danger to the townsfolk than the Turkish troops, who were still lurking nearby, having unsuccessfully besieged the town only two years before.

There was plenty of noise, with dozens of soldiers milling around in the streets, some on duty but others rowdy or drunk, alongside the usual cacophony made by people selling their wares, among whom the fish sellers were the most vociferous.

In this not entirely pleasant or salubrious atmosphere, a rumour began to circulate that the English aristocrat Lord Byron was on his way to help the people of Messalonghi, and perhaps the whole of Greece.

Lord Byron, in self-imposed exile from England, had found his life's mission: to ally himself with the liberation of Greece from Turkish occupation. For many years a philhellene, the poet believed passionately in the right of this country (where the very notion of democracy had been born) to an independent future and of its oppressed people to be free.

Through a significant financial contribution (mostly earnings from his bestselling poetry), he had supported Alexandros Mavrokordatos, the Commander-in-Chief and Governor of Western Greece. In Byron's eyes, he was the most stable of the Greek leaders and was popular for having successfully resisted the first siege of Messalonghi.

Mavrokordatos lost no time in spreading the word of Byron's arrival in the city, and of writing extravagantly

to him, until Byron's head must have swelled with self-importance.

'I am depending on you to secure the destiny of Greece,' Mavrokordatos wrote.

When messengers arrived to confirm the day of his arrival, the city began to hum with excitement. Every household counted the days.

'I want to go and see him. *Please* . . .' Despina Dimotsis begged her father, a wealthy merchant.

Everyone – even sixteen-year-old girls – was in a frenzy at the prospect of his visit. In this grey coastal town, such a colourful event was eagerly anticipated.

Despina's younger sister, Fotini, was nagging, too.

'The streets are no place for young women,' their father said firmly.

Only when he realised that his wife, Eirini, was as keen to be a spectator as their daughters did Emilios Dimotsis relent. He would be close by, with a group of local dignitaries in a welcoming party, and their mother and a maid would

accompany them. It was, after all, a historic occasion. Lord Byron's massive donation to the armed forces might save Greece from the Turks. He might turn out to be the saviour of their country.

'He's not just a celebrated poet,' said his wife with a playful smile.

One day, early in January, a vast crowd gathered at the quayside. There were ordinary townspeople, merchants, governing officers, priests and soldiers, and all were eager for their first sighting of Byron. Soldiers fired muskets into the air and there were artillery salutes as the poet stepped off the boat.

The rules of etiquette had to be followed, with formalities and official greetings, and Byron was gracious, despite an exhausting journey and feeling ill. Short speeches were made and there were ripples of applause.

The two girls, Despina and Fotini, and their mother were in an area reserved for women. Being smaller than almost everyone there, all three of them had a very limited view and craned their necks to try to catch a glimpse of the entourage.

'I can't see *any*thing,' moaned Fotini.

'I can! I can!' boasted her older sister. 'I can see everything!'

Eirini stood on tiptoe and looked in the same direction. At a distance, she could see a man flanked by two others. They were several centimetres taller than him. Could this be the person they were all waiting for? He seemed almost insignificant.

Byron cast his eyes wearily over the assembled crowd but then remembered that he must live up to their expectations

and put on the performance they hoped for, elegantly smiling and waving.

The journey from Kephalonia had not been an easy one, and he had been unwell for some time. The roughness of the crossing had not helped. Happily, he was now on dry land and it was just a short walk from where he disembarked to the house that had been prepared for his stay.

'It's almost as if he is *crippled*,' said a woman standing next to Eirini Dimotsis, watching the famous poet move awkwardly towards them. 'Is he limping?'

'I believe he is,' Eirini replied. He was not at all as she had imagined him. Not at all.

Her daughters were not listening to this conversation. The excitement of the day, the colour and pageantry of the occasion, were not to be spoiled for them.

As he approached, and the crowd parted to let him through, the girls realised he was looking their way. In a striking red military jacket, with golden epaulettes, Lord Byron was even more dashing than they had expected.

Despina was not the only female in the crowd staring at him in admiration. Byron was accustomed to being the centre of attention and having the eyes of thousands devouring him. He encouraged it, basking in it and welcoming the adulation.

He liked to make a big impression. If this were not the case, he would not have dressed up as he did, would not have worn exotic headdresses or commissioned extravagant helmets in the style of great Greek warriors.

Byron loved to be loved, but even more important for him was to have an *object* for his love. He did not feel alive unless he had a place to focus this driving force of his. Even when he was confronted by a large crowd, he would single out an individual. Women had been known to faint simply from feeling the power of his brief attention.

His eyes, encircled with their dark lashes, darted around the crowd until they met Despina's. They rested on hers with a lascivious curiosity that he made no attempt to conceal.

As his entourage processed closer to where the women stood, Despina saw two limpid pools of light. In the background, the Mediterranean stretched out into infinity, and the eyes that locked with hers were equally fathomless. She found herself drowning in a mixture of blue and grey with splashes of violet. Byron's eyes were like a spring sky on a stormy day, in all its beauty, variety and passion. She did not look away but boldly stared back.

He drank in the sight of the creamy skin that had always been hidden from the sun, her tiny waist, the slight flush on her cheeks, which he knew was the result of his momentary focus on her. She reminded him fleetingly of his 'maid of Athens', a young girl with whom he had enjoyed a brief flirtation, and he feasted his eyes on her childish neck and tiny ears and nose.

The mind of Despina's younger sister had already wandered elsewhere. A short distance behind Lord Byron, Fotini noticed a slim, dark-haired boy. His expression was sullen, and it was hard to discern from his demeanour whether he was friend or servant. The teenager, who was carrying some bags, was in fact acting as Byron's valet. Though he was grateful for the charity that the English aristocrat had shown his family back in Zakynthos, he had begun to feel uncomfortable about being the object of Byron's relentless, amorous attention.

'Look! Look, Despina!' said Fotini, tugging on her sister's sleeve. 'Look at that boy!'

Despina only had eyes for the older man.

'His mouth,' she giggled, ignoring her younger sister. 'It says "Kiss me".'

Byron's shapely mouth was as remarkable as his eyes.

'Girls! Keep your voices down, please,' said their mother.

Even their maid seemed embarrassed by their comments. In such a public place, they were not decent.

Fotini had no interest now in the older man with streaks of silver in his hair and a slight limp. She was still staring at the beautiful, sulky boy who trailed along at the back of the party.

As Byron progressed towards his new home, he glanced over his shoulder to look at Despina again; he knew that she would still be staring. This time, her dark and treacly look penetrated him like an electric shock. He felt it still burning in the back of his neck as they walked away.

Was it that very moment? Was it that specific 'look' of admiration from Despina that cast a spell on Byron and was the turning point, the beginning of his end?

Fotini soon forgot about the 'little princeling', as she had nicknamed Byron's valet, Loukas, but Despina could not get the image of Lord Byron out of her head. For many days she languished, unable to sleep or eat, incapable of freeing her mind or body from the grip of a childish crush.

'Come on, Despina,' coaxed the maid. 'You must try to eat something.'

Not far away, Byron, too, was lying in bed, tossing and

turning. He had himself fallen into a fever, with fits and faints that began to weaken him by the day.

'It's the eye,' one of the servants darkly commented, as doctors fretted and frowned at his bedside. 'Someone has cast the evil eye!'

'But nobody here wishes Lord Byron evil,' snapped one of the foreign doctors who was desperately trying to save the ailing Byron. 'Only the Turks would wish anything bad on him!'

The servant held her tongue. An English doctor was not going to listen to an uneducated Greek woman. As far as he was concerned, casting the evil eye was always a matter of jealousy, or of willing bad on someone. It was a simple curse, easy to comprehend. He knew well enough that Byron had even mentioned it in his poetry ('I know him by the evil eye, That aids his envious treachery'). What was unknown to him was that the *mati*, the eye, was not only cast by an envious or malicious look.

'It's all the adulation, you fool,' she muttered under her breath. What the doctors and most of Byron's entourage did not understand was that it could also be *admiration* that opened a door for the devil. When the doctors were out of the room, she took the small glass of water that was by the poet's bedside and put into it a drop of oil. It sank immediately, confirming what she already knew. The evil eye was there.

During March, Byron was in pain, with constant headaches and sweats. The doctors attending him were in despair and could think of no other way to treat him than with frequent bloodletting. This weakened him further and, as his condition worsened, panic, argument and ineptitude did little to improve matters.

Each day during these awful weeks Despina sat at her window, hoping and waiting. She once glimpsed Lord Byron in the distance, on horseback, but she yearned for another sighting of him. Rumours that a delirium was keeping him bed-bound kept her awake at night.

One afternoon, in April, when both sea and sky were slate-grey and rain was beating violently at her window, she was in a frenzy of agitation. A gale whined and howled outside and seemed to penetrate the walls themselves. She paced the room, unable to settle either at reading or embroidery. An earthquake the previous month, and now this unsettled weather, created a sense of apocalyptic doom. Suddenly, a bolt of lightning cracked across the sky and into the sea.

When Byron's death was announced the following day, it shocked the entire city. Perhaps the person who suffered more than anyone was Despina. She had never experienced such loss, such emptiness.

For the third time in her life, she set eyes on her idol. This time he was lying in the church of Agios Nikolaos, inside his coffin. Once again, he was surrounded by a crowd, though now they were mourning his departure rather than celebrating his arrival. His closed eyes could no longer charm.

Grief swept through Messalonghi. Guns were fired from the fortress, Easter Week celebrations were cancelled, shops and public offices were closed and three weeks of mourning declared. On the intended day of the funeral, it was as though the heavens wept. Torrential rain meant that it had to be postponed. When it took place on the following day, thousands lined the streets to say farewell.

No one shed more tears than Despina. Her eyes were swollen with weeping, oblivious to the damage they had done. In the years that followed, there would be talk of Lyme disease, malaria, epilepsy, or simply the excessive use of leeches. The theories proliferated and were endlessly argued over.

Byron's maid maintained for the rest of her life that it was the power of the *mati*, but nobody would ever blame the innocent Despina. It had never occurred to anyone that such a 'look' had come from her, so she would never carry the burden of a crime.

'If they had let me do the *xematiasma*, to cast out the evil eye,' the maid said, 'our lovely lord might still be with us.'

If only they had listened.

I'm not sure that I believe in curses but the idea of the 'eye' as a form of protection appeals to me. It crosses various religions and several continents and cultures, and nowadays I always carry one on a keyring. Just in case.

I read a lot about Byron during my time in Messalonghi, and by the end of my stay I felt only profound pity and sadness for him. It was easy for him to get women to fall in love with him (he had an animal magnetism that few could resist), but his deepest emotions were saved for men, who often did not return his love. The last few months of his life were spent not just in a state of delirium and sickness; he was also torn apart by his passion for a teenage boy, a desperate love that was never requited.

Byron's breaking heart led him to thoughts of death. In past weeks, I have felt this tendency in myself and I am unashamed to admit that there have been moments when I did not want to live.

Byron wrote this in January 1824 and it was to be his last poem:

'Tis time this heart should be unmoved,
Since others it hath ceased to move:
Yet, though I cannot be beloved,
Still let me love!

My days are in the yellow leaf;
The flowers and fruits of Love are gone;
The worm — the canker, and the grief
Are mine alone!

Byron died three months after writing this. It was his
valediction to love and life. I wonder if his foolish love for
an adolescent boy weakened him to the point of dying. Who
knows? But it definitely caused him terrible unhappiness as
his life ebbed away. I thought about how love can give us
so much joy but, when unrequited, delivers misery in much
greater measure. Would I let rejection destroy me, as I believe
it helped destroy Byron?

The hotel I stayed in during my weeks there was almost
inspirationally seedy. It had been built during the military
dictatorship and had not been touched since 1970. I moved the
desk towards the balcony windows to get a view of the sea as
I wrote, and there was no television to bother me. The towels
were like sandpaper and the sheets grey, but at least they were
changed each day. In a perverse way, I grew to love it. What
more would anyone expect for twenty euros a night? The
main benefit of this enormous place, where only ten per cent
of the rooms were occupied, was the absence of anything to do
with Christmas (no mechanical singing Father Christmas, no
baubles and no piped carols). There was just a pretty model

of a ship made out of lights that stood in reception. In many places, this karavaki takes the place of a Christmas tree.

It was unsettling to spend Christmas Day itself alone. I rang my brother and could hear his children singing 'Jingle Bells' in the background. I felt so isolated. It was the one moment when I almost flew home and put an end to these travels. Fortunately for me, Christmas does not drag on in Greece in the way it does in England. For most people it's just a day off, and life goes back to normal soon after. Overall, my days in Messalonghi were productive enough, and I got plenty of writing done, glancing up every so often to look through the dirty windows at the sea.

It was the last day of December when I left Messalonghi. I ended up that night in a place I don't even want to name. New Year's Eve is an evening I detest even when life is good, but I managed to choose somewhere where even the birds did not sing. However low my mood, the world had been spinning towards another new year, and within a few days I knew that I too had reached a turning point.

A few days later, after a detour to the lovely town of Arta, I arrived in Preveza. It was late when I checked into my hotel, and the town was quiet, as are most places out of season. The following day, though, the place was transformed.

That morning, I was woken at dawn by the tolling of bells. They continued for some time and, when they finally stopped, a voice took over. It was a priest broadcasting the liturgy. I opened my shutters and saw the belltower just opposite my window and, fixed to its roof, a pair of huge, old-fashioned loudspeakers. Realising that there was no chance of going back to sleep, I dressed, wandered downstairs and went out into the square.

It was impossible to get inside the church. It was crammed, with hundreds of people outside, craning their heads to see what was happening within.

Needing a coffee, I wandered towards the sea to find a café. As I turned from the narrow, shadowy street, I felt an unexpectedly warm breath on my skin, and saw that sunshine was making the sea sparkle. Most of Greece had seen snow in past days, but in this little harbour town a warm west wind had brought a sudden rise in temperature. These are known in Greece as 'halcyon days', and in January no Greek is surprised when they are given this tantalising glimpse of spring which can disappear as fast as it arrives.

What a beautiful day it was. The crowd was not just in church; there were hundreds at the water's edge, too, gathering as if a big event was about to take place. Everyone had made an effort. Some men were in suits (though many had removed their jackets), and women had dressed to impress their friends. Only the fishermen seemed to carry on as normal, selling the previous night's catch straight off their boats.

It was 6 January, a public holiday throughout the country, and in the entire row of cafés along the seafront there wasn't one free table. I asked a couple if I could share and, though they were a little hesitant, they agreed. Once I had ordered my coffee, I asked them what was happening.

'It's the Theophania,' answered the woman, as if I should know.

'Like Epiphany?' I suggested. 'When the wise men came?'

'In the Greek Orthodox Church, we're celebrating a different event,' she said. 'We believe that it was when Christ was baptised. It was his first appearance as God. And today

the priest blesses the water by throwing a cross into the sea.'

Seeing that I was genuinely interested, she continued to explain.

'And they say that, during the Christmas period, there are goblins, the kallikantzaroi, who stir everything up and generally make trouble. Today, we clear the seas of them so that sailing can begin again.'

'The sea is of supreme importance to us, with all our coastline and islands,' added her husband sentimentally. 'It's in our souls, you know.'

As I looked across, there was growing activity on the esplanade.

'And what's going on by the water right now?'

'Leonidas will tell you,' said the woman, laughing. 'When he was young and handsome, he participated in this ceremony.'

She rubbed his fat stomach affectionately.

'I would sink like a stone now!' he joked. 'She cooks too well, my wife.'

I took a great liking to this couple. They seemed like equals, very easy in each other's company, and with a love that seemed alive.

Leonidas was a local lawyer, and eager to give me chapter and verse on the ritual. His wife, Dora, had been a teacher, and was retired now.

'Quite soon, the priest will throw a cross into the sea, and those boys over there will jump in and try to find it.'

'So it's like a religious swimming competition?' I asked.

'Yes, it is,' he said. 'I took part in my younger days! Just the once. And so did my best friend from school, Giorgos.'

162

'Leonidas . . . do you have to tell this story?' said his wife, putting a restraining hand on his arm.

'Why not, agapi mou? It does have a happy ending, one way and another.'

She gave him a kind but long-suffering glance.

'Look, matia mou!' said Leonidas. 'He's there! Can you see him?'

'Yes,' she said, pointing him out for me. 'In a black cap.'

A little way off, I could see a man looking out over the water.

'Poor old Giorgos,' she said.

The young men of the town were getting ready to plunge into the sea.

HOLY WATER

Clock Tower, Agios Haralambos, Preveza

CREECE

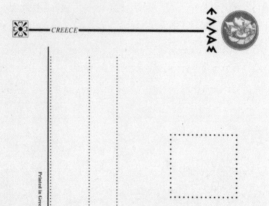

ΕΛΛΑΣ

Printed in Greece

HOLY WATER

It was 6 January 2010, and Giorgos Ziras was hovering near the entrance to the church. He could see past the dozens of heads to the far end of the aisle, where priests dressed in fine brocade and tall hats studded with jewels recited the ancient words. He had known the two older ones since schooldays and, even now, in spite of the long robes and frizzy beards, he saw them as boys. It seemed only a moment since they were all kicking a ball in the dust.

He watched young fathers enter the vestibule of the church, kiss the icon and then lift small children to do the same. Then they took candles from the box, lit them and planted them in a tray of sand, where they burned with a hundred others. There was standing room only in the church on that day. Only small children could weave their way between the plantation of adult legs to get to the front.

Outside the church loitered a small group of adolescent boys in ceremonial orange brocade. Scuffed trainers protruding from beneath hems and splashes of acne made them look less sacred and more profane. They were waiting for the moment when it would be time to bear the precious cross to the sea, but until then they kicked a stone around in the paved area outside. Nearer the water, a group of young men was waiting, ready to brave the waves.

On the same occasion, one year in the late 1970s, the church had also been overflowing. Everything was taking place as it always did, according to the rhythm and pace of the liturgy.

Giorgos had been into church earlier that morning to light a candle, his swimming trunks beneath his clothes. Now he stood outside, wrapped in a towel, waiting, shivering, along with his fellow competitors.

The group who stood ready to plunge into the sea that January morning had been carefully selected. They were members of the town's water-polo squad and, for several of them, it was their tenth year of taking part. A position in the squad gave them more status in the town than even being a member of the town council or police force. The chance to take part in the Theophania ritual, to dive for the cross the priest would soon throw into the sea, was just one of the privileges. But for Giorgos Ziras, the team's newest member, it was difficult to enjoy the prestige when the rest of the squad resented his arrival. He had been training with them for a long time, but once the coach had started picking him for key games last season, their dislike of him had become evident.

The joining of a new member usually meant the imminent departure of an existing one and, a few days before, Mihalis Nikopoulos had been told that he would not be needed that season. For a decade, he had been the backbone of the team, its highest-ever goal-scorer, and now he had been given the news of his dismissal. Without any sense of tact, the coach told him that he could have one last go at retrieving the cross but that, this coming summer, his ten years as captain of the team were over. Mihalis was a tough character, but the coach even more so. Mihalis betrayed no emotion, but a bomb inside him began to tick.

Giorgos Ziras's speed and agility in the water were much admired by the coach, and had won him the place in the team. Mihalis had the power of a small speedboat, but he was losing too many points for fouls and had become a liability to the team.

Palm fronds had been erected in an arch on the swimmers' platform, and the contenders stood beneath it. Giorgos was smaller and younger than the rest. Most of the others jostled about, having mock-fights, easy and familiar with one another. Many of them had been together in the team for several years. The majority were impressively well built, with powerful torsos that were the result of physical training or recent army service. Giorgos knew that he would never look like them. Even though he swam every day in the summer, any physical training just made him skinnier. Despite his grandmother's insistence that he was like a swordfish, the only sea creature he really resembled was a sea-snake, an eel-like creature that Giorgos had once seen in local waters.

Giorgos noticed Mihalis staring down into the water and not joining in with the joshing. Suddenly, he looked up and fixed Giorgos with a penetrating stare.

The younger man had never felt the power of such hatred and looked away immediately. He shivered, feeling his body temperature drop a few degrees, and drew his towel more tightly around him.

At the front of the ever-swelling crowd stood Margerita Ziras, holding her son's clothes. Giorgos glanced across at her, needing his mother's reassurance, but he could see that she was as nervous as him, her face taut and tense. She managed a half-wave.

Everyone was out in the streets that day: more than a thousand people dressed in their best, some almost in wedding finery, coiffured, perfumed, on parade. This was a social occasion as well as a religious one. Sunlight fell dazzlingly on the water, and the spectators who lined the water's edge put up a hand to shield their eyes. Some even donned a pair of fashionable sunglasses that made the men look mafioso (something they did not mind) and the women a little more Jackie O. For a few, the opportunity to greet each other and to calculate the cost of a neighbour's jewellery was enough to bring them out on to the street.

They heard the town band coming closer, as the priests, their attendants, the mayor and other municipality dignitaries processed from the church. There were local representatives from the army and navy, too. Anyone who had a uniform put it on that day, and wore it proudly.

Giorgos looked around and, over the heads of the crowd, he could see the top of a priest's hat and the flash of brass instruments behind. The column of people finally appeared and continued down towards the sea. With great difficulty, encumbered by the weight and volume of their robes, the clergy climbed into a small fishing boat. There were gasps of consternation as one of the priests, who weighed nearly two hundred kilos, tipped the boat almost to the point of capsize.

The youths on the platform knew that their moment was coming. Soon, the most senior priest would throw the cross into the water and the contenders would dive in, racing to be the one to retrieve it. The winner would be specially blessed but, more importantly, would achieve a hero's status in the town. For ten years, Mihalis had been that winner, effortlessly lapping through the icy water to find the cross.

The friendly pushing and shoving on the swimmers' platform had stopped now. Towels were dropped to the ground, goggles pulled down over their eyes. The boys watched as the little motorboat, dangerously low in the water, with its holy cargo and the fisherman at the helm, made its way across the sea.

Finally, the boat came to rest. The priest stood and began to speak. It was nearly time. Giorgos felt his heart pounding with nerves, with fear, with anticipation of the cold. He also felt a sharp stab in his back. It was one of the swimmers elbowing him out of the way. Everyone was jostling for a position at the front. He felt himself being nudged towards the side. Jumping into the water early would mean instant disqualification, and his toes gripped desperately on to the edge of the platform.

The priest held up the cross, and the crowd fell silent. All eyes were focused on the glint of gold. The priestly incantations continued, almost drowned out by the spluttering of the boat's engine. The cross was attached to a long ribbon and the priest hurled it into the water, then pulled it up again. Once. Twice. On the third immersion, he released the ribbon and the cross flew free. This was the signal. Giorgos felt another firm shove in his side that pushed him off the side of the platform. His leg grazed against the splintering wood as he fell clumsily into the sea.

Even as he swam, he felt a foot in his stomach and another in his face. His goggles were slipping off his head and into the water, and he felt the salty sting in his eyes and realised that he had lost them. The sea was opaque, green, and with the froth of a dozen swimmers around him it was impossible to

see. He came gasping to the surface, coughing, foolish, blind.

Ahead of him, towards the priest, there was an eddy of water. All the swimmers must have dived beneath the surface now, so he took a lungful of air and went under. With small movements of his feet, he glided towards the blurred outline of the group that he could make out beneath the water. It was a mass of pale flesh apparently joined into one body, a many-legged monster beneath the waves. The youths must be somewhere close to the cross.

He had heard rumours that the 'winner' of the cross was always prearranged, but he dismissed the idea, knowing that he was the fastest swimmer and had to be in with a chance. By now, the other swimmers were running out of breath and, one by one, they were making their way to the surface. Giorgos continued to dive. He saw a glint, the corner of the cross. There was another swimmer still down there. A broad body, with a gold chain around the neck. Mihalis. As Giorgos approached, he swam off, displaying the row of dolphins that were tattooed up his back and neck, visible even in the murky, underwater light.

He must be going up for air, Giorgos thought. Now was his opportunity. He had only a second or two left. This was his chance.

The cross was held captive, wedged beneath a rock. What the other swimmers had not done was try to shift the rock. They had just pulled at the cross. Giorgos stood on the floor of the sea and leaned. The rock rolled, and he nudged the cross with his toe. It came free. In one swift movement, he took the ribbon and jerked it upwards. He felt a burning sensation in his lungs, a roar in his ears and a sudden claustrophobia.

He kicked his way to the surface, holding the precious cross above his head so that it would appear first, so that the crowd would see it. He came up, gasping, inside the circle of a dozen or so swimmers.

Some embraced him and kissed him on both cheeks to acknowledge his victory, but he could sense the half-heartedness of their response. He had not been expected to win.

It was impossible to see their expressions behind goggles, but a break appeared in the circle so he swam towards the little boat. The priest leaned down to receive the cross.

Then Giorgos made his way back towards dry land. By the time he reached the platform, the other swimmers were all standing there. A hand reached out. It belonged to his schoolfriend Leonidas. Exhausted and weak, he struggled out of the water. His mother was standing there, offering him his towel.

As he rubbed himself dry and looked around, he realised that someone was missing from the platform. Suddenly, he was aware that a name was being repeated all around him.

'Where is Mihalis?'

'Did you see him?'

'Was he down there?'

Questions came flying at him from all directions.

'He was . . . I saw him . . .'

Nobody was listening.

Three or four swimmers dived back into the water and swam towards the area where the cross had been found. One of the swimmers swam across to the boat to alert the priest. By now, a few other boats were circling, and everyone in them peered down into the water.

People were exclaiming and shouting and pointing. A wave of consternation passed through the spectators, too. Giorgos heard the inconsolable wails of Mihalis's mother and sisters. Soon, a message was being sent to a diver in a nearby town.

Giorgos searched the surface of the waves, his eyes replaying those last moments when he had seen Mihalis. He remembered how he had swum off just as he approached, and it had not been towards him but away from him.

People were crowding around him again.

'Was he there?'

'Did you see him?'

'What happened down there?'

'Did he have the cross?'

'Did he get it first?'

With a sickening sense of fear and panic, Giorgos could feel the rumours already beginning to circulate. It was well known that he and Mihalis were rivals in the team and that he had displaced the stronger, older man. Mihalis had successfully turned the rest of the team against him, and this was obvious both when they were in the water and when they were out of it. It was something more than rivalry. It was bitter acrimony, especially after the previous season, when Giorgos had outshone the more experienced player's goal performance. Now they were looking for Mihalis's body, and they knew that he must have been the last one to see him.

For three days they searched. Teams of residents patrolled the shores of nearby beaches in case he'd been washed up on one. Prevailing currents meant that he might be found further north, on one of the stretches of sand. Nothing. So there was no funeral, no finality to the story, and Mihalis's father made it clear to everyone in the *kafenion* on whom the suspicion fell.

The police talked to everyone, and to Giorgos last of all. By this time, they had built a picture of the relationship between the two men. In spite of the gossip that Mihalis had been involved in various local crimes, no one wanted to believe ill of their sporting hero. They ignored the armed robbery in mid-December in which two men had been killed. Mihalis's brother and uncle had been caught in the act and would soon be on trial for murder. Witnesses had all mentioned a third man and some had been expecting Mihalis's arrest. Giorgos had never been in any sort of trouble, but no one cared about that. Instead, they painted an image of him as a ruthless competitor who was capable of doing anything in order to win. With no body and no evidence, he could not be arrested or formally charged, but the community had made up its mind who was to blame.

Giorgos could not leave town. It would have been an

admission of guilt to flee like a fugitive, and to arrive somewhere else, without family, friends or past. Nobody did that unless they had something to hide. He even began to wonder himself if he was guilty in some way.

'What people don't want to hear, they won't listen to,' said his friend Leonidas.

The coach apologised to Giorgos when he told him he would have to drop him, but without the full support of his fellow team members they could not cohere as a team. His former team-mates went on to great glory in the national championships, and three of the players took part in the next Olympic Games.

Giorgos got himself a job an hour's drive away in a company that packed and exported feta cheese. He continued to live with his mother but never showed his face in the centre of town. From April to October, he would stop on his way home to swim alone on a deserted and inaccessible beach, but in the winter months he went straight home.

Three years after the 'death' of Mihalis, a service was held at the church. The congregation matched the Theophania crowd for size.

For nearly forty years Giorgos had lived in this way, like a shadow. He existed, but had no presence. Perhaps the most painful part had been to watch the decline of his mother. They never spoke of the event, but Giorgos knew that she felt the weight of her son's unprovable innocence and the stigma that had surrounded the family since that January morning. It had affected her everyday life, too.

Coming to the Theophania was his way of reinforcing

his innocence. It was the only day when it mattered to him to hold his head high. The swimmers were now the children and grandchildren of his own generation, but many of the spectators were the same.

He could not ask one of these robed clerics to forgive him, as there was nothing to forgive. In order to seek absolution, you had first to offer the sin. Four decades on, he still stood alone, feeling simultaneously guilty and innocent. A criminal without a crime.

This year, as always, Giorgos looked about at the people in the crowd to ensure he was not uncomfortably close to anyone who knew him. He particularly avoided the men who had swum on the day of Mihalis's disappearance.

As he looked to his left, something caught his eye. It was the back of a man's neck. Peeking out above the collar of a cheap leather jacket, he saw the snout of a dolphin. The owner was virtually bald, so it was particularly noticeable. Tattoos had become more popular than ever in recent years, but it was less usual to see one on a man this age.

A strong sense of ill-ease swept over Giorgos and he felt a sweat break out on his back. The man in front of him was wearing semi-opaque sunglasses and a dark blue cap, and his features were obscured by its brim. He stood on the edge of the crowd. Could it be him? Could it really be Mihalis Nikopoulos, after all these years? In height he seemed the same, but his bulk seemed a little reduced.

Whether or not it was the man who had invisibly destroyed his life, Giorgos's instinct was to create a distance between them. His shaking legs slowed him down in his attempt to get away. As he walked, he encountered one of the few people with whom he still communicated. It was his loyal schoolfriend Leonidas, who had never once doubted Giorgos's innocence.

'Giorgos . . . *ti kaneis?*' he asked. 'How are you?'

Leonidas studied his friend with concern. Giorgos's face was drained of all colour.

'Are you all right?' he persisted, touching Giorgos's elbow.

'You know . . .' Giorgos replied, his voice quivering. 'The same as ever. And you? The children? The grandchildren?'

'*Ola kala,*' said his friend. 'All's well.'

The cross had just been thrown into the water and the crowd surged forward slightly to watch the frothing water. The turnout was bigger than ever this year and, these days, the words of the priests were amplified. A voice boomed out across the water and Leonidas had to shout to make himself heard above it.

'*Did you hear?*'

'Hear what?' shouted Giorgos cupping his hand.

'About old Markos Nikopoulos. Died yesterday.'

It gave Giorgos a jolt to hear the name. He had glimpsed Mihalis's father from time to time but had always managed to avoid coming face to face with him.

'His funeral is—'

'Today?'

'This afternoon. I just saw the notice.'

So the son had returned for his father's funeral. It made sense. It was the only event that would bring a man back under such circumstances, even if he discreetly remained in the shadows on his visit so that nobody else was aware of his presence, except perhaps close family. Giorgos knew beyond doubt that the man he had seen was Mihalis Nikopoulos. He *knew* he was alive.

The tears rolled down his face.

Leonidas was baffled. Why was his friend showing such grief at the death of the Nikopoulos father? It did not quite make sense.

The relief almost tore Giorgos apart. Exoneration. Vindication. Absolution. The words circled in his mind.

He was sobbing uncontrollably now, and Leonidas held him in his arms to support him.

Therefore with joy shall ye draw water out of the wells
of salvation.
Let us beseech the Lord for this water that it may be sanctified
by the power and virtue and descent of the Holy Ghost . . .

Like a mighty tidal wave, the words of the priest rang out over the sea.

The ritual of the Theophania was so dramatic, so bold,
so unexpected. To see people in the sea on a January day
was surreal, and it left a deep impression on me. The sheer
physicality of the athletes, performing with an accompaniment
of music and chanting, made me wish that the traditions of the
Church of England were more colourful.

Even the back of Giorgos's head, which I saw only in
the distance, seemed to speak of his years of continual, silent
suffering. All those decades of existing in the shadow of a bad
memory and an unspoken accusation must have taken an
enormous toll. He had lost more than half his life living in the
twilight, but the reappearance of Mihalis Nikopoulos gave him
the opportunity for renewal, a second baptism.

There was a moment as I was listening to this story when
I told myself that I must not let the years drift by, that I must
seize life and start again — and with conviction. During these
warm, early days of January, I felt myself begin to thaw.
The 'halcyon days' really are intoxicating, and Leonidas
told me why they are so called. According to Ovid, Alcyone,
the daughter of Aeolus, who ruled the winds, hurled herself

into the sea when her husband drowned. The couple were transformed into kingfishers (halcyons) and when Alcyone made her nest on the beach, her father calmed the seas in order to protect her eggs. These days of winter serenity are said to be for these nesting birds, and I admit that they gave me a wonderful sense of peace, too. I stayed on in Preveza to enjoy them, eating each night with Leonidas and Dora. Dora, as her husband had boasted, was a great cook, and she was determined to fatten me up. I had lost several kilos in the weeks after your non-appearance and my clothes were hanging off me, but by the time I left Preveza I was beginning to look healthy again.

I drove eastwards from Preveza towards Karpenisi. I took the wrong road at one point and found myself completely lost, on an unmade road high up in the mountains. For many hours, I was alone, far from civilisation but exhilarated by the solitude. The route was accidental, but it took me into magical landscapes which I would not have seen if I hadn't made a map-reading error. I began to wonder about serendipity. Can mistakes turn out to benefit our lives? Can the things that seem like disasters actually lead to better things? I wanted to hope so. At least I was beginning to consider the possibility. Up in the wilds of those mountains, I had moments of feeling free and light.

Ellie put the notebook down. She had been in Greece for four days now and was enjoying every moment of her time. During the day, she swam and sunbathed on the beach of her hotel in Tolon and, mid-afternoon, took a bus into Nafplio, where she explored something different each day (a castle, a church, a museum – it was a town rich in beauty and history, just as Anthony had described), before having a drink in the square and catching a bus back in time for dinner. On her second day, she wrote a postcard to her mother, knowing that she would be hoping for one. It seemed so old-fashioned to write it and then stick on six stamps, that left almost no space for the address. She smiled as she wrote her enthusiastic description of Nafplio. 'It has something special about it.' Without the evidence of Anthony's cards, she would have had little belief in it reaching its destination. To her friends, she just sent texts, with a selfie against a backdrop of the sea.

Ellie saved Anthony's notebook for the evening, reading a few stories a day on her balcony. She wanted, as atmosphere, the stillness of the night, the bright stars, the rhythmic noise of cicadas, the gentle lap of the waves on the beach. It seemed the right way to read this stranger's thoughts, privately and quietly, without the sound of pop music coming from the bar or the metronome beat of people playing beach tennis. Several times she had looked up on her map the distance between Nafplio and somewhere else that Anthony had visited. Her ideal would have been to go on a day-trip to Preveza or Patras, but enquiries at reception led her to the conclusion that a return bus journey even to Kalamata would be impossible in a day. She would stay put. Both Tolon and Nafplio were so delightful that she did not mind. Anthony's descriptions would have to suffice for now.

Greece was becoming more familiar to her both through his writing and through her own experience of being there. The scents of this country, the sound of its language, the flavour of its food and the smiles of its people were already sinking in, and she understood why Anthony had decided to go on his travels rather than return to London to face that dreary autumn. It had been one of the wettest on record, and she was glad for him that he had stayed away. His mood would not have been helped by the relentlessly grey days.

Ellie had never had a serious relationship and certainly not one that had caused her so much anguish. Girlfriends of hers had faced these traumas, and she had been a willing shoulder to cry on, but she had never imagined these emotions from a male perspective, and the bitterness Anthony described seemed very strange and strong.

Ellie's solitude on holiday was not so different from her day-to-day life. She knew that other guests in the hotel found it curious that she always ate alone, but she wanted to wear a badge advertising that she did not care. One night, a very nice couple in their sixties insisted that she join them for dinner but, even before the main course arrived, she knew more than enough about their granddaughter's exam results and a Caribbean cruise they had taken the previous year. Solitude was infinitely preferable and, for the rest of her stay, she retreated swiftly to her balcony as soon as dinner was over, with a glass of wine in hand.

That night, sitting on a simple plastic chair, her bare toes resting on the metal balcony railings, she thought about Anthony's sense of feeling 'free and light'. Perhaps the chilled wine had helped. She felt as if she were floating and, in that instant, there was nothing that troubled her. It was a precious moment, a rare and fleeting feeling. Calm and inquisitive, she read on.

I almost run out of words to describe the beauty of this country. Perhaps people who are born here, particularly those who have not travelled outside Greece, assume that the rest of the world looks like this, or perhaps they get so used to it that it no longer has an effect on them. I have had so many moments of love at first sight in Greece, so many instants when I have felt the lightning strike, the 'keravnovolos'. I am like an addict, waiting for the next time that my heart will almost be stopped by an unexpected view.

It is clear from their sculpture and architecture that beauty mattered to the Greeks in ancient times. When I look inside a glass case containing artefacts from five thousand years ago (Cycladic sculptures, for example), I can see that these are not purely functional objects. Not only did they understand aesthetics, they worshipped them.

Perhaps this is why I am so shocked when I see something ugly in Greece. I am often stopped in my tracks by beauty, but sometimes by ugliness, too. As in all things, this country wins the prize for extremes. There are landscapes that have been destroyed by the presence of huge concrete structures, put up and left half complete to stand perhaps for another thousand years: hotels, factories, office buildings simply abandoned midway through construction. Even with finished buildings, I sometimes look and just wonder 'why?' as I stare with horror at nine floors of orange-tinted windows and cracked concrete. In some areas, regulation seems not to exist. Styles, colours, materials clash together like anarchists and riot police.

One day towards the end of January, I saw a dam. A massive, abandoned dam. The rusting mechanism by which electricity should have been generated, the tonnage of concrete, the graffiti that is now daubed everywhere are a violation, a glimpse of hell. It will be there for ever like an open wound, the worst rape of a landscape I have ever seen. Millions of euros have been squandered and made someone somewhere very rich. I imagined visitors in another two thousand years trying to make sense of it all: the Acropolis, the dam across the Achelous. In the same country? What went wrong? It will be as mysterious as the Phaistos Disc.

I stopped there for a while. It was somehow impossible not to.

I felt like a tourist, as much as I had in Nafplio, but instead of taking in beauty and history, I was looking at destruction on a scale I have never seen before. Finally, I drove on. I wanted to put as many kilometres between me and this place as I could before darkness, so I drove and drove and drove, as if running from the devil, heading west again towards the sea.

Eventually, I came to a village that I liked the look of. I discovered later that it wasn't far from Dodoni, an ancient sanctuary. The village was mostly comprised of old traditional stone houses, but there was a pretty square with one kafenion and one taverna, and I spotted a bakery up a sidestreet. As I parked, I observed a dozen funeral notices on a board next to the small church. For some reason, I always stop to read them. They are the most obvious public notices in any place you go. People have to react quickly if they see the face of someone they know, because the funeral will be either that day or the next.

I find that learning who has died and how old they were tells me something about the place itself. If they are mostly in their late eighties or nineties, it is sad but comforting. Here, though, among the octogenarians posted up that day, was a much younger man. His name was Constantinos Arvanitis. He was sixty-two.

As I walked into the taverna, I realised the owner had been watching me loitering by the noticeboard.

'Gnorizeis kapio?' he asked. 'Someone you know? Costas Arvanitis?'

I was wearing a black T-shirt and black jeans that day, so perhaps he thought I was there for a funeral.

The people in the taverna were friendly enough and happy to have some business on a quiet Tuesday evening. It was called To Tzaki, which means 'fireplace', and in the corner was a huge log fire which the owner kept stoking. Even though the days were warm enough, the temperature plummeted at night and this cheerful glow was a welcome sight.

'We were all surprised by that one,' said the wife. 'Arvanitis was fit and healthy, always at his smallholding. Never missed a day there. Slim, vigorous, not a spare kilo on him.'

She brought a jug of water and some cutlery and set them

down on my table, continuing to talk as she did so. Her comments were addressed more to her husband than to me.

'Personally, I think there should have been a post-mortem, but his wife said no. So what can you do? The doctor wrote the certificate, and that's that. But I don't like it.'

'Eleni . . . you mustn't say that.'

'Agapi mou, it's too quick. A man dies suddenly. The wife doesn't shed a tear. Then he is in the ground. No questions asked.'

'That's normal here,' he said, turning to me. 'The funeral happens within twenty-four hours. It's tradition. It was a necessity I suppose, before the days of the morgue.'

'Yes, but we have refrigeration now, Oreste mou,' his wife chipped in.

'Eleni!'

'Anyway, there is the funeral tomorrow. And everyone will come back here afterwards. The menu is a bit limited today, as I'm getting the fish all ready for the makaria, the lunch afterwards.'

'Don't worry,' I said. 'I'll have whatever is easy.'

When his wife went into the kitchen, the man leaned over and said quietly:

'My wife won't believe it, but trust me, there was no foul play.'

He seemed very sure.

'Costas's wife had got suspicious because he kept being late home, and she asked me to find out whether he really was spending all that time at his kypos . . . so I went to check.'

The man was obviously keen to talk, but somehow reticent at the same time.

'You'll be gone soon, won't you?'

Satisfying himself that I wouldn't repeat it in the village, he told me what had happened.

IN LOVE
WITH LOVE

IN LOVE WITH LOVE

There had been little rain that winter, so the ground was hard. It was taking longer than usual to dig over, but Costas Arvanitis was glad to be out in the twilight, just at the time when the sun was going down and the moon was rising over the hills. The cypresses stuck out of the hills like blades.

He had been working in his smallholding all day, digging and digging, in an attempt to get the soil ready for planting. There were a few hectares, with half of them taken up by orange and olive trees. At about eight, he was ready to stop.

It was not love at first sight, but at first sound. His spade struck something. It was not the metallic *chung* of spade on flint, which set his teeth on edge and was a common sound in this rocky terrain, where he was endlessly sifting soil to rid it of stones. This was another tone. A bright *ching* that rang out like a musical note, a clear, ringing, bell-like sound, one that he had never heard before.

It was almost dark now, but he bent down to see what was beneath his spade. It was impossible to make anything out clearly, but he picked a little soil away with his fingernails, revealing what looked like a large white stone. He tried to lever it out of the earth, but it was stuck. It would have to wait until tomorrow. He gathered his tools, stood up and leaned backwards to bend his back. He could feel his bones creak. His body found the hours of labour a huge strain, but this little patch of land was his reason to get up in the morning, his life.

He ambled through the adjacent olive grove, flicking his cigarette lighter to illuminate the path through the trees. His *kypos* was almost a kilometre from the gravel track where he parked his truck, and it was getting to be a struggle for him to carry all his heavy tools. It took him half an hour in the darkness.

He was in no hurry. Twenty minutes later, he was in the village, and even then he stopped off first at the kiosk and then at the *kafenion* to delay his homecoming.

The nights were still cool and a wind had got up. He felt a chill on his lungs and the warming effect of the firewater that the owner immediately put on the bar in front of him was welcome.

'*Stin iyeia sou*,' said the *kafetzis*, putting a glass on the bar and filling it with clear liquid. 'Cheers.'

Costas tipped his head back and drank it in one, gently putting the glass back down on the bar for a refill.

Four men were playing cards in the corner and had not looked up when he entered. Few words or smiles were exchanged. Peace and quiet was valued in this place. The screen of the small television high up on the wall was blank.

Nobody took much interest in anyone else here. Everyone got on with his own business, and all had the same stories to tell. Most had children who had left the village, and wives waiting for them at home. They did not discuss politics because they shared the same views, and those with right-wing opinions went to the other *kafenion* in the village. It left little to talk about, and silence to fill the air.

The moment he stepped into his home, Costas heard a shrill voice:

'Where have you been? Why are you late? Dinner is cold! Did you bring onions? Couldn't you get here earlier? Have you been at the *kafenion*? Have you been drinking?'

His wife was shouting at him from a small scullery adjacent to the living area. The barrage of questions scarcely deviated each day, and neither did his grunted responses to each one.

Grey-haired, and as wide as she was high, Stella waddled into the room and put a plate down in front of him, and a second at the far end of the table.

He proceeded to eat, head bent over his plate, scooping food into his mouth without lifting his eyes. They had no conversation. This same pattern repeated itself every day, and had done so for many decades. He looked at the food but not at his wife. She slopped and slurped her way through her dinner. With only four or five remaining teeth, it was difficult for her to chew, and yet she continued talking, spraying pieces of meat and vegetables towards him as she kept up her assault of slurping and noise.

The television was on at full volume, with the screen split into eight squares. There was one woman and seven men, each politician stating his or her view of an economic problem to which there was no solution. No one listened to the others; all voices were raised, each person trying to be heard over the cacophony. The debate began in the morning and went on until night, on one channel or another.

Costas's life had two parts. Day and night. Tranquillity and noise.

Once he had eaten, he was ready for bed. The shower and WC were outside, just as they had been for all six decades of his life, and the water was unheated. Cold showers had never bothered him, but for Stella it was an excuse to avoid washing. Sometimes her skin was dark with dirt, but a lack of strong lighting and mirrors in the house meant that she was unaware of this. Like many women in this village, she had not seen herself for years. There was one small mirror in the outside shower room that Costas used for shaving, but it was too high for her to use. The burnt meals proved that she had no sense of smell, something he was reminded of each night as he climbed the stairs to the concrete-based bed they shared.

She was already under the thin blanket, tossing and turning and muttering in her sleep. He took his place next to her and gazed at the ceiling, a shaft of light penetrating the gap between the curtains and casting a beam on the faded marriage crowns that were nailed to the wall behind them.

Eventually, Costas fell asleep, waking the next day with the dawn to the eerie sound of his wife grinding her teeth. He slid out of bed, picked up his clothes, stole downstairs and grabbed his car keys from the shelf by the door. Within a few moments he was out of the house and starting his truck, praying that the coughing of its cold engine would not wake her.

It was only just light, but by the time he reached his *kypos* the sun would be above the line of the hills. Though his joints still ached, he was eager to get back to his digging.

His was the only vehicle on the road. In the twenty-minute journey he passed no one. Even with his foot hard down on the accelerator, the needle on the speed gauge

scarcely reached thirty kilometres an hour. Normally, this did not bother him because he was not in a hurry to reach a destination; there was never any pressure of time, nobody he was in a hurry to meet, nothing he was in a hurry to do. Except for today. Something felt different today.

When he turned on to the rough road, he found his heart beating. At last, he pulled up at the side of the dirt track. All his tools were kept under a tarpaulin in the back of the pick-up. He pulled out a large spade and reached inside for a trowel. In the dashboard, he kept a small bottle of brandy and, tucking it inside his top pocket, he began walking purposefully to the *kypos*.

When he got there he looked at the ground, and his eyes rested on the pallid stone. He would work on that first. There could be no sowing until he had removed it. During the night, the wind had disturbed a few more millimetres of soil and, as he approached, he could see that more of the stone had been exposed. He brushed some away with his hands and realised it had a pearly sheen. The spade now seemed too brutal. Whatever it was, this stone looked special, and he did not want to damage it.

All morning, he scrabbled with his hands to reveal more and more of this shape. It seemed that it was a flat expanse with no edges. How his tomatoes, courgettes and *fasolia* could have grown for so many years with such an obstacle beneath their roots he had no idea. There had been some seismic movement in the area lately, and this must have shifted the soil and brought it to the surface. His vegetables could only benefit if he cleared it from his land.

Then, suddenly, the stone seemed to rise and he felt a

small mound beneath his big, gnarled hand. He picked up his spade again to dig down, and managed to lever huge clods of earth away from the sides. An hour or so later, the soil was piled up in hillocks all around him.

It was two o'clock in the afternoon. His back ached and his hands were blistered. Some hours earlier, he had dropped his jacket on to the ground and now his shirt was saturated with sweat. He ambled over to the row of orange trees and sat slumped beneath one so that he could lean against its trunk. All that had sustained him during the past hours were regular sips of brandy.

The task was going to take longer than he had anticipated, but he was determined to continue, even though his heart was beating fast from exertion. He carried on for several more hours before calling it a day.

He had no time to go to the *kafenion* that night, and went straight home. As soon as dinner was swallowed and he had washed his plate, Costas went out into the yard for his final cigarette of the day. His wife had kept up a barrage of complaints at his lateness but, outside, there was a welcome silence.

At noon on the third day, still spurred on by that first musical note he had heard, his suspicion that this was no ordinary piece of stone was confirmed. It was something smooth and sculpted. By mid-afternoon, he realised he was looking down at the plump cheeks of a woman's bottom. He laid his hand on her curves and felt the cool marble beneath his palm. By three o'clock, he had brushed away more dirt and, from the dent between the buttocks, his finger could follow the subtle indent of a spine.

By six o'clock, grimly determined, he had revealed an expanse that was perhaps forty centimetres by eighty. It was only when he stood up to stretch and looked down at his morning's work that he appreciated for the first time what he was seeing.

It was a whole body. A woman's. Her entire back was now exposed to the air; her legs, behind, neck and the edge of what must be her hair. He picked carefully at the soil with his fingers now. She was lying face down and, as he brushed away more and more earth, he could see that one of her arms rested by her side. The other ended at the elbow. For Costas, born and bought up in a rural village, such a sight was unfamiliar. In his whole life, he had never visited a museum.

He realised how wrong it was to be using a spade and ran his hand over her very cautiously, very lightly.

The memory of touching a woman's body was so distant that he felt almost sinful. It had been more than thirty years. Perhaps thirty-five. He could not be specific about when it was that he had last touched his wife, or had any desire to do so. She had been ravishingly beautiful at eighteen when they married, still lovely at twenty-five, but by the time they had had two children it was as if she no longer cared.

Her weight gain was not the only issue (Costas had got used to the idea that his wife was heavier than him). It was her abandonment of hygiene that upset him. Her hair was unwashed for many months, and he could not tell if it was her skin or her hair that gave off the odour that filled their bed. By forty years old, she had looked sixty, had lost her teeth and had sprouted hair in all sorts of new places. Costas did not look at other people's wives, but he did not look at his own either.

Several more hours went by as he scraped away, just with his fingernails now, picking individual clods of earth to try to loosen the hold that the ground seemed to have on her body. It was almost impossible to believe what was emerging. By ten o'clock that night, he was exhausted, and darkness was hampering his efforts.

When he got home, there was a plate of food on the table and his wife was already in bed. The gristly meat had gone cold, but he swallowed it almost without chewing and then took his nightly shower. Today he had to scrub his fingernails especially vigorously. Each one was packed hard with dirt from his labours in the *kypos*.

When he came out of the shower, he gazed into the darkness and an unfamiliar sense of contentment came over him. As he smoked his last cigarette of the day, he heard the hoot of an owl.

The following morning, he was gone before dawn, taking with him a small brush from the kitchen. He would use it to sweep away the dirt from his discovery.

Perhaps he would see her properly today.

He worked more like an archaeologist than a gardener now. He had even forgotten about the need to sow.

That morning, he felt the stone shift slightly again. He wanted so much to see her face, but it was going to take some time until her whole body was free and even then she might be too heavy to turn over.

For many more days, he worked meticulously and carefully, treating the woman as though she were the most

208

precious thing on earth. At this moment in time, she was.

As he worked to remove the earth from beneath her body, he found a long, slender object. At first he imagined it might be an animal bone, but then realised it was a finger. It was slightly curved, with a perfectly shaped fingernail and creases for the finger joints. He put it carefully in the breast pocket of his shirt. A while later, he found the remainder of the hand. It was so fine, so fragile, and he held it gently, resting it on his palm. It had survived, almost intact, presumably for many, many years, but he treated it as though it were made of porcelain. He took it over to where his jacket lay and rested it on top. Forgotten feelings of tenderness stirred inside him.

In the early hours, during the third week of excavation, Costas was awoken by the sound of heavy rain on the roof. He leapt out of bed, managing not to disturb his snoring wife, dragged on his clothes (checking that the forefinger was still in his shirt pocket) and left the house.

The truck outside roared to life. Costas crunched it into gear and drove off. He should have covered his woman up the day before.

When he reached his plot, he could see the area that he had exposed in the past few days was covered once again. This time in damp sludge. He felt guilty for not having protected her. As the sun rose, he used a cloth to clean her up and then continued. Now that the earth was damp, he could make faster progress and loosened it clod by clod from around the torso, then began on the legs. It was painstaking but a process that he did not want to hurry. The anticipation was a pleasure in itself.

With each tiny new space on her thighs and calves and ankles revealed, his obsession with her grew. She was taller than him. From the top of her head down to her heel was almost two metres.

Four or five more days of meticulous work, and she was almost free.

The other men in the *kafenion* noticed that Costas arrived later and later each night. As the days lengthened, so did his hours of excavation. They also noticed how thin he was getting and how wild his hair was (he did not make time for a weekly visit to the barber). They also noticed how happy he seemed. Unkempt, but contented.

Even though they were usually silent, these men began to murmur and mutter among themselves.

'Looks like he has a girlfriend,' said one.

'Costas?'

'What else makes a man change his habits?' said another.

'But his appearance . . . ?' said another. 'He's losing his grip.'

Costas Arvanitis was a man in love. Of this there was no doubt. He was in love with Aphrodite. He did not even know her name, but that's who she was. She had lain there for millennia, waiting to be found and, like an ancient Sleeping Beauty, needed to be revived. The effect of her beauty was a powerful force. Many thousands of years before, as all craftsman had when they were depicting the gods, the sculptor not only believed that she represented the goddess, he also believed that she actually *was* the goddess. Costas was experiencing the potency of this conviction.

Finally, she lay there, face down, in her entirety. Naked, perfect, sensual and strong. The goddess of love and beauty.

Costas gazed at her. His curiosity about her face was immense, but he would wait until the following day to try to turn her.

At around midnight, he covered her with a blanket.

'*Kalinihta, agapi mou,*' he whispered in the darkness.

Between that moment and the following day, he thought of nothing but this woman. His dreams were filled with her image. Suddenly, life had something that transcended the day-to-day struggle, the sound of a grumpy wife and bickering politicians, the sight of the long-suffering faces in the *kafenion* whose deep-set lines revealed the misery that had become a habit. An absence of joy was replaced by the presence of love.

The sun was just peeking over the mountains when he reached the *kypos* the next day. Even as he approached through the olive grove, Costas's heart was beating fast. He set his tools down and pulled away the blanket. There she was, in all her perfection. The first rays of the sun made her seem whiter and purer than before. There were even hints of crystal in the marble that made her sparkle.

Using a series of wooden planks that he had dragged from the truck, and some rope, he would have to lever the body to turn her. This was work for half a dozen men, but he didn't want to share his woman with anybody. He was determined to do it alone. It took some time to get everything in position and the first attempts failed. Throughout the process, he was terrified of her breaking.

Finally, at about three in the afternoon, the arrangement of all the various parts came together. As he leaned down on his lever, the woman rose slightly from her sleeping position.

Just for a second, before she fell, Costas caught sight of her face. It was just a brief glimpse of her profile, but it was enough.

He saw a strong nose, full lips and the edge of a perfectly oval eye. With the lightest touch from his chisel, the sculptor had indicated the lines of a smile at the corner of that eye.

Not only was her body without flaw, but so, also, was her face.

Costas gasped. As Aphrodite fell once more face first into the soil, he felt the full force of her erotic power, just as every mortal before him who had ever looked at her.

He gasped again. His shortness of breath continued and was soon followed by a tightness around his chest and pains in his arms. He knew he had over-exerted himself in trying to lift her.

Costas lay down, hoping that this would alleviate these unfamiliar aches and pains, stretching himself out close to the statue and putting his head on her shoulder. She was surprisingly soft, and his cheek fitted into the nape of her neck.

Costas never got up again.

By the time Orestes reached his friend's *kypos*, it was too late to do anything. He noticed that his friend had a smile on his face. With sadness, Orestes carefully moved Costas's body to one side and, while doing so, felt the hard piece of stone in his top pocket. He removed the finger and then wrapped Costas in the blanket that had been used to protect Aphrodite.

Orestes knew that the discovery of an ancient sculpture in a field, or even in a city, was in the interest of only the very few. It could cause serious disruption to day-to-day life. All over Greece, building works (the Thessaloniki metro was a good example) took ten times longer than they should have if there was any suspicion of ancient remains in the vicinity. Nobody in the village would welcome the discovery of this artefact. Who knew what else might be under there? The last thing anyone wanted was archaeologists crawling over their land and banning development or agriculture.

He covered the sculpture once again with layers and layers of soil. It took him an hour or so to replace all the earth and to build it up again, perhaps a little higher than before, and to smooth it over.

He drove at full speed back to the village and went to see Stella.

'It must have been a heart attack,' she said.

The doctor agreed. Orestes called in at the *kafenion* and, with two other men from the village, loaded a wheelbarrow on to a truck and went to collect the body. The funeral would take place the following day, but before the burial Orestes would visit Costas's home, where his friend would be lying in an open casket, and discreetly slip the precious fragment of Aphrodite into the breast pocket of the deceased's only suit. He knew that Costas would want that.

Perhaps another man, in years to come, would be digging the ground and make a similar discovery. It was possible that Costas had not even been the first . . .

I have an image of Costas, happy and fulfilled at the moment of death. Maybe this is what really matters. I think that, for those few weeks, his feelings for Aphrodite gave him a zest for life that he had lost. The Greeks recognise that there are different kinds of love and that one word does not fit them all. The boundaries between them are blurred but, broadly, agapi (perhaps the most cerebral) is for God and family, filia is for friendship and erotas is for sexual attraction. Erotas had been absent in Costas's life for so many years and, for a brief while, he felt its full, enriching power once again.

In many mountain villages that I passed through, where older people have lost their teeth, their hair and their interest in what they look like, it is difficult to imagine what attraction still exists between the sexes. Given that the appreciation of beauty seems to be something innate, one wonders why nature blesses so few people with it, and even then for such a brief period.

I am not scornful of Costas's worship of beauty. He was overcome by Aphrodite's power. I have realised in these past months that appreciating beauty and being seduced by it are two different things. In the future I will be more cautious, knowing that it can make us lose our minds. Socrates said: 'Beauty is a short-lived tyranny.' He was right.

I went to Costas's funeral, and his family welcomed me to the lunch afterwards. I did not feel in the least like an intruder. I watched Stella, all dressed in black, and noticed that she did not seem to be grieving any more than I did.

Orestes and Eleni rented me a room above the taverna and I ended up staying for many weeks. It felt like home. I even became fond of the nagging cats who wrapped themselves around my legs as I ate each night – and, with great reluctance, I usually left a mouthful of Eleni's delicious cooking for them. I was writing all day and spending most of each evening in the kafenion. One of the men there (he had gone with Orestes to carry Costas home) patiently taught me the three variants of backgammon that they play in Greece: plakoto, fevga and portes. I forgot everything else while I was playing, since it was crucial not to lose concentration even for a moment. Tavli, as it's known here, seems to me the best metaphor for how life works. Luck dictates how the dice land (maybe a double six, perhaps a one and a two), but then it's down to the player to decide what happens next. At the moment your fingers slide the counters from one triangle to the next, good fortune, skill, experience, wisdom, stupidity, carelessness and concentration can all play a role. I even began to get the odd game off him.

Almost two months after arriving in this village, I had reached the midway point of drafting my book and, in spite of Eleni and Orestes's protestations, I felt that I should move on. Eleni was quite determined to introduce me to her unmarried niece.

'She's a schoolteacher,' she said. 'And she'll be coming from Arta at the end of March for a holiday. She's nearly thirty-

five. You two would have so much in common – and you need a good woman!'

'She won't want someone my age,' I insisted. 'I'm forty-five.'

'Well, you're still a handsome man,' said Eleni, stroking my cheek affectionately.

I had to be tactful, but the last thing on my mind was another relationship. I was neither ready nor interested.

Apart from anything, there was much more of Greece yet to see. On the wall above the table in the taverna where I always sat for dinner, there was an old poster. It almost looked like a photomontage. It was an old monastery perched on top of a pillar of natural rock and must have been completely inaccessible from the ground.

'You must go there,' insisted Eleni. 'Akseizi ton kopo.'

'She's right,' said Orestes, uncharacteristically agreeing with his wife. 'It's worth it.'

Promising them both that I would return in the future, and that I would bring them a copy of the book I was writing (Orestes and I had spent many hours talking about the power of sculpture), I packed my bags and, at ten o'clock one morning, with great sadness, left the village. I had found real peace there.

My next destination was more planned than the previous one.

The poster had not really prepared me for the strange, otherworldly landscape of Meteora. I felt as if I had arrived on another planet. Meteora means 'suspended in the air', and this is how the monasteries seemed, far above my head, on pinnacles six hundred metres high. Around twenty-five million years ago, when there were waters at the height where the monasteries sit now, a gap appeared to allow them to pour *through the rock and into the Aegean. Wind and rain has since moulded a landscape that is both mystical and sublime.*

Over one thousand years ago, the first ascetics, in order to deny themselves the pleasures of the world and the flesh, climbed up to the caves which had been eroded within these rocks. Away from the world, above the clouds, they sought a state of ecstasy that connected them with God.

A few hundred years later, in an almost impossible feat of engineering, some monks lifted rocks to the top of a pinnacle and built the first of twenty-four monasteries. Six of these remain today, with small communities of monks kept company by nothing more than painted images of the saints. They live far from the world and closer to heaven.

Having climbed a very steep path to visit the highest of the monasteries, Megalou Meteorou, I wondered about the effect of this isolation on the few monks who live there. Does it still give them peace of mind?

In Kalambaka, the town close to the monasteries, I met a priest. We were both waiting in a long line at a cash machine, which seemed incongruous. We got talking, first of all about the restriction on withdrawals from Greek banks (it was still continuing, many months after having been instituted). 'Personally, I can easily manage on sixty euros a day,' he said to me. 'It's more than I get through in a month.'

I imagined this was true. I asked him about the monastic way of life in this remote region, and he told me that solitude and separation from the world do not suit everyone. With a slight incline of his head, indicating the monastery that was visible above us, he told me about something that had happened there a few years ago.

MAN ON A MOUNTAINTOP

CARTE POSTALE

Meteora

The phone rang in the living room, and a tall, muscular man, around forty-five years old, snatched the receiver from its cradle. The line went dead, but he knew who had called.

'*Giannis!*' he shouted into the other room. 'Get in here, now!'

Giannis appeared.

'Tell that girl to stop ringing,' he said angrily. 'You see enough of her at school.'

He cuffed his elder son roughly round the ear.

'Why can't you be more like your brother?'

Dimitris, who was reading quietly in the corner, had announced his intention to join the priesthood some time before. A teacher at his school had taken a group of boys to visit one of the monasteries on Mount Athos, which was a mere fifty kilometres from where they lived. After the visit, Dimitris had never been the same again.

'I have been called,' he told his parents. Unlike Giannis, who was older, Dimitris had never kicked a ball, was diligent with his studies and did not think about girls. Now, his main preoccupation was God.

Their grandmother, who lived with them, continually crossed herself, on trains, buses and in the street, her hand mapping out Father, Son and Holy Spirit across her chest. It was an obligation whenever she saw a roadside memorial, chapel or church, and it was hard to go more than a few hundred metres without seeing one. Before Dimitris's visit to Mount Athos, this was the closest the boys had to a living experience of religion, apart from when this same *yia-yia* took them to church at Easter. Their father's religion was clear and liquid. If he did not want his wife to go to church, she did not dispute it. She had been a victim of his drunken abuse on so many occasions that she did not want to add further provocation.

When she heard of Dimitris's decision, however, *Yia-yia* reacted as if she had been slapped:

'*Thé mou!* My God!'

She was a devout woman herself, but for her own grandson to devote his whole life to God? That was a different matter altogether. Where had he got such an idea? It was insanity.

'You shouldn't have left that picture of Mount Athos on his wall,' she said to her daughter. 'You shouldn't have let him go on that trip in the first place. The whole business! It's not normal for a child of his age.'

His mother thought it was an adolescent phase. She had one son who prayed and had a Bible tucked down the side of his bed, and another with acne and dirty magazines beneath his mattress. She hoped that both boys would grow out of their respective habits. Her husband threatened to beat them if they did not.

After a few years, Giannis stopped getting spots, but Dimitris went to study for the priesthood and was eventually sent to a place far from where his family lived. Meteora was a long way from the sea, and the twenty-four monasteries (only a few of them still functioning) teetered precariously on pillars of limestone, one thousands metres up in the sky. It was as if the priests lived between this world and the next, suspended somewhere between earth and heaven. The houses in the shadows beneath them never saw the sun.

Every year, Giannis would make the long journey to see his brother. For him, this annual visit was the only day when he came into contact with the sublime. As he tore along the straight road from Karditsa in his latest sports car, he felt a surge of adrenalin. It was not brought on by the first glimpse of the monasteries, remote and mysterious, up ahead. It was being able to put his foot down on the almost empty road.

Every time he went to Meteora he was driving something a little flashier. In the early days of his brother's time in the mountains he had arrived in a Nissan. He had progressed to a BMW and, this year, it was a red Porsche. Sadly, his younger brother never saw his car, as he was obliged to park some distance away.

Giannis usually came early in the year, when the weather was misty, and this month snow had fallen heavily in this part of Greece. As he locked the car, he realised with annoyance that he had forgotten to bring a change of shoes. His suede loafers were totally unsuitable for the climb to the monastery, which involved a long ascent through a forest of ancient trees whose leaves formed a damp carpet underfoot.

He had to focus on each step. Dense mist obscured everything beyond five metres, but as he reached the top of the hill he saw that he had emerged above the clouds.

He could now see the monastery and, in a few more minutes, he reached the cobbled path that took him to its main door. He stood there and looked out above the landscape of undulating grey fog. At that moment he saw a figure emerging, floating effortlessly through the sky.

Giannis smiled. Dimitris seemed to be arriving in some kind of spaceship.

Dimitris stepped out of the small cable car and walked towards his brother. He was holding a secular blue plastic bag full of provisions, left down below by a local shopkeeper each week.

Giannis leaned forward to embrace him and caught a whiff of his brother's unwashed skin and stale-smelling hair. He saw that his beard was matted. The hand-knitted black cardigan that he wore over his habit had several holes in it and the habit itself was flecked. With soup? With milk? It could have been anything. He was shocked by the change in his appearance from the previous year.

'That's a nice way to travel,' commented Giannis. 'I thought it was God arriving.'

'A bit safer than the old method,' smiled Dimitris. Before the cable car was built, the monks used to hoist each other up from below in a net.

As they walked up to the door together, Giannis noticed that his brother was limping.

'Your foot . . . ?' he enquired.

'No, no. It's just a broken sandal. I need to sew it.'

The strap had worn and snapped, and his brother was dragging his foot to keep it on.

Giannis remembered with annoyance that his own shoes would probably have to be thrown away. Even his socks were saturated, and he could feel his toes going numb.

Beneath the volumes of dense black hair on Dimitris's head and face, his brother's skin was pale and pure, saved from the elements by the high walls of the monastery, where daylight never shone. He scarcely had a line on his face. In spite of the beard, he looked childlike.

Drink, drugs, smoking, late nights and exposure to the sun were among the pleasures and vices of the life that had aged Giannis. Added to these was the constant anxiety of working out devious ways to avoid paying debts and taxes, of ducking and diving, wheeling and dealing. His body, by contrast, was in good shape. Despite a decadent lifestyle, he always made time for regular visits to the gym, where he lifted weights, and he occasionally ran half-marathons.

Dimitris did not study his brother. All he noticed was the garish logo emblazoned on Giannis's jacket and, as they walked through into the monastery, that the smell of candles that burned all around them was not enough to obscure Giannis's strong aftershave.

Dimitris put the bag of provisions down in a small scullery next to the entrance, and the two brothers walked through the chapel.

The wall paintings were among the most rare and precious in Greece, executed by an artist from Crete four hundred years earlier. Theophanis had also painted at Mount Athos, and the faces that surrounded them now bore the same mixture of joy and sadness, the *harmolipi*, that had so affected Dimitris on his school visit.

There was a large plate of holy bread cut into cubes on a low table in front of them. Suddenly hungry after the long climb, Giannis resisted the temptation to take a piece.

Dimitris noticed his brother's left foot twitching nervously up and down and how the little gold stirrup on the shoe caught the light each time he moved. He was conscious that Giannis was in need of nicotine.

'No change in the rules, I suppose?' asked Giannis.

It was ironic that, in a place where precious sixteenth-century wall paintings were gradually darkening and disappearing in a haze of candle smoke and incense, smoking a cigarette was not allowed, even outside, where ash could be flicked hundreds of feet into the void beneath.

'Alas, no,' answered Dimitris, raising his eyes to heaven.

'God's rule?'

'No,' said Dimitris. 'The one above Him.'

'The bishop?'

As Dimitris moved further into the chapel and sat down, Giannis watched him more closely. In contrast to his youthful face, Dimitris had a protruding stomach and stooped posture; to Giannis he looked like a man who had gone to seed. Giannis was proud of his own physique.

Dimitris's own turning circle was smaller than a prison yard. Members of his flock could arrive at any time, and they did not expect him to be out. Since the lift that brought him up and down the rock had been installed, even the minimal exercise he used to take had been reduced to walking a few metres a day.

'How are our parents?' asked Dimitris.

'The same,' answered Giannis. 'Nothing changes. Father still drinks. Even more now that *Yia-yia* has gone. At least she tried to discourage him.'

'So he still raises his hand against Mother?'

'Of course he does.'

'Can't you *do* anything?'

'Can't *you*? Pray harder . . . ?'

Giannis still did everything to provoke his pious brother, just as he had when they were small boys.

'I live above them, so I hear what goes on sometimes. But when I get downstairs it's usually all over and done with. There they are, sitting watching TV as if nothing has happened. Mother sniffing. Pretending to have a cold.'

A moment passed. Giannis wondered if Dimitris was praying, but he soon interrupted the silence in any case.

'*Gamoto!*'

The sound of swearing in this sacred place jarred, but Dimitris did not respond.

'Mother made you some sweet biscuits . . . I left them in the car.'

'That's nice of her. But it's Lent. So not to worry. You can eat them on the way home.'

Dimitris was well used to his family being out of touch with the Church calendar.

Giannis could not ask his brother what he had been

doing, because he knew the answer. Reading the Bible, praying and meditating. Even now Giannis was not sure if there was a difference between them. Perhaps hearing confession was the one thing he would have been interested in. He was always intrigued by what people might offload on to his brother and how someone who knew nothing of sin could respond.

'How is business?' asked Dimitris.

'In spite of everything, it's going well,' answered Giannis. 'People will spend their very last cent on an espresso. They'll be drinking coffee as Greece collapses around them!'

Giannis was now running five outlets of a coffee franchise. During the recent crisis, he had offered the lowest prices in Athens and there were queues every morning outside every branch. He was doing very nicely.

'Let's say, I am offering a public service . . . a bit like you.'

Dimitris was a man of few words. His brother's sarcasm bounced off him.

'You know what I mean . . . confession? Coffee and confession? Don't you think they have something in common? A quick fix of something to make people feel a bit better?'

Dimitris folded his hands in his lap and looked down at them. It would be better not to rise to his brother's bait nor to find himself debating the differences between a caffeinated drink and one of the sacraments. Silently, he prayed to God for the strength to keep calm, digging the fingernails of one hand hard into the other. Giannis's mention of 'confession' stirred unutterable torment in him.

The woman. She was always on his mind.

A couple had visited the monastery a few months before. It was during August, when large numbers of people made the journey to Meteora. Many of them were standard tourists whose chief interest was in taking pictures, but others came on a more spiritual quest.

A large coach party had arrived one day. Most of them were in their seventies, and for many it was a considerable struggle to reach the monastery.

There was also a younger couple. Dimitris had realised that they were not part of the main group.

The woman's husband had wandered off to the museum, and she remained behind in the room where they were now seated. It was a hot day, so it seemed natural for anyone to want to rest.

She had long, curly blond hair that Dimitris noticed immediately. All the women in the coach party had stiff, short styles, specially coiffured by a hairdresser for their outing.

None of the older people had any interest in speaking to Dimitris, but he could see this younger woman was trying to catch his eye.

'Excuse me,' she said quietly. 'Is it possible to say confession? I need to do it as soon as possible.'

A pair of dark green eyes looked pleadingly up at his. She seemed small and vulnerable and yet there was a wildness about her, accentuated by her lion's mane of unruly hair.

It was odd for someone to be in a hurry over such a thing, but he realised afterwards that she wanted to do it while her husband was looking around the museum.

'Come with me,' he said.

They went into the chapel, and Dimitris led her into the sanctuary, where he took the *epitrachelion*, the holy stole, from its hook and put it round his neck. It transformed him into someone with the power to absolve her of her sins, and at the end of the confession he would place it over her head and read the prayer of forgiveness.

They sat opposite one another and she began to speak. Her voice was so quiet he had to lean forward to hear her.

'I'm so ashamed,' she said. 'My sins are heavy.'

'God will forgive you,' Dimitris told her. 'God will wash away your sins.'

'I don't think He can,' she whispered. 'Because I can't get rid of my desire.' There was a breathless urgency in her voice.

'He forgives every imperfection, purifies you of every transgression.'

'But every minute of the day, every hour of the day, my mind is filled with such desire, with such a powerful urge that I cannot resist it . . .'

The woman's voice was husky, full of sexuality. It stirred something in his memory and he began to sweat profusely as he listened. Her words faded in and out as he tried to focus on what she was saying. The temperature in the small, airless space seemed to rise and rise until he was gasping for breath, his head swimming. He was struggling to remain sitting, holding on to the edge of his desk to stop himself collapsing. With a sudden, terrible realisation, he knew that it was he, Dimitris, whose sin could never be washed away.

When he came to, he was lying on the cold stone floor. The woman had gone. She had fled as soon as Dimitris fainted and alerted a visiting novice, who was now mopping his brow with a damp cloth. The stole was twisted beneath him.

He lay still, agonised by the memory of his teenage transgression, which he had tried every day to suppress and which at that moment had come flooding back.

Only once, a year or so before he had left home to go to Theological School, Giannis had persuaded him to go into their grandmother's room. *Yia-yia* was away with their mother, at a funeral. There was a telephone extension in her room. Not for the first time, Giannis called a 'hotline' to talk to someone called 'Natalia'. He had talked to her before, but this time he had bullied Dimitris into taking a turn to hear what she would like to do to an eager adolescent. The feeling of desire that came over him was unfamiliar and overwhelming, and when Giannis thrust a porn magazine in front of him the image of a naked Natalia appeared in his imagination, pearly skinned, huge-breasted, wavy-haired, bottle-blonde.

The encounter was interrupted by the slam of the front door. Dimitris dropped the receiver, but their father was already in the room.

Over by the window, Giannis stood smirking. Dimitris, meanwhile, was hastily doing up his flies, red-faced. His father, who had come straight in from the bar, extracted enough information from him to justify a severe beating on his naked behind.

Talking to Natalia was the closest Dimitris had ever come to any kind of sexual encounter, but the shame of being 'caught' had lived with him, even haunting his dreams. The woman on the phone was still the subject of his regular fantasies.

This voice that he had heard in the sanctuary was the same as the voice that had troubled him for the past fifteen years. Just like Natalia's.

The woman's confession had taken place a few months earlier, but every day since he had been tortured by the memory of her voice, lying awake until two or three in the morning, then getting up to spend the rest of the night on his knees, praying until his back was sore and he shed tears of pain from kneeling on the stone floor.

He sought confession for himself, but nothing shifted the burden of his sin or silenced his obsession. For months Dimitris struggled, and the expression on the faces of the icons that surrounded him no longer seemed kind. They were reproachful.

Giannis glanced at his Rolex.

'I need to get back,' he said.

Dimitris stood up.

'Thanks for coming,' he said.

'It was good to see you,' said Giannis, backing away from, rather than moving towards, his brother.

'Send my love to our parents,' Dimitris murmured.

The solid wooden door closed behind him. Giannis felt relief to be leaving. He had been there for an hour, and it was more than enough. He slipped and slid back down the hill. It was even harder going than the ascent. It took him more than forty minutes but, eventually, he could see his car, gleaming like a ripe tomato on the road below.

At last he reached it, got in and sat for a moment, leaning

over to the passenger seat for the sweet *koulouria* that his mother had made for Dimitris. He ate five, one after the other, then lit a cigarette.

Not long after Giannis left, the doors of the monastery had opened again. Dimitris hastened out. He could no longer endure the gaze of the saints who looked down at him from walls and ceilings, nor the images of heaven and hell that were portrayed around him. They taunted him. The certainty of salvation had left him. He was no longer sure that, when the time came, he would be with the sheep rather than the goats. Coffee . . . confession . . . Perhaps his brother was right. Perhaps they had as little value as each other.

He could not find God within the walls of the monastery. He had sometimes spent the night in one of the nearby caves where hermits had gone to meditate and be away from the world, but there he only looked deeper into the blackness of his own soul. The words of Jesus, from the Gospel of Matthew, followed him there and seemed to echo around the rocky walls:

'Whosoever looketh on a woman to lust after her hath committed adultery with her already in his heart.'

As darkness began to fall, he ran, almost tripping as he went, down a hidden pathway from the monastery, taking a detour to climb a mountain nearby, one that had never been built on by monks. Its summit was clear and free. There were no angelic faces, no images of the Last Judgement. This was the place.

The mist encircled him.

By now, Giannis had flicked the butt of a second cigarette out of the car window. Out of habit, he glanced at himself in the rear-view mirror, then inserted his key into the ignition. The engine roared into life and he sped away.

As he came round the corner, he glimpsed the monastery, unlit and lonely. The image of loneliness did not compare, however, with what he saw next. On a neighbouring mountaintop, he spotted the figure of a solitary man. Mist

was swirling around him, and clouds constantly formed and re-formed as the wind blew. There was a moment when the fog obscured him completely and, a few seconds later, when it had dissipated, the man was gone. The mountain was empty.

Giannis turned up the volume on his radio and drove on.

Such isolation. Such misplaced guilt. Such tragic consequences. It can't always be easy for priests who have taken a vow of celibacy. It must have profound psychological and physical effects on them.

Meteora is a spectacular place to visit, and it made me think about the difference between loneliness and solitude. The Greeks have one word for both: monaksia, which explains why some of them, when they see a man alone, pity him. In some situations, perhaps they had cause, but as time has gone on I have grown stronger in my solitude. I now know the difference between this and loneliness.

I spent a few days in Kalambaka, and went walking every day, allowing the landscape to get under my skin. On these long walks, I couldn't help analysing our relationship, and looking for clues that might have indicated things were not right. Things I must have missed at the time.

At the end of my stay, I had had my fill of tranquillity, so I left for Thessaloniki, which was three hours away on a good, fast road. I was excited about feeling the warmth of a crowd, hearing some loud music in a bar, catching the smell of souvlaki in the street.

It was 25 March, and a warm spring day. As soon as I had checked into my hotel, I went down towards the sea to walk along the esplanade. I found myself surrounded by flags. They fluttered from balconies and public buildings, were waved in the roads and sold in the squares. I was soon absorbed into the crowds that lined the streets, and people cheerfully told me why we were all standing there, watching thousands of schoolchildren, soldiers and people in national costume marching by. It was their Independence Day parade.

I learned how history and emotion (perhaps inseparable in Greece) are bound up with the flag, and I also heard a story that showed how strongly the symbolism of this flag is rooted in the Greek soul.

Greece is haunted by two periods of occupation. The more recent one, by the Germans in the twentieth century, was for three years. The earlier one, by the Turks, was for nearly four centuries, and it is their liberation from this that the Greeks mark every 25 March with a huge parade.

This is also the Feast of the Annunciation, the Evangelismos, the day when the Archangel Gabriel told the

Virgin Mary that she was to have a child. During a lull in the parade, a fiery old man standing next to me told me how the arrival of Jesus Christ and the departure of the Turks are linked, leaving me in no doubt that the war against the Turks to achieve the liberation of Greece was seen as a holy war.

'We were outnumbered by the Turks, hopelessly outnumbered,' he told me proudly. 'But God was on our side, and that's what mattered.'

Although he was with his family, I could see that he was happy to have, in me, a new audience. His wife and daughter had heard his stories so many times. I listened intently and nodded. Old men like him need little more than this as encouragement. He relived the events from the past as if the battlefield were still wet with the blood of Turks and Greeks.

'After all those centuries, the Turks thought we had given up! But we have fire in our hearts. We never relinquished our language, our traditions, our religion! And it was a bishop who chose this day for us to rise up and fight.'

He raised aloft the small flag in his hand. People all around him were turning to listen to his rhetoric. A young woman next to us held her small child close and nodded with approval.

'He chose this day, the day of the Evangelismos, to raise the Greek flag and to proclaim our freedom. It was the beginning! For nine years we fought. And then we were free!'

The old man was almost hopping with excitement; it was as if he had taken part in this nineteenth-century fight himself.

'Look! They're coming,' said his middle-aged daughter, patiently touching him on the arm.

Then she turned to me and said discreetly:

241

'I'll tell you a story later, if you have time when all this is over. We'll be going to have some lunch, and you're welcome to join us. We eat a special dish for the Evangelismos.'

'And it's our pappou's name day, too,' said one of her teenagers. 'So we have a huge cake!'

Her grandfather's name, she told me, was Vangelis.

'That's so kind,' I answered, 'but I'm a total stranger.'

Their mother shrugged her shoulders, as if to say, 'What does that matter?'

'We live just there,' she said, indicating the ugly, grey concrete apartment block behind us. 'My name is Penelope, by the way.'

A group of women in short, embroidered, red velvet jackets, their heads ornately wrapped in scarves, heavy necklaces of gold coins jangling around their necks, began to file past, and my attention reverted to the parade. The colour and variety of the regional costumes was spectacular – men in extravagant knickerbockers and long boots, others in full white skirts and shoes with enormous pompoms. The parade had turned into theatre.

Two hours later, I was settling down with Penelope, her father, husband and two teenage children at a table in their living room. There was a clear view of the sea. A huge dish of bakalarios skordalia, salt cod with garlic mash, was set down in front of me. I helped myself, and ate hungrily while, with regular interruptions from her father, Penelope told me a story of love and war.

'She's making it all up,' said her father, leaning in conspiratorially, but I was not so sure . . .

JE REVIENS

CARTE POSTALE

POSTKARTE — POST CARD

'JE REVIENS'

It was so wet that the parade had nearly been called off that year. The streets were glassy, and the awning to protect the mayor and other VIPs was lashed with rain, each downpour making the canvas sag ever more dangerously. The musicians in the band played on, their fingers stiff with cold beneath their white gloves. Only the drummer, beating time vigorously for many hours, was able to keep his circulation flowing. The road along which they marched followed the seafront and a cool wind blew in across the Gulf. Mount Olympus had disappeared in a grey cloud.

There were spectators from every generation: babies with pompoms sewn to their soft-footed shoes, toddlers in *foustanella* fancy dress, students from the university, office workers happy to be having the day off, mothers, fathers and grandparents. They were all out in force. There were plenty of people watching from their balconies along the seafront. Everyone wanted to see the parade.

Among the crowd watching from the pavement, an old woman remembered the day long ago when she had

been a flag-bearer. If you were top of the class, you had the privilege of carrying the national flag in the parade. Though Evangelia's moment of glory had been many decades before, she relived it each year. Now her heart swelled with pride in anticipation at seeing the granddaughter who bore her name also bearing the flag.

A man came by selling small plastic flags for just seventy cents. She could tell from his accent that he was Albanian, and his worn shoes had absorbed so much water that his socks and his trousers were wet to the knee. His fingers were slippery with rain and he struggled to give Evangelia her change.

She looked at her flag, its simple blue-and-white design full of meaning, the nine horizontal stripes each recalling the nine-syllable rallying cry used by the Greeks to rid their country of the Turks.

'*El-ef-the-ri-a i Tha-na-tos!* Freedom or Death!'

As did many, she believed that God had been on their side in the fight against the Turks. With His help they had rid themselves of Ottoman oppression; the flag itself embodied their motto.

Wave after wave of teenage girls and boys walked past the crowd, awkwardly trying to march in step. '*Ena, thio, ena, thio, ena sto aristero.* One, two, one, two, one on the left.'

The old lady flicked her flag back and forth, trying to match their rhythm.

In spite of the academic achievements that were being recognised by a place in the parade, many of the girls looked as if they would rather be somewhere else. In their unpolished shoes, flesh-coloured tights, short black skirts and white shirts, they were damp and cold. All of them. The only effort they had made was the lavish attention they had given to their hair, rivers of it, now beginning to form into rats' tails. Most looked sulky.

The ranks of boys seemed to be enjoying themselves, exchanging smirks as they passed by in a shambolic parody of a march, sporting asymmetrical haircuts that had been assembled with gel and the barber's razor. Again, at the front of each group of fifty or so, one boy had been singled out to carry a large flag, which he did with pride.

It was tiring, waiting there in the drizzle, and Evangelia hoped her granddaughter would appear soon. At ninety years old, it was a huge effort to stand for so long. She noticed that the flag seller was taking a break and was now spectating, his flags lowered to his side.

At that moment, she caught sight of her granddaughter in the sea of faces.

'Evangelia! Evangelia!' she called, trying to attract the girl's attention. 'Congratulations, *agapi mou*! Bravo!'

The sallow, dark-haired, seventeen-year-old looked ahead, concentrating on balancing the weight of the flag and its heavy pole on her hip. She did not turn her head.

Neighbours of Evangelia who were standing nearby joined in with the applause. They had known the girl since she was a baby.

'Bravo, little Evangelia! Bravo!'

The old lady beamed with pride.

Then came the representatives of another school, led by the boys. Out in the front was an exceptionally handsome youth with high cheekbones. He was black-haired and taller than the boys behind him, and he carried his flag with great conviction.

Evangelia's neighbour lowered her own small flag, muttering.

'It's wrong,' she said. 'It's all *wrong*. He shouldn't be bearing our flag.'

Another one, close by, picked up on her theme.

'Albanian . . .' he said darkly, and under his breath.

Another man heard the word.

'A *foreigner* carrying our flag?'

'It's not *right*. Not right at all,' agreed his wife. 'Only a pure Greek should have this honour!'

Evangelia glanced at the flag seller, who clasped a bunch of fifty or so flags in his fist. His eyes glistened.

The conversation continued around him.

'He's top of the class, Dimitri,' said another woman. 'That's why he's carrying the flag. You might not agree with it, but that's how it is.'

There were grumbles of discontent all around and silence in their section of the crowd. Nobody around cheered the group.

The boy came level with Evangelia and glanced over in her direction. His face creased into a dazzling smile, then he turned to face the direction in which he was marching, waving the flag so that it floated, blue and white, unfurled, liberated to flutter in the sky.

She looked at the man who was standing silently next to her. The flag seller's eyes were full of tears, and Evangelia realised why the boy had looked their way.

'Congratulations,' she said quietly, turning to the man. 'You must be proud.'

He nodded in acknowledgement, unable to speak. His eyes were still following the group from his son's school, but all he could see now was the top of the flagpole his child held.

When Evangelia next looked round, the man had shuffled away and melted into the crowd. Almost immediately afterwards came troops of soldiers and young conscripts. Their boots hard and crisp on the tarmac, they marched along the street. Their chants were loud and fierce, giving the impression they were battle-ready.

I will fight for you,
Give my life for you,
Write in blood for you,
Use my heart for you,
To say 'I love you.'
Ell- a- d- a mou, Ell-a-da mou!!!
I will fight for you,
Give my life for you.

It seemed they were ready to die for their country.

The conversation around Evangelia had moved on to other things, but she thought of what the Albanian might have heard (and prayed that his Greek was too poor for him to have understood). As the soldiers began to pass, she found her shame deepening, and not just because she should have supported the woman who objected to her neighbour's comments.

If the Albanian boy had no right to carry the flag, then neither did her granddaughter. In all the world, she was the only one who knew this, but it was as true as the flag was white and blue.

Like the father of the boy who had passed before them a few minutes before, the father of her own child had spoken little Greek. Her granddaughter was by no means 'pure' in blood.

What had taken place had been so many years before, but the secret still endured.

Evangelia was eighteen years old when German soldiers marched into her city. At the time, her father owned a café, *Je Reviens*, close to the port. It was a convenient situation in a busy location and he was forbidden by the Germans to close it. The bar quickly became an establishment popular with the occupying soldiers.

Evangelia's mother refused to have anything to do with it, and her brothers had managed to get out of the city to join the resistance. This left only Evangelia to help her father, which she did by washing glasses and cleaning the tables. She was not allowed to speak to the soldiers.

Many of the men were drunk and ill-disciplined when they were off duty. Evangelia hated them all, except for one, who always sat quietly on his own as if keeping an eye on his fellow Germans. When any fights got out of hand, he disciplined the perpetrators and threw them out on to the pavement. He was of a higher rank than the others and never drank with them. Instead, he sat and read.

As Evangelia carried a tray of glasses through one day, one of the young corporals touched her bottom. Her father saw and came from behind the bar to confront a table of

jeering soldiers. One of them stood up to her father and drew his gun. For a few seconds of pure terror, Evangelia imagined that both she and her father would die. Their lives had no value for these young conscripts. Suddenly she was aware that the soldier who always sat quietly in the corner had also stood up. He barked something in German and the younger man immediately put away his gun. The group of offending soldiers never reappeared in the bar. From then on, Evangelia always felt safe when she saw him sitting, almost unnoticed, in his usual corner. Her father never charged him a drachma for his coffee or occasional glass of raki.

A few days after the incident with the gun, when the café was almost empty, Evangelia noticed that the man was reading something in French. It was one of the subjects in which she had excelled at school. Despite being under strict instructions to keep her distance at all times from the clientele, she could not resist speaking to him and seized the opportunity given by the book.

'*Merci*,' she said. '*Vous avez sauvé mon père.* Thank you for saving my father.'

He assured her that it was purely duty to act as he did. They then had a brief conversation, both of them happy to speak a language they loved. He told her that his name was Franz Dieter and she told him hers.

To hear him speaking the musical language that she associated with poetry and literature transformed him in her eyes. The guttural sound of German had not suited him.

Over a period of some months she had small conversations with him in this language that was foreign to them both and incomprehensible to everyone else in the bar.

257

'*S'il vous plaît, n'imaginez pas que tous les Allemands veulent la même chose, pensent la même chose . . .*'

It was a polite request, his plea for understanding. He wanted her to believe that not all Germans were the same, with identical desires and beliefs. To state any more would have been enough to have him court-martialled. He was simply asking her to see him as an individual.

Later on, as their conversations continued, she discovered that he had not chosen to be a soldier; he had wanted neither to give up his post teaching French in a university nor to leave behind his home in Dresden. None of these things had been his choice.

Over the following year, Evangelia looked out for him each day. When he was going to be away on duty, he always told her in advance. He knew – they both knew – that an attachment between them was growing. Inside the formality of their conversation, much could be expressed, and only the two of them shared the significance of the day when he first asked if he could use *tu*, the informal 'you'.

Evangelia's French rapidly improved, and her father could not object to their conversation as it was clear that Franz offered some kind of protection to the bar.

Three years after they had marched in, the rumour began to circulate that the Germans were defeated and were to leave Greece. There was quiet celebration at the news, but many would not believe it until they saw the back of the soldiers. One night, Evangelia learned that it was true.

The café was empty. Something was definitely taking place. She stood alone behind the bar, polishing glasses. Her father had not yet come down from the first-floor apartment for the evening. She replaced the glasses carefully and straightened the bottles on the shelf, her back to the door. The bell gave a brisk *ting* as someone came in.

Evangelia span round. It was Franz. In his hands was a small pile of books. He advanced towards her.

'They are for you. You know we are leaving?'

Evangelia came out from behind the bar. He held out the well-worn books to her and she took them from him, glancing at their spines and blinking back her tears.

Balzac, Flaubert, Racine, *Poèmes d'Amour*.

They were all the books that he had been reading in these past months. She looked down at them and then up at him, her emotion undisguised.

'I can't take these with me,' he said.

Evangelia spontaneously put the books down and threw her arms around him, feeling the metal buttons of his uniform through her thin dress.

Franz instinctively tried to pull away, aware of what would happen if her father or another soldier appeared, but her innocence and the flowery scent of her hair intoxicated him. In all these years, they had never even stood close and the human contact and sweetness of a feminine embrace were unfamiliar. As she looked up into his face, he bent down to kiss her.

Evangelia's feelings for this young soldier poured out in her response. This was the last time she was ever going to see him and great waves of sorrow, even of grief, washed over her.

For both of them, there was a sense of discovery but also of panic.

259

'*Vous allez revenir?*' Evangelia asked, barely concealing her desperation. 'You will come back?'

Franz did not answer.

They stood in the middle of the café looking at each other, until Evangelia took his hand and led him into the shadows. Her need to kiss him one last time was urgent.

Gone was the timidity of their first embrace. In its place came the raw passion of a farewell kiss. This fair-haired soldier had never been her enemy and, now that his country had been defeated, there seemed nothing more natural than to show him her love.

In the darkness of a small storeroom, Franz laid down his jacket for Evangelia to lie on and, until the sound of her father's footsteps disturbed them, they made love in the darkness.

Wordlessly, but holding Evangelia's fingers until the final moment when he had to let go, Franz left quietly through another door. This moment in both their lives passed as quickly as any other.

Having straightened her clothes and tidied her hair with her fingers, Evangelia went out into the bar. The books were still lying on the table.

'Whose are those?' asked her father gruffly.

'They're mine,' she said, quickly picking them up and holding them tight to her chest.

Over the following months, Evangelia's family struggled, as did every other ordinary family in Greece, to rebuild their lives. There was great joy that the Germans had gone but, as the Greek people surveyed the devastation they had left in their wake, there was little celebration. It was a matter of survival and reconstruction. Evangelia's brothers were swept up in a new wave of fighting between Left and Right, and it was several years before either returned to Thessaloniki.

Greece was in chaos. Hundreds of thousands of Greeks had died during the occupation, many of them from starvation. Everyone was undernourished. Perhaps for this reason, it was only in her seventh month that people outside the family noticed Evangelia's pregnancy. Both her parents accepted it (they had no choice), and it was easy for the family to fabricate the story of a fiancé who had never made it back from the front – and, in any case, a fatherless baby was not so unusual during these dark days of loss.

When the baby was born, she was adored by everyone around her. To have new life in the midst of the dust and the rubble was a blessing, they all said.

Efi was never told the identity of her father. She grew up in a period of relative peace and, in time, had her own children, naming her eldest daughter after her mother.

Nature kindly made the decision that Efi should look exactly like her mother. There was not a trace of her father's blond, Teutonic looks and it was in this way that the secret had been kept.

Later, on the afternoon of 25 March, Evangelia went to church, as she always did on her name day, and lit a candle to her lost Franz. He had not promised to return but she had always hoped that, one day, she would see him again. Whenever she saw a party of German tourists she scanned their faces, looking for his sapphire eyes and gentle smile.

After her ritual, she went by taxi down to the port and stood outside the now abandoned café. Just as she did every year on this day, she took an old and battered book from her handbag and silently read a particular poem. Even now, she longed to see the man she loved. Even now, she dreamed of his return.

Présence de Dieu
Max Jacob

Une nuit que je parcourais le ciel amour
Une nuit de douce mère
Où les étoiles étaient les feux du retour
Et diaprées comme l'arc-en-ciel
Une nuit que les étoiles disaient:
'Je reviens!'

In the Presence of God

One night as I surveyed a lover's sky
A gentle mother night
When the stars were lights to guide a homecoming
Dappled like a rainbow
I read into the stars these words:
'I will return!'

I looked up Max Jacob as soon as I could. He was a Jewish poet and painter, a friend of Apollinaire and Picasso, and he died in March 1944 en route to Auschwitz. I imagine Evangelia found that out, too.

The German occupation left the country completely stripped of resources and money. The troops (perhaps Franz Dieter included) destroyed as much as they could on their way out of Greece when they retreated in 1944. I met plenty of people on my journey, old and young, who believe that Germany should pay what they still owe.

The 'unpaid' cost of Nazi war crimes, damage to the infrastructure and the forced loan extracted from the Greek banks are said to amount to the equivalent of nearly 300 billion euros today. Such a figure would help pay off the debt that cripples Greece now.

Thessaloniki itself is particularly scarred by the Holocaust. More than fifty thousand people, the majority of Greece's Jewish population, were forcibly deported by train to Auschwitz. Very few escaped this horror. Perhaps some of them might have met Max Jacob, if he had not died on his way there. The hardship that Thessaloniki faced is almost impossible to imagine on a sunny day in spring, but the memories still linger.

I stayed in Thessaloniki for many more days than I had planned. It is a beautiful and fascinating city, lively from dawn until dawn. The huge university fills it with vibrancy and youth. I became friendly with a curator in the Archaeological Museum who invited me to a series of lectures and events, and I was even asked to give a seminar. I was rejoining the world, and even had the energy and inspiration to finish the first draft of my book.

One afternoon, when I was ambling through the cobbled alleyways of the Ladadika (an area of the city full of old olive-oil warehouses), I heard a sound that took me back in time. It would have been very familiar to the teenaged Evangelia, before the German jackboot marched in.

It was somewhere between piano and stringed instrument, with the occasional ting of a bell, like the chime of a triangle. It reminded me a little of rebetiko, the music that originated in Asia Minor, and I felt the stirrings of a strange, deep nostalgia for an era that I had not even lived through, a homesickness for somewhere I had never been.

As I turned into the square, I saw the source of the music. It was a big, decorated wooden box on wheels, with a handle that its player was turning to make the noise. A laterna. The player was around seventy years old and very smartly turned out. Once I had dropped five euros into his upturned tambourine, he had all the time in the world to answer my questions.

Tassos was his name, and he told me that laternas, barrel

pianos, had been ubiquitous in the days before the gramophone and were the first mechanical way to produce music. For a century, they were glamorous and popular. The first ones were crafted in Constantinople by an Italian, hence La Torno, 'the thing that turns'. Production more or less came to an end after the 1950s, and now they are a less common sight.

He lifted the lid so that I could see the mechanism. As the handle was turned, a wooden cylinder pierced with hundreds of steel pegs rotated. When a peg came into contact with one of a row of spring-loaded hammers, the hammer rose, before falling back on to a string to sound the note.

It was finely crafted, but what intrigued me more than anything was the black-and-white photograph framed by carnations on the side of the box.

'They always have a picture,' Tassos told me. 'But this picture is very sentimental. It meant a great deal to the owner . . .'

'So you aren't the owner?' I asked.

'I am now,' he said. 'But originally it belonged to Panagiotis.'

'Who was he?'

'The happiest man I ever knew,' he replied. 'The story really begins in 1954, but I'll start in 2010. Our country's finances were already in a mess. I was going around the tavernas selling packets of tissues and cigarette lighters and, suddenly, people didn't even have cash to spare for those. The only person for whom the coins kept flowing was my friend Panagiotis — the sound of his laterna always got people to dip into their pockets.'

LATERNA, POVERTY AND HONOUR

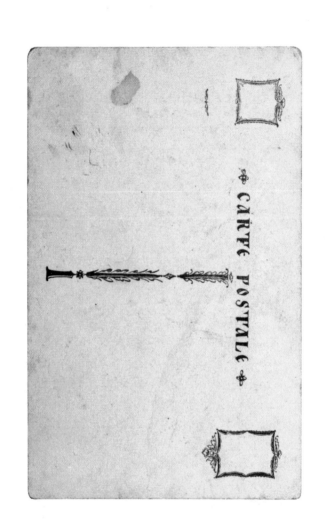

CARTE POSTALE

'LATERNA, POVERTY AND HONOUR'
'Λατέρνα, φτώχεια και φιλότιμο'

The streets of Thessaloniki thronged with people, but the *salep* seller was doing very little business. Only a few tourists stopped to buy the thick, sweet drink that he served from his wheeled cart. Most of them couldn't get through a whole cup of it. Made from orchid tubers, it was an ancient recipe and an acquired taste, only bought to satisfy curiosity.

'The young these days,' the seller muttered, 'they just want their frappé.'

Watching the streams of people strolling hand in hand along the esplanade, the *salep* man had grown bitter. His father had given him the trolley with its big metal container forty years earlier. It had been a family business, but he felt ever more certain that it would end with him. Nobody wanted his drink any more and, year by year, sales dropped. Coffee had always been a rival, but the culture surrounding it these days was obsessive. Hot in the winter, cold in the summer. He had no chance.

'They need three hands here, these kids,' he said. 'One for the cigarette, one for the girlfriend and a third for the coffee.'

The chestnut man did slightly better. A cheap snack of freshly roasted chestnuts appealed to almost everyone. With a seeded *koulouri* bun from the seller on the corner of Aristotelous and Niki Street, a handful of warm chestnuts had always been considered the perfect breakfast. Nowadays, though, the huge student population of the city preferred fast food.

Greece seemed to be going through a period of transition, as far as the older generation was concerned. They moaned about the way their country had changed, how traditions were disappearing, how they didn't recognise their own *patrida* or the people who lived in it.

The only person working on the streets who never complained was Panagiotis, the *laterna* player. The one consumer habit that did not change was a desire to recapture the past, and what he was selling was like an aroma, something intangible, a glimpse of the 'black and white' era. He lived in the past himself and reminded other people of theirs, and passers-by were very happy to toss him a coin. Many coins, in fact.

Most thought he was simple because he seemed happy travelling from the old town to the new, from square to esplanade and back again, trundling his precious *laterna*, but he regarded himself as an artist, a *kalliteknis*. This belief sustained him in his solitary life, along with the coins that people left in the upturned tambourine at his feet.

His passion for the *laterna* was born when he was ten. It was in the early 1950s, when the country was learning to live in peace again. The sun seemed to shine every day and Panagiotis and his friends could hang around in the streets

of Athens, disappear for hours in a game of hide-and-seek and take over an alleyway to play football. They never tired of these activities, but one day in the summer of 1954, their routine was interrupted.

'They're making a *film!*' Panagiotis's best friend said gleefully. 'They're shooting round the corner in the square now – but next they're coming *here!*'

The five boys, all in short trousers and around ten years old, stopped their game and sat on a wall waiting, swinging their skinny legs in time.

Eventually, two men came, both in suits and trilbies, one of them fatter and older with a handsome moustache. The younger of them had a *laterna* strapped to his back. Behind them came a group of more than twenty, burdened with cumbersome equipment. Three men carried a huge camera, and others had heavy lights and microphones. In addition to the porters required to carry all of these, there was a team for costumes and make-up, and then of course the director himself.

The children looked on, instinctively keeping quiet while the filming took place. Two men talked, then a man near the camera shouted, then they talked again. This process went on and on, with one repeat after another. The children kept hearing the word: 'Cut!'

When they finished filming the scene, the actors and crew strolled away, presumably for lunch, leaving the street empty. The boys all simultaneously leapt off the wall.

As well as all the other filming paraphernalia, Panagiotis noticed that they had abandoned the *laterna*. It was lavishly painted, decorated with flowers and, in pride of place, there

was a black-and-white portrait of a glamorous couple. He ran towards it. He could not resist. As always, the other boys followed their ringleader.

Panagiotis reached out and touched its wooden case, which was warmed by the sun. Then he grabbed the handle and began to turn it. Music rang out, sweet and melodic, its notes ricocheting off the walls and filling the little sidestreet. The other boys pranced around, jigging up and down to the tune.

The actors and crew were returning from their break.

'Hey! You!' shouted the cameraman. 'Leave it alone.'

The director had seen them, too, but his momentary irritation vanished when he realised the potential of this mischief on film. He wanted to capture the boys' childlike delight in music.

'Stop! Stop!' he called, as the boys tore off down the street. 'Wait!'

He sent his assistant to run after them, and he soon returned with the five boisterous children. For a whole afternoon, they shot and re-shot the scene of the boys gathered round the *laterna*, with Panagiotis and a younger boy turning the handle before being chased off like street urchins.

During a break, Panagiotis lifted the lid to see the working mechanism of the *laterna*. It was more complex than anything he had ever seen. He was spellbound by the minutely coordinated set of actions that resulted in the magical production of music.

The film *Laterna, Ftohia kai Filotimo – Laterna, Poverty and Honour* – was released the following year and was an enormous success. It told the story of two itinerants who meet a rich girl on the run. They forego the chance to gain a huge ransom by handing her in, preferring to help her rather than betray her.

On a warm summer's evening in 1955, Panagiotis and his parents went to an open-air cinema to see it. They were full of anticipation. There on the screen they saw the familiar sight of Plaka, their neighbourhood. Every door, every step, every window was glamorised by its transition to the screen.

When their son's face appeared, Panagiotis's parents burst into applause. He blushed with equal measures of embarrassment and pride.

At that moment, he realised that this was what he wanted to do with his life. After the film, he told his parents that he had something to tell them.

'I know what I want to do when I grow up,' he said.

They held their breath. An actor's career was not really what they wanted for their son.

'I want to be a *laterna* player,' he announced.

From that day on, Panagiotis lobbied his father.

'This is what I want to do,' he said to him. 'You won't have to worry about my future!'

'A life on the road?' said his mother, wringing her hands.

'Making people smile and making them dance!' said Panagiotis. 'What could be better? I'll need a *laterna*,' he added.

The charm of the film lay in the combination of the actors' exuberance, the images of Greece and a happy-ever-after story. Panagiotis wanted to inhabit the world it portrayed, where people needed little to be content and honour prevailed.

A *laterna* cost far more than his parents could afford, but over a period of three years, they kept aside everything they could. Panagiotis's father had always hoped that his son would help him in his foundry when he left school, but you could not make a boy who wanted to play a *laterna* solder iron for railings. He respected his son's strong sense of vocation.

Eventually, he and his wife had saved up enough. They covered it with a blanket and, that night, they waited up for him to come home before the great unveiling. He was as thrilled as they had hoped. It really was his dream. As was the tradition, Panagiotis dressed up in a tailored suit and put a flower in his buttonhole. He was aged seventeen and ready to go on the road.

Just as he knew from watching the film, it was an itinerant life, and his heart beat faster when he looked at a map and saw the names of other cities: Larissa, Lamia, Tripoli, Ioannina, Thessaloniki. He planned to visit them all.

Certain lines from the film had always lived with him:

O kalliteknis then einai ekeinos pou pezei violi i flaouto,
O kalliteknis einai etho.

Panagiotis often repeated them to his audience, who were all familiar with the film:

The artist is not the man who plays violin or flute,
The artist is here.

And with the final words, he pointed to his heart.

The couple whose image decorated his *laterna* were Jenny Karezi and Alekos Alexandrakis, the romantic stars of *Laterna, Poverty and Honour,* but people who stopped to listen soon knew that he had been in the film, too. Everyone remembered the scene with the small boys. Panagiotis became a celebrity and played up to his role, dressing grandly and making sure that people knew of his connection with the 'big screen'.

After a decade on the road, this dapper figure decided that Thessaloniki was the ideal place to make his home. There was a constant influx of newcomers to the city so his potential audience was always refreshed by tourists, students and travelling salesmen. Gramophones were already in production but there were still plenty of people who preferred to dance to a *laterna*. He rented a small house in the old town, with a place to store the *laterna* on the ground floor, and settled into a pattern of playing in different squares and streets around the city.

Sometimes he would get a whole group dancing around him in Aristotelous Square, and then another circle would join on the outside, and then another. Eventually there might be three or four concentric circles. It was good for everyone when that happened and sales of everything benefited: *salep*, chestnuts, *koulouria* and even paper tissues.

Even as the years went by and the world began to see the *laterna* more as a form of begging than of culture, Panagiotis continued to believe in himself as an artist and people continued to throw coins and notes into his tambourine. The sound evoked a memory of innocence and they happily rewarded him for it. He took the money as his due, but spent only what he needed on his modest and simple life.

Over the years, he gained a reputation as the happiest man in Thessaloniki, untouched by the worries that caused his fellow street sellers such pain. Then one day, when he returned from a successful evening near the White Tower, he could see that his door was already open. When he reached it, he saw pinned to the frame an official-looking envelope. It was a warrant for his arrest.

He parked his *laterna* on the ground floor and, as usual, wearily climbed the stairs. Giving the door a huge shove to move an unseen obstruction on the other side, he made his way in. The whole floor was thickly carpeted with coins, and once he was inside Panagiotis tipped the day's earnings

on top of the rest. He then lit a candle that was sitting on a battered table and crunched across the carpet of coins that covered his floor to reach the sink. Having filled a cracked mug with water, he crunched over to his bed. The flicker of the flame caught the gold and silver edges of the coins and created a glittering pattern on the ceiling. Much of it was small change, not enough individually to buy a *koulouri*, but collectively it added up to millions. It was a treasure hoard. Panagiotis could hear a few coins trickling down through the floorboards, and he made a note to retrieve them in the morning.

The following day, the police returned with a search warrant. Panagiotis was already out somewhere in the city, turning the handle of his *laterna*. There was so much money in his house they would have to return with a truck. The judge would demand it as evidence.

It was decades' worth of earnings. The police report that was printed in the local newspaper said that the coins were almost a metre and a half thick on the floor in some places. One of the taller officers had to stoop in order to avoid hitting his head on the ceiling. There were layers and layers in every denomination, millions of them, and it took a team of three police sergeants two weeks to count them all.

For sixty years, Panagiotis had not paid tax. Not even ten cents. By more or less ignoring his earnings, he believed he had retained his principle of noble 'poverty' (even if 'honour' had been compromised).

There was a long court case, during which he had no heart to play his *laterna*, even in the evenings. The tonnage of euros that was being stored in a bank until the case was over gradually dwindled and by the time the lawyer's fees, tax and fines had been paid, all he had left was the *laterna* itself. Panagiotis's main fear had been a prison sentence, but the judge felt that a financial penalty was the most appropriate one. 'This is the punishment that best fits the crime,' he said, signing papers that effectively took everything from the old man except his musical instrument.

'I am still an artist,' said Panagiotis outside the court, hatted and suited, with a carnation in his buttonhole. 'And my *laterna* is all I need.'

When he died, a few years later, in the same bed in which he had been sleeping for nearly fifty years, his landlady found a note in his room saying that the *laterna* must go to his friend Tassos. She thought this must be someone among the street sellers, and it didn't take her long to find the right man.

For Tassos, it was definitely a step up from selling paper handkerchiefs, but it wasn't his vocation, as it had been for Panagiotis. He didn't have the visceral connection with the *laterna* and he didn't play with a smile. He could not take people back to a lost time.

As Tassos finished his story, a Ferrari roared by. The music that blasted from its open windows drowned out all other sound.

'I miss the old days!' he yelled above the din. He wasn't just referring to the easy availability of any music, any time, any place. He was talking about the government wanting even street vendors to pay their dues now.

We ended up having a heated discussion about paying tax. I had never imagined that I would have such a debate in a Greek square with a man who busked for a living, but I learned a lot about the way in which some people here view the tax system. They simply don't see themselves as part of it (just as Panagiotis hadn't). This man, Tassos, did not feel that he should be obliged to pay even a cent of his earnings, however small the percentage. There was no connection in his mind between himself and the schools, hospitals, roads, street cleaning, and so on that have to be paid for.

His view was simply this: all politicians are corrupt and the money he would pay to the government would go straight into someone's pocket. This attitude runs through the veins of the Greek people – and not entirely without reason. Billions have been stolen, wasted and squandered by people in high places over the past few decades, further deepening the vast, unpayable debt that now burdens this small country. So I partly understood why he felt as he did, but I couldn't help asking him, 'How will things ever get better?'

He didn't have an answer, and the shrug of his shoulders gave me the impression that this individual did not care for society but only for himself: he was a one-man band in more ways than one. Until a new culture of transparency sweeps through the country, from top to bottom, what chance is there?

As our encounter came to an end (it reached an impasse very rapidly), I noticed that, close to where we stood, there was a set of overflowing bins. On the ground next to them lay a man. It was hard to tell if he was sleeping or dead.

I could not help making the connection in my mind between Tassos's sense of himself as an individual without responsibility and the man lying on the street to whom the state can offer nothing. By the end of our conversation, I resented having given him even a euro.

In Greece, there are said to be places (as well as people like Tassos) that exist totally outside the law. People talk of towns and villages that are never visited by the police and run themselves almost as independent kingdoms. Perhaps they are pure legend, but I don't imagine that all the stories are fabricated.

There was news coverage not so long ago of a village on an island that had been left alone by the police for many years. When a new regional head of police was appointed, he decided to pay a visit. The villagers put up barricades and shot and wounded several police. When the officers finally went in, after days of siege, they discovered dozens of cash-point machines which had been wrenched from the walls of banks in towns all over the island, scores of Porsche Cayennes and many children who had never been to school. A thriving economy based on a highly lucrative drugs trade meant that the place had become a law unto itself. Such a village is rarely on a tourist map.

On my own journey, I occasionally arrived in a place that was a quintessential carte postale – and yet there was something not quite right about it, something that made me dislike it, a gut feeling, perhaps. Similarly, I went to places that were scruffy, but charming. Of course, this might have something to do with the time of day I arrived, the smile (or scowl) of a shopkeeper or the way a waiter greeted a traveller such as me. Whatever it is that makes a place welcoming or hostile is initially hard to define, but there is often an explanation.

After my stay in Thessaloniki, I took a week or so to make my way slowly down the east coast, passing through Katerini, Larissa, Volos and Lamia.

One day, not a great distance from Lamia, I visited a fishing village that was so pretty no painter could have done *it justice. To get there, I drove down a bumpy road (little more than a track) through verdant meadows and past rows of ripening crops. Oranges and lemons were so plentiful that they lay in mounds, ungathered.*

The village was ideally located, south-facing, with a sheltered natural harbour and colourful fishing boats moored in a tidy row. There was even a delightful sandy cove for swimming close by with pine trees right down by the water's edge. Ancient olive trees with gnarled silver trunks grew in abundance on neighbouring hillsides. The residents seemed to have more than enough of everything.

As far as I could see from the displays in the seafront restaurants, compliant fish swam into nets to feed a population that had little or no interest in tourism. Everyone eating in them looked like a local and several gave a dismissive 'tut' when I asked if there was a table free. Evidence of their lack of interest in foreign visitors was that not a single shop sold sun lotion, straw hats or even a postcard. That's unusual enough for a Greek seaside place. But the total lack of hotels, pensions or even signs saying 'Rooms' was almost beyond explanation.

This was a place truly lacking in filoxenia, hospitality. I swam, strolled around the village and, for the first time on this trip, felt like taking out my camera. I remembered how much pleasure I used to get from capturing a place on film. The familiar weight of my Nikon was comforting and I felt less conspicuously alone in a place which, like most, seemed entirely frequented by happy couples. Once it was dark I had an overpriced dinner (reluctantly served) and then drove out.

When I got to the main road, I did not stop for another fifty kilometres and, when I did, it was midnight and I was in a workaday town. I picked the first hotel I came to. Two stars, twenty-five euros for the night, and the crispest linen and most comfortable bed I have ever slept in. Breakfast was complimentary and included the best coffee I had tasted for weeks.

'Will you be staying another night?' enquired the owner, cheerfully bringing me a second espresso, before I had even asked for one.

'Yes,' I decided spontaneously. 'I would love to.'

'Excellent,' he said. 'You don't have a fixed itinerary?'

'No,' I replied, 'I'm just following my nose. It's the best way.'

'Alone?' he asked.

I nodded, but less sadly than I would have done a month or two before. The word had slightly lost its sting.

He seemed genuinely interested to know where I had been, so I described a few of my favourite places (many of which he had never visited himself). I told him about the previous day, about the strangeness of the place in which I had found myself. When I said the name, his reaction was immediate.

'You went there?' he said incredulously. He shook his head in disbelief. 'Nobody goes there. Certainly not tourists.'

'Why on earth not?' I asked him.

'It's said,' he replied darkly, 'that something terrible happened there.'

What he told me more than explained my sense of unease.

HONEYMOON

POST CARD
CARTE POSTALE

HONEYMOON

Voyage de Noces

'Jean-Luc, isn't that beautiful!' Sylvie said to her new husband as they drove past an old stone house. 'Look at that gorgeous little cottage, with all the creeper, so roman*tique*!'

With no knowledge of what had left these buildings in such a bad state (vendetta, death or tragedy were common causes), visitors saw only what they wanted to see, and such dereliction could charm, forming part of a tableau. Even the wrecks of wooden boats, once intended for repair, looked delightful in the sunshine.

'Look at that! It's almost *sculptural*, isn't it, *mon cher*? Like a fish skeleton! *Extraordinaire . . .*'

Jean-Luc, who could not take his eyes off the road for fear of disappearing down a rut, grunted in response.

Sylvie and Jean-Luc, intrepid French young professionals, preferred to take a route other than the one well beaten by most holiday-makers. It was their third visit to Greece, and their honeymoon. They followed what was little more than a track down towards the sea. It was part of a satisfying illusion that they were discovering

somewhere very few people had been. They wanted to dive beneath the glossy surface of the postcard and find themselves the 'real thing'.

After their flight from Paris, which had been delayed, they were so eager to get on the road that neither of them noticed there was only a dribble of petrol in their hire car. By the time the light had alerted them, every petrol station was closed. Their top-of-the-range jeep finally juddered to a halt by the side of the road with the sun beginning to disappear behind the mountains.

They would have to find somewhere for the night. The road map tucked into the dashboard showed no signs of habitation for many kilometres ahead, but Jean-Luc consulted Google Maps, which indicated a few houses at the very end of a small turning off the main road a short distance ahead.

'It's a ten-kilometre walk, *ma chérie*,' said Jean-Luc. 'We'll manage that, won't we?'

The question was rhetorical. They had both walked up Mount Kilimanjaro the previous summer (it was where Jean-Luc had proposed). Ten kilometres was nothing.

They set off on foot, stuffing a change of T-shirt and their toothbrushes into Sylvie's Hermès bag. After almost two hours of walking along a neglected, pot-holed road, they came to the houses. The windows were dark, and there were no cars parked outside.

'I don't think they are inhabited,' said Jean-Luc.

There had been no signposts of any kind en route, nor had there been any turnings off the road. They took it in turns to illuminate the way with the flashlights on their mobiles.

'Are you *sure* there's anything down here?' asked Sylvie.

'The road wouldn't be here unless it led somewhere,' said Jean-Luc, with impeccable logic. 'There's definitely something there.'

As they walked, he consulted the vintage Patek Philippe on his wrist, a gift from Sylvie's father when they got engaged. It was gone nine thirty.

Another group of houses came in sight not long after. They had reached the edge of a village.

'Strange that it wasn't on the map,' commented Sylvie. It was almost a small town, by Greek standards.

Sylvie was charmed by the elegant pastel-coloured houses with pretty wrought-iron balconies and huge pots overflowing with basil. Her energy and enthusiasm for their adventure returned. Jean-Luc, however, was in a bad mood. He blamed his wife for the lack of petrol and the fact that they did not know where they would sleep, but most of all, for his hunger.

They came to a small street with some shops, but the butcher's, baker's and greengrocer's were all closed.

'Why is everything shut?' Sylvie asked her husband. 'It's a Friday night!'

They would have expected most things to be open at this hour.

'How should I know?' Jean-Luc answered grumpily. 'Your guess is as good as mine.'

He pressed his nose up against a wine shop.

'Looks like they have some excellent vintages,' he said. 'Pity it's closed.'

The sight of some St Émilion *premier cru* in the window

had almost cheered him up. Someone in this town appreciated good wine.

The village was strangely empty for a Friday in late April but they could not read the signs in the shop windows that explained why.

Even a *kafenion* they passed was shut and, in their walk through the town, they had so far not seen even one small *pension*.

Sylvie pointed at a sign. 'I think that says "Police Station",' she said.

A small arrow pointed up to the first floor.

'Maybe they'll be able to help,' she said. 'I'll just pop up and ask them.'

Sylvie had learned a few words of Greek and had her phrasebook tucked in her bag.

At the top of a long, narrow staircase she found a single door. As she knocked, the force of her hand pushed it open, and she found herself in an empty room. There was not a table or even a chair. It was just a high-ceilinged, windowless space painted light green with a noticeboard nailed to the wall on which were pinned some black-and-white mugshots. She shut the door and went back down into the street.

'Any luck?' asked Jean-Luc as she emerged.

'Well, there can't be much crime here,' she said. 'But maybe there are no hotels either.'

'*Merde!*' said Jean-Luc. 'It looks like we're going to be walking all the way back to the car and sleeping in it.'

He then felt obliged to state the obvious, simply to accentuate the misery of the situation.

'And there are clearly no petrol stations in this town.'

'Let's try and be positive,' said Sylvie, taking her husband's hand. 'It might be lovely under the stars . . .'

It wouldn't be too bad, she thought. The evening was still warm.

This out-of-the-way community clearly economised on street lighting, and the moon was new so it did not light their path.

Despite the darkness, Sylvie realised that they had passed the same pastry shop more than once.

'We must be going round in circles,' she said in frustration.

They continued on for a few more minutes.

'Why the hell didn't you check the petrol gauge . . . ?' she suddenly said.

He did not respond for a moment.

'Me?' he retorted, implying that he regarded it as his wife's responsibility.

Trying to calm down, he changed his tone of voice. They had got married only two days earlier, after all.

'Look, let's keep looking for somewhere to eat,' he suggested.

The village was a complex network of small streets and they turned a corner and, without expecting it, found themselves in a square. Sylvie noticed that the doors of a nearby church were open and, as they approached, they could see that it was full, with the congregation almost overflowing on to the street.

'At last!' said Sylvie. 'A sign of life!'

'What's going on?' she whispered, as they stood at the door.

Jean-Luc was tall enough to see over the heads of the congregation. At the far end of the aisle he could see several priests and a crowd of people standing around a large, flower-covered coffin. All the blooms were white.

'It looks like a funeral,' he said quietly.

They both backed out, feeling that they might be intruding. Hunger was beginning to get the better of them both now. There had to be some restaurants.

At the end of the next street they spotted a shop with a light on. It was a general store, the *pantopoleion*.

'I forgot to bring any toothpaste from the car,' said Sylvie. 'They're bound to sell some here.'

Ignoring her husband's protestations of hunger, she pushed open the door. Jean-Luc stayed outside. Although the shop front was narrow, the shop itself went back further than they could see. She started perusing the shelves at the front of the store to see if they sold what she was looking for.

The *pantopoleion* had a bizarre range of goods on its shelves, and it was hard to tell if things were new or second-hand. Some of them must have been sitting there since the 1970s – everything from hair-ties with plastic bobbles, cassette tapes, eyeshadows in bright blues and greens, cotton bras for old ladies (one size only) and brown plastic shoes (one style only). Sylvie was bemused by a range of faded coats and handbags and an odd selection of jewellery. There were even some tattered German–Greek phrasebooks and an old Nokia phone. She noticed everything from Tippex to flat-packed doll's clothes. Every shelf was filled from front to back, and there were things hanging from the ceiling.

From the gloom, a deep, nicotine-tarry voice asked, '*Ti theleis?* What do you want?'

Sylvie jumped as a broad, imposing figure emerged. Assuming the owner might only speak Greek, Sylvie did a mime of cleaning her teeth with her forefinger.

'Toothpaste?' the woman answered gruffly. 'No. No toothpaste. Try the pharmacy.'

The shopkeeper was rattling some keys, indicating that Sylvie should leave. She was only too happy to do so, though she imagined that the woman knew as well as she did that the chemist's was closed.

Before she was ushered out, Sylvie managed to ask her why it was that everything was so quiet.

'*Megali Paraskevi!* Good Friday,' she hissed.

Outside, Jean-Luc had lit a cigarette and was pacing up and down.

'Well, she wasn't very helpful,' commented Sylvie. 'No toothpaste.'

'*Allons-y*,' said Jean-Luc irritably. 'Let's go. If there's nowhere to eat, you won't need to clean your teeth anyway.'

As they walked, Sylvie told him what the shopkeeper had said.

'But Easter was in March. And it's now nearly May,' said Jean-Luc. 'She was making a fool of you.'

The couple had not understood that the date of Greek Orthodox Easter was different from the Catholic one. The only person they had spoken to since landing was the monosyllabic car-hire man, and he had not mentioned it. He had certainly not pointed out the additional premium charged by the company for holiday weekends.

Jean-Luc spotted a small taverna not far from the general store. He grabbed Sylvie's arm and led her there.

'Have you booked?' asked the owner.

The tables were all empty, both inside and out, so the question surprised them.

'No,' said Jean-Luc. 'Did we need to?'

'It's Easter,' said the man coldly. 'You should always book at Easter. Especially on Good Friday.'

Sylvie and Jean-Luc looked at each other. Sylvie could see that Jean-Luc was going to protest.

'You can have a table just for an hour. Until the *epitafios* has been taken round the streets and back to church. Then you will have to go. That's when everyone will arrive.'

They asked for no further explanation and took one of the tables on the pavement.

'So it *is* Easter,' said Sylvie. 'The woman in the shop was telling the truth. It must be why the church was so full.'

The waiter brought a number of dishes. There was no menu. No choice. They were served with squid, octopus and taramasalata (none of which they would have ordered) and drank water only. Jean-Luc was fussy about his wine and it was only available from the cask here.

'I could really do with some meat,' said Jean-Luc. 'Or even some decent fish.'

'I suppose it must still be Lent,' said Sylvie, chewing on some *kalamari*.

While they were eating, Sylvie got her phone out and looked up 'Greek Orthodox Easter'. Briskly, she paraphrased:

'So, tonight they parade the icon of Christ around the town, tomorrow they burn an effigy of Judas and on Sunday they celebrate that Christ is risen. According to this, the Greeks eat only seafood tonight. On Saturday it's some kind of soup made from lamb guts and on Sunday it's lamb on a spit.'

'Well, I don't plan to stick around for the roast lamb,' said Jean-Luc grimly.

As they were finishing the meal (the dishes had come in quick succession), they heard the sound of a band. They looked over towards their left and saw a procession. At the front, four men carried what looked like a funeral bier. It was covered with thousands of white flowers and the frame on which it was borne was also adorned with flowers and foliage. It was the 'coffin' that Jean-Luc had seen in the church. Behind it processed a dozen or so clergy, followed by altar boys, then a band (thirty-strong) who played a doleful funeral march. After that followed various people in military uniform, some sailors, boy scouts, girl guides and then the people of the town. They moved at a slow, dignified pace. A few people who had come to stand not far from the taverna threw petals in the road in front of them. Everyone then began to sing a hymn. As the bier passed, Sylvie and Jean-Luc caught the sweet scent of lemon blossom.

'That must be what he meant by the *epitafios*,' said Sylvie.

The waiter put the bill down on the table in front of them.

'I think we're expected to leave,' she said under her breath.

Jean-Luc pulled a fifty-euro note from his wallet and slammed it on the table.

When the waiter returned with five euros change, Sylvie enquired about hotels.

'There aren't any,' he said bluntly.

So far, this town was showing them none of the Greek hospitality they had experienced on their previous trips.

Sylvie and Jean-Luc's table had been completely cleared. The waiter had even removed the paper cloth that covered it. He could not have made it more obvious that he wanted them to go.

'Come on,' said Sylvie quietly. 'I hate this place.'

'What about a petrol station?' Jean-Luc fired a final question at the taverna owner.

'There's one about twenty kilometres from the junction with the main road. Back towards Athens.'

'Let's just go, Jean-Luc.'

They could see that this man was determined to be unhelpful, and the congregation from the church was now arriving en masse to take up their tables. Sylvie noticed how sombre everyone seemed. Nobody was smiling or talking.

'I suppose Good Friday is quite melancholy,' she said. 'If you're religious.'

'So what's our plan?' said Jean-Luc, as they got up and made their way back up the street.

Sylvie noticed that the general store still had a light on.

'Why don't I ask the woman there if she knows of any rooms – or even if she has a can of petrol she could sell us,' she said hopefully.

The owner was sitting at the till when Sylvie walked in. It was as though she was expecting her.

'Do you know of anywhere we could spend the night?' asked Sylvie.

The woman glanced up from her crossword puzzle.

'We're stuck, you see,' said Sylvie. 'The car has run out of petrol and there is nothing we can do about it until tomorrow.'

The woman's eyes passed from Sylvie to Jean-Luc.

'There is a room up at the police station,' she said, still looking at the young man. 'It's all I can suggest.'

'The police station?' repeated Jean-Luc. 'Where you went earlier, Sylvie?'

'It's just for a night,' said Sylvie, appealing to her husband. 'Anywhere will do. I am so tired.'

'*Efharisto poli!*' she said enthusiastically to the woman, not wanting the invitation to be rescinded.

'My brother is the local policeman. I am sure he won't mind.'

Jean-Luc looked uncomfortable.

'I can't believe we're spending the night in a *gendarmerie*,' he said so only Sylvie could hear.

'We don't have an option,' said Sylvie, and they followed the woman's ample bottom through the streets.

When they got to the police station, the shopkeeper led them up the stairs.

The first room was as Sylvie remembered, but she had not noticed the door at the back. This led into another room.

'It has two single beds,' said Sylvie brightly when they walked in. 'And, look, there's a sink in the corner.'

Jean-Luc didn't speak. He hung back resentfully.

Sylvie threw her bag on to one of the beds as if she were in a smart hotel. Jean-Luc poked at the mattress of the other with his finger.

'The first night of our honeymoon . . .' Sylvie laughed.

'I suppose when you're this tired, a filthy blanket won't stop you sleeping,' he said, assuming that anything they said to each other in French would not be understood by the Greek shopkeeper.

Sylvie looked round to thank the woman, but she had already gone and the door had shut behind her.

'We must go and thank her in the morning,' said Sylvie.

Sylvie cleaned her teeth in the sink (without toothpaste), splashed water on her face and then lay on her bed. Jean-Luc was already asleep. Within seconds, so was she. It had been a long day. Exhaustion had overcome them.

The following morning, Sylvie woke first. The room was windowless, so it was not the light that stirred her but a raging thirst. The squid had been very salty. She had a small bottle of water that she had picked up in the restaurant, and she refilled it at the sink.

Jean-Luc was still fast asleep. She glanced at her mobile and saw that it was already midday. Coffee would be nice, she thought, so she decided to pop out and see if there was anywhere that did a takeaway.

The door handle seemed stiff. It would not move more than half an inch up or down. She rattled it, tried it gently, then more forcefully. It would not move.

Jean-Luc slept on. Sylvie could feel anxiety rising in her. The high-ceilinged room suddenly seemed claustrophobic in a way that it had not on the previous night. And now it felt airless, too.

She tried the door handle one more time, then turned back to the room, breathless with panic.

'Jean-Luc, Jean-Luc!' She was shaking his shoulder now. 'It won't budge, Jean-Luc. We're stuck in here. We can't get *out!*' she screamed.

Jean-Luc rubbed his eyes.

'What . . . ?' he asked sleepily.

'We're stuck in here,' she repeated tearfully.

Jean-Luc calmly swung his long legs over the bed.

'Let me try,' he said. 'I don't suppose it is actually stuck.'

He grasped the door handle firmly and pushed it down. Then did the same a second time with more force. The whole thing came off in his hand.

'Jean-Luc! Look what you've done!'

'It's not my fault, Sylvie!' he snapped.

His wife had begun to weep.

'We must stay calm,' he said. 'We won't get anywhere by panicking.'

He walked over to the sink, drank thirstily straight from the tap and patted his face with water.

As he did this, Sylvie began to hammer on the door with her fists.

'*Au secours! Au secours!* Help! Help!' she cried out.

Taking Sylvie's hands, Jean-Luc made her sit down on the bed next to him.

'Do you have any charge on your phone?'

Sylvie reached out for her handbag and removed her phone. There was some charge, but no signal. Jean-Luc discovered it was the same with his.

'So we just sit here? Until someone comes to the police station? Supposing nobody does?' said Sylvie.

'Somehow, because it's Easter, it seems less likely, doesn't it?' said Jean-Luc.

'So . . . what now?'

'Do you have a nail file?'

Sylvie fished around in the bottom of her bag and produced a metal one.

'I am just going to see if I can do something with this.'

For an hour and a half, Jean-Luc fiddled around with the file and the mechanism. Sylvie lay on her bed staring at the ceiling, nervously fiddling with her wedding band, rolling it round and round, as if this would help pass the time.

Suddenly, she heard the crunch of the mechanism and sat up. The door was opening!

'Jean-Luc!' she cried, leaping up with excitement as it swung wide.

Her pleasure turned to dismay when she saw what lay on the other side of the door. Bars. They must have been flush with the wall and been quietly slid across after the door itself was shut.

'We're in a cell,' said Jean-Luc quietly. 'And look . . .'

Sylvie walked forward.

'Look at this padlock,' said Jean-Luc. 'We're not supposed to get out of here.'

Someone had locked them in.

Sylvie was visibly shivering.

'Why?' she said faintly. 'What did we do wrong?'

'I just don't think we were meant to come here,' answered Jean-Luc.

To the frustration at being confined was now added an almost paralysing fear.

For a moment, they just held on to each other, then Jean-Luc looked around the room and up to the ceiling. There was an air-conditioning vent high up in the wall.

'There is no way of getting through these bars, but maybe one of us can get through that,' he said, pointing upwards. Jean-Luc was tall and lean but had very broad shoulders. It was obvious that only someone more petite would fit. Sylvie.

The only way of reaching the vent was to turn the metal bed frames into ladders. One on its own would not give enough height. With huge difficulty, using all his might, Jean-Luc heaved the second bed into position on top of the first and lashed them together with the dirty blankets.

He could see the fear in his wife's eyes.

'It's our only hope of getting out of here,' said Jean-Luc

pleadingly. 'Here. Take the nail file. You'll need it up there.'

Sylvie silently put the file in her jeans pocket and began to climb. Once she reached the vent, she began to work on the screws, eight of them, that held the grid in place. They had all rusted.

'I can't shift them,' she said, in a small, terrified voice.

'You have to keep trying, darling . . .'

After almost three hours, the grate clattered to the floor. Now she had to try to crawl through the hole.

'Jean-Luc . . .' she said, looking down at her husband. 'I can't.'

'Please, *ma chérie*. Please. For both of us, please try.'

With all her strength, Sylvie hoisted herself up into the narrow space. Her feet disappeared and Jean-Luc was left alone in the cell. He called up towards the dark hole, but there was no reply.

On the other side of the wall, Sylvie had tumbled head first on to a balcony. Two plastic chairs had slightly cushioned her fall, but she was winded and bruised.

Slowly, she got up and looked around her. Jean-Luc was relying on her so she told herself to be brave. Darkness had already fallen and, in the gloom of the street below, there was not a living soul. The houses were unlit. Sylvie worked out that she could climb along a row of balconies and then down into the street. From there she could find her way back to Jean-Luc.

Ten minutes later, stiff with bruises, she was ascending the stairs inside the police station once again. This time, the solid outer door was locked. She banged on it and called, hoping that her husband might hear her and know she was safe.

Inside, Jean-Luc sat on the floor, fruitlessly trying to get a signal on either his or Sylvie's phone. Both told him that it was now nine in the evening. His hunger from the previous day was nothing compared with what he was feeling now. Outside, fear was driving Sylvie on. She needed to find help to free him.

She wanted to avoid the *pantopoleion*. It must have been the owner who had locked them in. Perhaps if she got to the seafront there might be some other tourists who could help her. Perhaps even someone French.

The streets were winding and did not seem to follow any logic, but she knew that, if she followed any gentle downward incline, sooner or later she would reach the sea.

A dog ran at her from the shadows, stopped only by a huge chain. Involuntarily, she let out a cry of fear. From then on, her heart was pounding.

Suddenly, in the darkness, she stumbled into a low bollard. Instinctively, she put out her hands to break her fall, and heard a distinctive crack. Her knees fell hard on the cobbles but it was her left wrist that she had broken. Within moments, it swelled and her fingers began to stiffen. Just before it would become an impossibility, she pulled off her wedding ring and slipped it into her jeans pocket. Soon, her fingers were as fat as sausages. Sitting on the kerbside, she rocked back and forth in pain, weeping with the agony that now swept over her. She vomited into the gutter.

'*Zut!*' she exclaimed, clutching at her wrist. '*Zut! Zut . . . !*'

Blood was oozing through a tear in her jeans. Her knee was badly cut. She sat for several minutes to overcome the nausea and then, trying not to faint, used the bollard to pull herself up. After taking a few steps, she realised that she would have to sit again. Sinking back on to the pavement, she put her head between her knees, all the while trying to suppress her sobs of pain and frustration.

After a while, her head was slightly clearer, so she got to her feet again. She must keep going. It was at least an hour since she had left Jean-Luc. Holding the wall for support, she edged down the street. In the distance was the seafront, and she could see movement there. She approached it cautiously. Not for a minute did Sylvie forget that there were people in this town who did not want them there.

She could now see, up ahead, that a crowd was flowing along the esplanade. The end of the road was still a good hundred metres away and her going was slow. As she approached, she saw that the crowd was lining up along the water's edge. There were no street lights and no lights in the cafés or tavernas by the water.

A thousand people stood there: men, women, children. In the darkness, she could see that each one of them was holding a single long, white, unlit candle. A priest was chanting, but the crowd was silent, their faces expressionless.

What are they doing? Sylvie asked herself.

Very discreetly, she joined the edge of the group. Everybody had their eyes set on something out in front of them, ignoring the people they were standing next to. Sylvie realised that something was taking place in the water itself.

Beside her, a child was pointing upwards to a bright light in the sky.

From a cliff on the other side of the harbour came an

orange light. It was travelling at a steady speed, apparently in mid-air, above the water. It was a fuse.

A split second later there was an enormous explosion. The sound ricocheted back and forth from the rocks opposite. A conflagration had been ignited right in the middle of the harbour.

Black against the dark blue of the sea, the silhouette of an island that had been built in the middle of the water rose. It resembled a stork's nest and the whole thing was now alight, with flames licking up into the sky.

On the island was a structure. It had been hard to make out at first, but now that the fire was raging she could see it clearly. It was a scaffold. A gallows, from which hung a limp figure.

She remembered what she had read the day before about the effigy of Judas being burned on Easter Saturday.

At that moment, there was a deafening series of explosions as fireworks went off in the sky above her and bangers were let off all around. It was like being on a battlefield. She flinched.

Next to her, both left and right, the candles were being lit. One person passed a flame to the next, until all one thousand were glowing. All along the waterfront, flames flickered and danced, illuminating faces from beneath. People seemed happier than they had done the previous night.

A woman thrust a candle into Sylvie's right hand and lit it with hers.

'*Christos Anesti!*' she said gleefully. '*Hronia Polla!*'

Sylvie did not have the slightest idea what she meant, nor

did she appreciate that the flame with which her candle had been lit had been brought from Jerusalem that afternoon. It was a holy light. Christ was risen.

Many people in the crowd were turning away now. It was time for their meal.

Sylvie continued to watch the effigy, mesmerised. It was taking its time to burn, given the intensity of the fire, and its lanky shape made her think of Jean-Luc. Pain must be making her delirious.

From one moment to the next, the wind changed and the flames licked in the direction of the quayside. A smell drifted her way. It was the distinctive scent of cooking meat, which was strange, given that nothing would be roasted until the following day.

'*Mon Dieu* . . .' said Sylvie under her breath, numb with shock. 'Oh my God! Oh my God . . . !'

After a few minutes, the flames died down again. The charred body smouldered. She stood motionless as the vertical support of the gibbet slowly keeled over and fell into the sea. Whatever remained of 'Judas' went with it. The island and everything on it had been incinerated, and all that remained were some blackened shreds of straw floating on the surface of the sea.

The rest of the crowd had dispersed now, and she was afraid to be standing alone. She had to get back to the police station, but not to find a policeman. Sylvie already knew that this was futile. She took one last despairing look at the water and turned away.

She hobbled as fast as she could, supporting her broken wrist with her right hand. Every step was agony. There were a few more lights in the houses now and, eventually, she saw the familiar sign.

ASTINOMIA. POLICE.

With dread, she dragged herself up the staircase. The door at the top was open.

The outer room was unchanged, but the inner door had been closed. The bars that she had not noticed on her first visit the previous afternoon had been slid back.

'Jean-Luc! Jean-Luc!' she called out, almost too weak to speak. 'Jean—'

The door handle moved easily. She opened the door. The two beds were just as they had first seen them, with the grey blankets neatly tucked in. The air-conditioning vent was back in position. There was no sign that anyone had slept in the room. And no trace of her husband. She looked under the bed, in case there was a car key, his toothbrush . . . anything. Any piece of evidence that they had ever been in the room had gone. It was as if they had never been there.

Adrenalin fuelled Sylvie's flight from the village. The only thing of which she was certain was that she had to leave. The walk to the main road, however, took twice as long as it had done the previous day.

The jeep, of course, was still locked. And it had no petrol, in any case. At around four in the morning, a truck passed, but it would not stop. The driver was probably drunk. She sat by the roadside in despair, shock paralysing her, her wrist and knee throbbing. At one point she reached into her pocket. Somewhere in the past hours, her wedding ring had fallen out. As the day broke, a farmer came by and gave her a lift. All he understood was that she had a broken-down car and a cracked wrist.

He did not speak a word of French or English, but she was happy with silence. He took her to the next big town, fifty kilometres away.

At the hospital there was a doctor who spoke French fluently. She was hysterical, almost incomprehensible in any language now, but she managed to relay her story. A number of other doctors and nurses gathered round her as the doctor translated. Several of them nodded. They, at least, believed her. Everyone in that part of Greece knew of the rumours surrounding that village and how, in past centuries, its inhabitants had used the occasion of Easter Saturday to hang a criminal. Few knew that it was a tradition that had been reinstated. Jean-Luc and Sylvie had been in the wrong place at the wrong time. In other words, without knowing it, they had broken one of the Draconian, if unwritten, laws of the village. They had intruded.

There was no corpse, no evidence, no witness to support Sylvie's story. To her horror, the young woman found herself under investigation. Everything went against her. Even the fact that she had 'lost' her wedding ring just days after being married suggested that a terrible altercation had taken place that had led to her injuries. The police and the local people closed ranks. In the end, only the absence of a body meant that murder could not be proved.

The Greek press were briefly obsessed by the case but after the trial the story was soon forgotten. Some time later in the window of the *pantopoleion* appeared two simple wedding bands, nestled between a multi-pack of plastic combs and a cracked Patek Philippe.

My blood ran cold, thinking that I had eaten dinner overlooking that same harbour, and I had a nightmare about Jean-Luc that night.

I spent a few more days in this comfortable, cheap hotel and then decided I should move on. I had been travelling for nearly nine months now and, though I was beginning to think less about you, other worries were beginning to creep in: firstly, my financial situation, and then the related anxiety over when I would have to return to London. I decided to put these things aside, at least for a while longer. First, I wanted to celebrate Easter, perhaps to rid myself of the images of what had happened to Sylvie and Jean-Luc. I ended up spending this important religious festival in a mountain village, where I was adopted by some hospitable strangers for a few days. I saw the burning of a Judas effigy for myself, shared their magiritsa (the lamb-gut soup) and stayed up until three in the morning listening to live music.

The village was near Thermopylae, which is famous for the heroic last stand of three hundred Greeks against an invading force of more than one hundred thousand Persians (some

*historians think many more). I stopped in an empty car park by
the huge monument there and I was moved by this memorial
to an extraordinary feat of bravery, even though it took place
more than two and a half thousand years ago. Next to a
magnificent statue of King Leonidas wielding his spear were the
words: Molon Lavay! – 'Come and Get Them!' This was his
response to a demand to lay down his weapons. His defiance
was uncompromising and impressive.*

*Another car drew up while I was standing there and an
elderly couple got out. They were probably in their early
eighties, small in stature like most people of their generation,
and very smart, in contrast with their battered old Toyota. The
old man touched his cap in greeting and the three of us gazed
quietly at Leonidas, silhouetted against a blood-red sky. The
man turned to me and began speaking: 'Filé mou, ehoume
akomi sto ema mas tin andistasi. Etsi, alloste, ehasé ti zoi tou
kai o aderfos mou. Kapii apo emas dev . . .'*

*I loved hearing the flow of passion that poured from
him, but felt I should tell him I was a foreigner and did not
understand everything he was saying.*

*'Sorry, sorry my friend!' he said. 'I was saying that it is
still in our blood to resist! My brother lost his life that way.
Some of us will never give in to the Germans!'*

*Perhaps that's why this memorial is still so affecting, because
Greece is such a small country and has often been outnumbered
and outgunned. There are strong memories of resistance against
Germany and the Turks, and brave acts such as Leonidas's have
become the stuff of legend. Plenty of people feel that the country
is suffering oppression by Germany even now and, though it is
in an economic sense, the will to resist is strong.*

As the sun went down we went our separate ways.

The evenings were distinctly warmer now. Summer was almost here.

Although I had travelled very freely, there had always been one very specific place on my itinerary. It was somewhere that I had planned to take you, but now I was ready to go alone. I woke that morning and compared how I was feeling now with that black day in mid-September. The clouds had lifted. I realised that I would go to this place without sadness. And that I am no longer writing this for you.

'Delphi: Beautiful and mysterious.'

When I went there on a school trip, decades ago, these were the words I scribbled in the margin of an exercise book. It was not just the ancient stone pillars, amphitheatre and stadium that ignited my imagination. It was the atmosphere. It possessed something mystical. As a teenager, I responded to it, and I always wanted to go back to see if there was really something supernatural there – or had it just been in my adolescent mind?

In the ancient world, great leaders took major decisions only after consulting the Delphic Oracle. A priestess sat in the Temple of Apollo, of which very little remains these days, and her utterances, once they had been interpreted by a priest, guided them. There are various theories about what induced the trance-like state in which she spoke. Her strange ramblings and hallucinations are now thought to have been brought on by the natural fumes that came up through a crack in the ground (perhaps ethylene or methane).

For thousands of years, Delphi was a religious epicentre. People came from miles around to make sacrifices and seek

*advice. Then they gradually stopped believing and began
finding alternatives, seeking truth through prayer, interpreting
the stars, reading Tarot cards, gazing into crystals or, in
Greece, examining the patterns in coffee grounds. There is just
as much interest today in the search for enlightenment as in the
past, though we look in different places.*

*Sometimes when you revisit a place that made an
impression it seems smaller, or in some way disappoints, but
Delphi was more extraordinary than I remembered. The
location seemed even more spectacular and there is now an
elegant museum housing its glorious sculptures. On that
dazzling day in May, I felt its magic again.*

*The night after my visit to Delphi, I stayed in a small
hotel in a nearby fishing village. At breakfast the following
morning, there was a young woman eating alone. The silence
was awkward in the empty dining room, so we started talking.*

*At first, I didn't realise she was Greek. I imagined she
was a tourist like me. She had short, well-groomed hair, an
expensive jacket and a camel-coloured handbag with some
kind of designer tag. When she introduced herself as Athina,
however, I guessed her nationality.*

*'I'm just here for the weekend,' she said, in perfect, slightly
clipped, English. 'I live in Germany.'*

*This explained why she hadn't quite seemed to fit my
image of Greek women, and when I realised she was a young
professional who had made a home in a northern European
city, her cropped hair and chic, androgynous clothes were
explained.*

'How do you find living in Germany?'

It seemed polite to ask. I didn't have to ask why she had

moved there. She was one of many thousands of economic migrants from Greece who had left to find employment elsewhere.

'It's OK,' she replied, in a non-committal way. 'Banking is pretty well paid.'

I didn't ask her any more questions. The conversation turned to Delphi, what had impressed us, whether we liked the layout of the museum, and so on.

Out of nowhere she said something so acutely personal I was completely lost for words.

'I came to find myself.'

She looked up from her plate and smiled for the first time in our conversation.

'You know the words that were supposed to have been carved above the doorway into Apollo's temple?' she continued. 'Gnothi s'eafton: Know thyself.'

I nodded.

She was pushing a piece of tomato around her plate but suddenly looked up and made eye contact with me.

'For the first time in my life, I think I understood myself,' she said.

Her eyes were shining with excitement. Her serious demeanour had gone and, as she told me her story, she became more and more animated. Less Germanic, more Greek somehow.

'I saw into my future!'

KNOW THYSELF

DELPHI

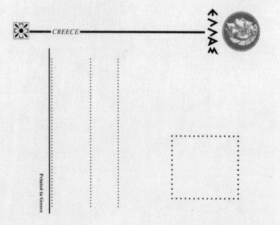

CREECE

ΕΛΛΑΣ

Printed in Greece

'KNOW THYSELF'
'Γνωθι Σαυτον'

Just a month earlier, Athina had been on the twenty-eighth floor of an office block in Düsseldorf, gazing out of a tinted window at a view of other tinted windows. The entire area was dominated by gleaming glass towers and, in Athina's eyes, they seemed to exist merely to reflect each other. The occupants were international corporations whose bankers, lawyers, brokers, hedge-fund managers and financiers existed to service each other in a self-perpetuating cycle of activity.

The words 'refinancing', 'blue chip', 'tax restructuring', 'due diligence', 'off-shore' and other similar phrases floated above the boardroom table. She pondered the language of business. Whether in English, German or Greek, it was not hard to master, it was *how* you said something rather than *what* you said that seemed to count.

In front of each executive, next to a notepad and a sharpened pencil, was a cup and saucer full of weak filter coffee which had gone cold some time before. These items that cluttered the table were as lacking in purpose as the meeting itself: everyone made notes on an iPad and sipped takeaway cappuccinos.

Athina surreptitiously glanced at the time. The meeting had lasted almost two hours but they were only halfway through the agenda. She stifled a yawn. She had already given a presentation on a new telecoms company that needed refinancing, and now a colleague was taking the floor, using PowerPoint to present some financial forecasts. He was the latest recruit to the team, over-eager and over-prepared.

What am I doing here? Athina asked herself. The first few weeks of living in Düsseldorf had been exciting, but once the novelty had worn off this question had surfaced in her mind every day. It had been more than a year now.

Why was she living in a foreign country, in a cold climate, far from friends and family, doing a job she did not even enjoy? How had this *happened*?

When the meeting finally ended, it was eight thirty in the evening. She threw her laptop into her briefcase and slipped out of the room without saying goodbye to her colleagues. The only way she had found to calm herself and to silence this inner scream of hers was yoga. Bikram, Ashtanga, meditational. She had tried them all, and there was a kind of brief solace to be had. She wondered if it was the only thing keeping her sane.

If she didn't run, she would miss her class.

For an hour, incense and Indian mantras successfully wrapped her in their embrace, but it was for the 'moment' only. Once the caressing sounds of running water and wind-chimes had faded away, along with the scent of lavender and bergamot, all the benefits vanished, too. Well-being was just another commodity, sold by the hour. A poster on the wall outside the studio instructed: 'Find yourself', but if there was one thing she knew, it was that her 'self' was not to be found on a yoga mat.

Afterwards, she walked back once again through the city's treeless centre, peering upwards through the concrete towers to find the stars. She hurried home. She was late for the weekly Skype session with her parents in Lamia, but knew they would have stayed up. From the closest station, it was a half-hour train journey home.

'*Agapi mou?* How are you? How is Düsseldorf? Is it cold?'

There was not a breath between the questions.

'I hope you are eating more than just sausages and schnitzel, my darling. I know German food is a bit heavy. I wish I could post you some nice *dolmadakia*. But I will send you some olive oil. Uncle Dimitris just finished his harvest and he says it's the best for ten years or more. We're so proud of you, darling. But we miss you. Aunt Georgia sends her love. It was her saint's day yesterday. Did you remember to wish her *Hronia Polla*? She says she didn't hear from you . . .'

'Mama . . .'

Her father's face appeared on her screen, jostling her mother to the side. Athina loved to see them both, and enjoyed the glimpse into her old home, so familiar and unchanged. It gave her a lump in her throat.

'*Matia mou*, your cousin Giannis just lost his job in the insurance company and he's taken work as a barman. And his brother has been applying for positions all winter. And there is nothing. There is no work here. He was offered a post in Katerini but . . .'

'Papa,' she said. 'Why isn't he taking the job?'

'We've told him to talk to you. Maybe you could find him something in Germany? Is there someone you could ask? He's a good kid. Do you think you could? Your aunt would be so happy. Things are really bad here now.'

'We're so *proud* of you,' interjected her mother, tipping her head on to her husband's shoulder so that her daughter could see her. It was true. They were both full of pride that their only child had excelled at school and gone to university. They were also happy that they had been able to afford to send her to the UK to do a Masters. Not everyone could do that.

Her father was determined to continue with the news update.

'The government seems to be making things worse at the moment. There was a demonstration today and there is going to be general strike next week. Syriza are in trouble. They've disappointed everyone. Even the people who voted for them.'

It was almost impossible to interrupt either her mother's stream of consciousness or her father's flow of gloom about the Greek economy. She did not even try.

'It doesn't look very cosy there,' said her mother, peering into the screen. 'Is it warm enough? Has it been snowing yet? How is your housemate?'

Athina's flatmate was a doctor who had placed an advertisement in a Greek newspaper, *Kathimerini,* for someone to share her place in Düsseldorf. She wanted to live with a fellow Greek, even though her hours in the hospital allowed little time at home. Athina herself had to leave at seven in the morning to get across the crowded city, and she often returned after ten at night, so the two young women rarely saw each other, except for brief chats outside the bathroom.

'She's fine,' answered Athina. 'Working long hours.'

'*You* work too hard, too,' said her mother ruefully.

She could not hear exactly what her father muttered in her mother's ear, but she thought she heard:

'Better than not working at all . . .'

The push and pull of her father's pride and ambition for her and her mother's strong desire to bring her only child back into the nest was something that had for years been a conflict. She reacted against both, and the conversations were exhausting. She had to conceal so much from them, and to try to avoid drowning in their well-meaning but sometimes bullying instructions. At least in Düsseldorf she was not stifled by them, as she had been in her home town.

She had told her parents that she was paid 1,600 euros and had never been able to bring herself to correct their misconception that this was her monthly salary. In fact, it was her weekly salary, an astronomical sum by Greek standards. Initially, she could not believe how generous the bank was, but of late she had begun to regard her earnings as compensation. Some days it felt as if she had sold her life to this faceless corporation.

The following day, at the early-morning conference, she gazed out at the usual view of the soulless city, with its kilometres of smug steel and glass. She realised she had to get away.

There was a long weekend coming up and she had nothing to stay in Germany for. An embryonic relationship with a colleague had fizzled out, which was probably a good thing, as it was frowned upon to date someone in the firm.

Before the conference had even ended, she had booked a return flight to Athens on her iPad. But she did not plan to go home. Her father would be upset that she was not happy in Düsseldorf and her mother might get false hopes about her coming back to Greece. She had another idea.

Those words on the poster, 'Find yourself', had brought back something she had learned at school. They were words that were supposed to have been engraved above the door of Apollo's temple in Delphi: *Gnothi s'eafton*: 'Know yourself'.

She had never been to Delphi but, like every Greek schoolchild, she knew that for many centuries people had sought guidance there about their future.

The priest and the prophetess were long gone, and yet plenty of people still visited the ancient site. She wondered why. At least going there might give her time to think, as well as to see some blue sky.

Athina killed time on the flight by reading her horoscope in the inflight magazine. If you followed the instructions and took the astrologer's advice, at least it would be a way through life. The writers always sounded so sure, wrote with such conviction that she, a Libran, had certain characteristics and must therefore do x or y with her life. Perhaps it was today's equivalent of consulting the oracle. It was simply a matter of faith, and she envied people who had it.

The moment she stepped off the plane, the fragrance of her country assailed her. Even the airport itself had a distinctive scent. It was probably just air freshener, but she wanted to fill her lungs with its sweetness. The whole airport seemed alive, and the cafés in Arrivals were thronging. Before queuing to hire a car, she bought herself an *elliniko metrio*, a strong, slightly sugared Greek coffee. She was like an addict getting her first fix after a long time.

'Having a good day?' asked the man on the Hertz desk.

Her smile was noticeable. Most people who came to hire cars were stressed, but this rather well-dressed young woman seemed at ease.

'Yes,' she answered. 'Very.'

'Going somewhere nice?'

'Somewhere I've never been before,' she said. 'Delphi.'

'Going to consult the oracle?' he said teasingly.

'Kind of . . .'

He handed her a key.

'Good luck!'

As she drove along the motorway it was as if the car knew the way. It was a simple route, almost a straight line to her destination. He must have upgraded her, and the sound system in her Audi brought the familiar voice of Giorgos Dalaras bursting into the luxuriously upholstered interior. It was as if he were personally serenading her.

S'agapo, yiati eisai orea,
S'agapo, yiati eisai esi.

I love you 'cause you're beautiful,
I love you 'cause you're you.

She had not allowed herself to listen to Greek music while

she was away because it made her homesick, but now she was 'home' she could indulge herself. She sang with him, shouting the words to the lushly forested mountains ahead of her.

The journey took her through a green landscape along a road lined with luminous yellow broom. The sky was azure. The spectacular valley through which she drove was almost enough to have come for.

Within two hours, she saw the first signpost to Delphi.

It was only the glimpse of a few columns through the trees that alerted her to the fact that she had arrived.

Having parked, she strolled in to buy a ticket for the site and the museum.

'Go to the Temple of Apollo first,' said the woman on the desk. 'Then the museum. It's best that way round.'

Dutifully, she did as she was instructed. The afternoon was sunny, but in late spring there were few other tourists. Athina wandered along the path, the 'Sacred Way', trying to imagine how it had looked two and a half thousand years before. There were remains of the treasuries where, in ancient times, people had left their offerings of money to be given to the priest in exchange for his predictions and advice.

At the site of the Temple of Apollo were some impressive pillars, but the archaeology was not enough for her. It was like looking at a human skeleton and trying to imagine a living, breathing person. She continually glanced at the reconstructions in her guidebook to build a mental image of how it had really looked. The amphitheatre and the gymnasium needed less imagination. They were intact, and the silver-grey stones seemed still to hold within them the cheers and murmurs of excited crowds.

She soon understood from the captions that the original site of the oracle had long been buried by an earthquake. It must have been a catastrophe for people to lose their source of wisdom and guidance, and she couldn't help feeling a pang of disappointment for herself.

Before going to the museum, where sculptures and other artefacts excavated from the site were displayed, she went to the café to buy water, and sat down on the terrace outside to admire the view. The rugged natural beauty of the location was a sight itself, even without the ancient artefacts.

Just before Delphi, she had stopped in Arachova to buy cigarettes. She had not smoked since her last visit to Greece over a year ago – in Germany, it was virtually impossible to do so without breaking a law. As she inhaled, Athina knew that the pleasure was more to do with the freedom to smoke than with the nicotine itself.

The smell of pines was strong and, with the warmth of the sun on her face, she felt herself begin to thaw. She closed her eyes. The previous summer, she had worn her winter coat every day. For the first time in eighteen months, she was without it. It was still on the back seat of her car, and the drabness of Düsseldorf, with its unrelieved grey skies, seemed far away.

She stubbed out the cigarette and got up. She was ready for the museum.

The moment she entered, she was bewitched by the spacious rooms that housed the most exquisite artefacts she had ever seen. All of them were thousands of years old, and most were in glorious golden stone. There were sections of friezes depicting scenes from the Trojan War: abductions, battles, lions, giants and gods. They were full of action and movement, telling stories as if showing them on a film reel.

There were also tiny statuettes only a few centimetres high, and more monumental works such as those of the Kouroi. The story of these powerfully built twin brothers was a tragic one.

Their mother needed to be taken by wagon to a temple and, as there were no oxen to pull it, the two young men harnessed themselves to it and dragged it. She was overcome at what they had done for her and prayed for them to be given the best a man could receive. They lay down to sleep and never woke again.

Athina was shocked.

A peaceful death, she thought. Was that really the highest prize?

The bittersweetness of the story's ending left her feeling empty.

Not far away stood the statue of Antinous, supposedly the most handsome man in the world, and beloved by the Emperor Hadrian. When he drowned in the Nile, the heartbroken Hadrian made him a demi-god. The statue was full of pathos, a lament to lost beauty and youth.

These images of early and untimely death haunted her. Not one of the three knew even the day before that their lives would end. Had they achieved what they wanted to achieve? She doubted it.

There were plenty of other memento mori in Delphi, but she needed little reminder that life should not be wasted. This was not a revelation. Death had been present even on her journey here. She had seen numerous roadside memorials to accident victims, several cemeteries and many trees on which were pinned the faces of dead men or women, to advertise a forthcoming memorial or funeral service.

What she really wanted was direction. Like the people in ancient times who had come here, she yearned for some advice, an insight into what she should do with her life.

Before leaving, she decided she would take a look at the Temple of Athina, the Tholos. It was just across the road from the museum.

It was past six now and all the other visitors had gone. The few coaches had left promptly at five. It was so deserted that she felt like a trespasser as she walked along the rough ground to the temple's ruins.

The profusion of yellow margaritas and wild grasses that grew all around the site gave it a look of total abandonment. A goldfinch sang tunefully in the nearby olive grove and an invisible cuckoo softly accompanied him. Other birds whistled and cheeped. The air was full of midges.

The intimate circle of pillars immediately enchanted her. There was a completeness about this temple, the Tholos, that other parts of Delphi did not have. Perhaps she felt connected with it because of its name? Athina passed nearly an hour sitting on the stones, listening to the birds and gazing at the landscape around her.

She had not even noticed the small house tucked away in the corner of the site, and the sudden appearance of a man almost next to her gave her a start.

When she saw he was in uniform, she relaxed.

'You work late,' she said.

'All night,' he answered. 'There's a healthy black market in antiquities. So we have to guard our treasures.'

'But it would be hard for anyone to steal those, wouldn't it?'

Athina pointed at the trio of lofty pillars that soared above them into the sky. Three out of twenty that once formed a rotunda had been restored.

'You'd be surprised what people nick,' he said.

'It's a beautiful place,' she said.

'In my opinion, this is the most lovely part of the whole site,' he said.

It seemed he didn't do this job just for the money. She could sense that he genuinely loved the stones for which he was the watchman.

'The Sanctuary of Athina . . .'

'*Pronoia?*' said Athina, reading from her guidebook.

'Foresight. Athina of Foresight.'

'She gave insight into the future?' asked Athina.

'Some believed so. It might not only have been from the oracle that people sought advice.'

'What is it like being here . . . when it's dark?'

She imagined that, at night, this area of fallen columns and grey, stone slabs might be rather ghostly.

'I'm used to it,' he said. 'But it has more than ample rewards.'

For a moment, Athina wondered what he meant.

'Look behind you,' he said.

Athina turned.

What she saw shocked her. It was a sunset of such strangeness and intensity that she gasped. The sky was pink and smoky, as if a volcano had erupted in the distance and sent its flames and ashes towards the heavens.

For a year, she had not seen the setting of the sun. In Düsseldorf, it quietly slipped away from the day, behind either clouds or buildings.

Only now did Athina remember its strength and power. Until she had gone to live in Germany, the movements of the sun, the moon and the stars had been part of daily life, always there, always visible. She had not realised how intensely she had missed the beauty of Greece.

The sunset seemed supernatural. She stood side by side with the guard, watching the extraordinary phenomenon, in silence, feeling its supernatural force.

'I never tire of it,' he said.

He liked to talk, as did anyone who spent so many hours alone, and she was happy to listen.

'Someone could take away the pillars, but nothing can take away the gifts of nature,' he said. 'We're blessed by them in this country.'

They strolled around the circular temple together while he continued.

'I sometimes wonder, for all the talk of Athina of Pronoia and the Delphic Oracle, whether the real attractions here are the landscape and the sunset. And can you imagine a full moon over all this? It's worth seeing, I tell you. It takes your breath away.'

Athina listened to every word he said.

'I wouldn't want to be anywhere else. They tried to

make me take a post at Epidaurus. But I didn't want to go. I refused. Sometimes you just know where you want to be. It's the place where you are really happy. Even if it's once a day, for a few moments. If life is worth living for those moments, then you have something. And here is where I want to be.'

He drew on his cigarette and gazed towards the west at the first star that had appeared, just at that moment, in the indigo sky.

In a moment of pure epiphany, Athina felt as if she had been set free. She knew where she wanted to be. Finally, the oracle had spoken.

Athina was very animated by the decision she had made. She certainly seemed independent enough to make a new start, and told me that she had saved plenty of money from her time in Germany. She would be comfortable in Athens, even if she could never again match the salary she had earned in Düsseldorf. Her parents would know nothing of her decision until she was back in Greece for good.

'It's much easier that way! I know it's the right thing for me,' she said, with certainty. 'But you can imagine the family discussions that will go on.'

I mentioned that, in the UK, most children don't really consult their parents about every life decision, and that they are encouraged to be independent.

'They try to interfere in everything here,' she said. 'They would even come into school to sit your exams if they could!'

We agreed that this mentality will probably never change, but that it does reflect something very appealing in Greek society: the strength of the family. Everything has its pros and cons.

'I'm twenty-eight years old, but in the eyes of my father I

*will always be a child,' she reflected. 'Ultimately, though, it's
my life. I have to live it.'*

I told her what I did for a living, and for the first time
confided in someone the reasons for my recent travels. I had
not shared any of this before. She didn't react or judge or give
advice. Her eyes showed that she sympathised with what I had
gone through. For both of us, Delphi was a turning point.

Athina had a plane to catch that evening and needed to
pack, so we exchanged email addresses in case I should be in
Athens at any time in the future. We paid our bills at the
same time and, though she resisted the gesture, I carried her
bag out to her car. A few hours later, I was on the road, too.

The weather was perfect now, with clear skies and
temperatures that were comfortable rather than enervating.
I wanted to read through the whole first draft of Cycladic
Sculpture and Modernity and visit some islands before my
travels ended. My money wasn't going to last indefinitely. It
meant going back towards Athens but, within a few hours, I
was in a queue for the ferry at Rafina, ready to take the ferry
to Andros.

The moment of departure on a Greek ferry is one of great
anticipation. I had experienced it so often, but the moment
when the last car has driven on, the ramp is pulled up, the
chains are loosened and the stern pulls away from the dock
always thrills me. That Friday late afternoon, there was a
party mood on board, hundreds of passengers looking forward
to reaching a common destination, sharing a journey over the
sea. The Aegean was very calm that evening, and I sat on
deck with the salty breeze enveloping me like a second skin.
Two hours later, we were back in our cars in the fume-filled

hold. We had arrived. Everything happened in reverse, and soon the ferry was chugging back towards the mainland, sounding a lonely farewell with its horn.

Whatever preconceptions I had about Greek island architecture (small, whitewashed houses, modest stone cottages by the water's edge), they were quickly dispelled. The first thing I noticed when I reached Hora, the main town, was the large number of enormous mansions: houses of such grandeur and elegance that they looked out of place, almost absurd. Many had pillars and loggias, some were pink or other pastel colours, others would have looked at home on the Grand Canal in Venice.

On an island where the population nowadays does not even reach ten thousand, it was intriguing that such wealth had once existed there. It was a striking anomaly. As well as the houses, there were impressive public buildings. A friendly shopkeeper, who knew every detail of the island's history, boasted that its economy had been based on huge maritime wealth and that Andros had been second only to the city of Piraeus in numbers of ships registered there. I noticed a very grand building (a hospital for the elderly) which had been given by one of the Embirikos family, who owned the largest steamship fleet in Greece. An inscription described the benefactor as 'Traveller and Returner', so it appears that the seafarers of Andros always came back to their modest but lovely island, even after long periods of travel.

I also discovered an inspiring contemporary art museum, built by the Goulandris family. It was an unexpected treat on this small island, with some stirring sculptures by Mihalis Tombros, an artist born on Andros, as well as some *magnificent paintings. I was sitting outside on a wall, looking at the view of the sea and rereading the catalogue, when a woman stopped to talk to me. I realised that she was the person who had sold me a ticket, though I hadn't really noticed her then. She asked me if I had enjoyed the gallery and I told her how impressive it was to find such great art on a small island like this.*

'Yes,' she said, 'but one of the best Andriot artists is not displayed.'

She told me that she was referring to a female artist all of whose work (including a portrait of her own parents) had been lost.

It was obvious that she wanted to tell me what had happened and I was more than willing to listen, not least because she was strikingly beautiful, like a painting herself.

THE LONELY WIFE

CARTE POSTALE

Correspondance   Adresse

Andros

THE LONELY WIFE

The marriage was a matter of practicality rather than passion. Antigoni was nearly thirty years old when her father accepted the proposal on her behalf. Her younger, prettier sister, Ismini, was already in demand, but tradition dictated that she could not marry first.

Down by the waterfront of Piraeus one spring afternoon, when the two women were out for a stroll, they stopped in a *zacharoplasteion* for coffee. Antigoni noticed a stocky, middle-aged man walk by and glance in their direction. Not once, but three times. She assumed that Ismini was the object of his attention.

Christos Vandis did not want a flighty, pulchritudinous bride whom he could not trust while he was away. A wealthy ship owner from Andros, he spent long periods at sea and was looking for a reliable wife, someone plain but not unattractive, to run his household. *Jolie-laide* would suffice. He passed through Piraeus fairly often, and this was not the first time he had seen this young woman with her fashionable short, dark hair and pronounced nose. He was now forty-five, his parents had both died and he had inherited their property. He must find someone to marry, and his time for the search was limited since he would soon be back at sea. A few discreet enquiries allowed Vandis to discover what he needed to know. The girl's father was a port manager. That would do. Christos wasn't looking for wealth.

Antigoni accepted the proposal more for her sister's sake than her own. She knew that she was a barrier to Ismini's fulfilment (her younger sister yearned to leave home and be married). Things might have been different if Ismini had not been flawlessly pretty, with light green eyes, fair silky hair, a radiant complexion and just the right number of freckles across her (small) nose. She was *koukla*, in other words, 'like a doll', constantly an object of male attention.

While Ismini was always thinking about the future, Antigoni was happy with her life in Piraeus. In the mid-1930s, it was a fast-growing city, with a population close to two hundred thousand and plenty of culture. There was always something new on at the theatre or cinema, and often an exhibition of art. Since the death of their mother, when Antigoni was fifteen, she and her sister had known great freedom in a place that pulsated with life.

Antigoni read a great deal and regularly sat at their open French windows and painted the view, usually a boat or one of the city's grand neoclassical buildings with the sea in the background. Occasionally, she sketched people in the street, and then in the privacy of her house applied colour. 'You should teach!' said Ismini, and she had started to do so, thereby giving herself a little income and independence.

The years were passing, however, and the vision of

herself as a schoolmistress, unmarried and living with her father for ever, was another factor in her decision to marry.

She knew there would be sacrifices to be made in becoming the wife of Christos Vandis, and that his wealth would be little compensation. In Piraeus, Antigoni had enjoyed the unbroken continuity of many friendships from childhood to adulthood. At her wedding to Christos she saw all the familiar faces but, when the day ended, she realised that this had been a farewell party.

Afterwards, she and her husband spent two days at the Hotel Grande Bretagne in Athens before returning to Piraeus and setting sail immediately for Andros. Her father, sister and three close friends were there to wave them off and, as the boat moved further and further away and they were reduced to tiny, faceless figures, she began to doubt whether the small shapes at whom she was looking were even people she knew, or just strangers.

Antigoni was glad that her new husband had gone to the bridge. Her chest and throat tightened as she watched everything she knew and loved – the people, the buildings and the ships still in dock – vanish from view. The handkerchief that she had been using to wave like a flag was now used to dab her eyes. Never had her feelings for Piraeus been stronger. Her heart was heavy. She knew it would be a long time until she saw her city again.

Her first sighting of Andros as the boat came into dock in Gavrio was through a porthole. She was lying on the berth in her cabin, wracked with nausea. Only when the boat was completely still could she open her eyes. She saw a

VICTORIA HISLOP

blue sky above her. Then, as her stomach ceased to churn, she was able to sit up. There were green hills and a row of houses by the water's edge. She steadied herself before drinking a glass of water that someone had thoughtfully put on the ledge above the bed, then looked at herself in a small mirror on the back of the door. A grey, waxy face looked back at her. Purple shadows ringed the eyes. She combed her hair and quickly applied some lipstick and rouge.

There was a sharp knock on the door. At the same time, the knob was being turned, then Christos walked in.

'Ready?' he said, oblivious to what she had suffered in the past hours. 'There's a car waiting to take us to Hora. Someone will collect your bags.'

She forced a smile and then followed him along the narrow, wood-lined corridor and up a polished ladder to the deck.

There were two significant similarities between the port city of Piraeus, where she had grown up, and Andros: sea and boats. In all other ways, Andros was entirely different from her old home. Christos talked continuously as they motored along the winding coast road. He was in the front with the driver and Antigoni sat quietly in the back. During the two-hour journey from Gavrio, her nausea returned and twice she had to ask the driver to stop.

As the car wound its way around the twists and turns of the road, Antigoni gazed out of the window, occasionally making a noise to show she was listening to Christos, who was telling her about the society into which she was moving. Through the haze of dizziness that kept enveloping her, she heard lists of names. Who was who, who was a relative, who was married to whom, who to like, who to avoid. It sounded to her as if the only people she should associate with were the wives of other shipping families.

By the time they drew up, outside an immaculate, cream-coloured, double-fronted mansion with fluted pillars and ornate wrought-iron balconies, she felt light-headed, as though her mind and body were disconnected. The chauffeur opened the car door for her and could see she needed to be supported. Christos had already gone inside the house, so the housekeeper and the maids' first sight of their new mistress was of a sickly looking woman leaning heavily on the driver's arm. This image would remain with them.

Many of the older Andriots had not travelled to the wedding, so the following week a reception was held in the mansion's large dining room for her to meet them. Under the oil-painted gaze of her husband's ancestors, Antigoni shook hands with a hundred well-dressed strangers. Some of the old men she met had faces that resembled those in the more austere portraits, and she wondered if they were relatives of her husband.

Over the next few days, with more of Christos's instruction, Antigoni was in no doubt over which of the eccentrics and mavericks of the island were to be avoided. Her husband clearly wished her to be safe, but she had the feeling that his real motivation was for her to be stored away, kept refrigerated for his return. It sounded as if he would rather she did not leave the house at all.

In late July, three and a half weeks after the wedding, Christos Vandis left for North America. Even with good sailing conditions, he expected to be away for a year. Antigoni felt a sharp pang of abandonment and loneliness. She was far from home, exiled.

The weeks went by and, without his portrait in the hallway, she would not have had any recollection of her husband's features. The memory of his touch had long gone, and the only thing she could evoke was his smell. She did this by going into Christos's dressing room and breathing in the scent of his suits, on which still lingered tobacco and cologne – or when she passed a *kafenion* where the men all smoked. A modicum of attraction had grown between them during the brief period that they had spent together, but for her it was now fast evaporating.

The summer months passed with temperatures that slowed life down. Her daily activity would usually involve a visit to (or a visit from) one of the other shipping wives. She rarely spoke to anyone else. Even her interaction with the maids was largely to tell them what she would like to eat, and that was very little during these weeks. Antigoni was lethargic, but her lack of activity bothered her less than she had imagined. The heat was enough to silence the streets and almost to stop the clocks. Languid days turned into sleepless nights.

As the days grew cooler and summer turned to autumn, Antigoni's energy returned. She could not stay inside, occupied with the management of household accounts. One of the things that she had brought from her old life was her easel and paints. On the first of October, she got up at sunrise and walked into the hills, her satchel thrown across her shoulder. On the way out she picked up a flask of water, a piece of cheese and a few tomatoes from the kitchen. The maid watched her silently. She had never recovered from the damaging effect of the first impression she had made on the servants. They saw her as weak, and as an outsider. Antigoni had no way of knowing what they did when her back was turned, and while she was away from the house it was impossible for her to know. All she knew was that the furniture was always thick with dust, and she imagined they breathed a sigh of relief when they saw her leave. It did not bother her.

Her paints became her company and a reason to explore this island. She had never painted such landscapes before, so it was an adventure, leading her to discover the network of ancient footpaths that criss-crossed the island, the pretty stone walls, the unexpected waterfalls and streams. It was an enchanting place.

She often completed a painting while she was up in the hills, liberally splashing deep green strokes across her landscape to represent the sharp spikes of the cypress trees and adding a little white church, a windmill or pigeonnier, to give the painting a focus. She never tired of domed churches in front of a blue sky, or the ruins of a castle silhouetted against the sunset.

By mid-November, although the days were bright, she could feel the cooling of the air. One afternoon the rain came and fell in such torrents that every brushstroke was washed away. Her charmed days of painting on the hillsides were over.

She returned home and spread the work she had done so far on to the floor in the dining room. Painting had chased away her loneliness, but now she needed new subjects. As she put some of the landscapes away in her portfolio, a picture of her sister fell out of it. She missed Ismini so much and the image brought her vividly to mind. Antigoni was critical of her own work but knew that her real talent lay in painting people's likenesses.

Emboldened by the sight of her sister's portrait, she set off the following morning to find a subject. The sour-faced maids would not do.

She wandered out towards the sea rather than away from it, as she had done in past weeks, glimpsing the little church and the ruins of the castle that had appeared in her work so many times. She found herself walking past a painted door that was built into a rocky cliff. It was bright blue and just like the door into a house, but this was a door into a cave.

As she was walking by, it flew open. A woman rushed out towards her, screaming and waving her arms.

'No! No! No! No!'

Antigoni froze. The woman stopped dead right in front of her and stared. Her eyes were as bright a blue as her door and her sodden, matted hair as dark as granite.

Both women stood still for a moment. The wild-eyed woman instilled terror in Antigoni. Then she repeated, but more quietly: '*No, no, no, no . . .*' and her voice died away in a whisper. 'Sorry, sorry. I'm so sorry. It must have been a bad dream.'

Antigoni shook her head to reassure her.

'Don't worry,' she said, taking a step back.

Christos had warned her about the 'wet witch' who lived in a cave that reached far into the rocks. The island was so well endowed with water that moisture literally oozed from its stones, poured out of the earth and left the walls of houses dripping. The floor of this cave was a puddle, and it was said that no liquid ever passed the witch's lips because she absorbed all the moisture she needed through her pores. She dripped, her transparent clothes clinging to her, and there was often a cluster of schoolboys hanging around outside her door, hoping to see the contours of her bottom and breasts. People said that she was able to deliver a cure or a curse, and to live on raw fish that she scooped from the waves with her hands. Most people kept well away from her; all except a handful of fisherman who knew that fish were too wily to be caught by hand and often took her the tiny *marida* that they could not sell. They hoped that in exchange for these they could come in to the cave for an hour or so. It was rumoured that she sang before and after making love to them in a pure, tone-perfect voice.

The woman was no longer tormented with her nightmare, and Antigoni could see that her face was chiselled and every feature in perfect proportion.

'Is this where you live?' she asked her, though the answer was obvious.

The woman nodded.

'You're new here?' she asked Antigoni in return.

'Yes, quite new.'

'I thought you must be,' she said and, after a moment's pause, added, 'Not many women stop to pass the time of day with me.'

I didn't have a choice, was Antigoni's thought, but instead she said: 'Well, it was nice meeting you,' and walked on.

All day a vision of the woman's face haunted her. It was so strong and so wild. She wanted to paint her.

The following morning, she went by at around the same time. A man was emerging from the cave-house. After a moment or so, she plucked up courage to knock on the door and, from inside, she heard a voice.

'Go away. I don't need fish today.'

Through the closed door, Antigoni explained who she was and what she wanted. After a while, the woman was coaxed into opening her door just a crack.

'You can come in, but not for long,' she said. 'I don't like sitting down.'

Antigoni went inside and, almost in darkness, rapidly sketched the woman's face. She could do the rest at home.

Her hands were damp and the pencil slipped through her fingers once or twice. In the shadows, the woman looked sinister but beautiful.

For the next few weeks she worked for hours every day on the portrait, absorbed and happy with what she was achieving.

Before she put the final touches to the painting, she had found another model.

On the feast of the Evangelismos, Antigoni went to the big church on the hill. She soon realised that she would be the only member of the congregation. Nobody else came to hear Father Minas preach because he had a reputation for subversive ideas. 'Just avoid him,' Christos had said. 'He is unsafe. He's another Kairis.'

Antigoni had seen a statue of the man to whom Christos referred in one of the town's squares. Theophilos Kairis, a son of Andros, had been a priest and intellectual who had advocated the separation of the Church and the state back in the nineteenth century. There were local people who still believed he had deserved excommunication and exile for such an outrageous idea, and some believed that this current priest had similar ideas to Kairis. Most kept away from him unless he was needed for a rite of passage: baptism, marriage or funeral.

Antigoni listened to what he had to say, but her mind was on the extraordinary face, the huge oval eyes, the flowing hair and beard that reached his chest, and his gesticulating hands, their fingers as fine as lace bobbins and longer than any she had ever seen. He was full of passion and his rich voice suited the liturgical chants.

Antigoni went several times after that to hear him, but took her sketchbook, too. While he was preaching she drew him clandestinely, trying to capture the expressiveness of his hands as well as his face.

She worked for weeks on his portrait. She could have painted him a thousand times and never tired of his expression. In the final version on canvas, Antigoni caught a moment when his palms were coming together, either in prayer or applause. It was ambiguous.

Her next subject was the schoolmaster. Theodoros Sotiriou had been at the secondary school for so many years that he had even taught Christos. 'It doesn't matter if he has the sayings of Plato on his wall or not. The man doesn't have an ounce of wisdom in his own mind. And besides that, he is no example for the children.'

Antigoni's husband had never explained what he meant and, in the rushed weeks before his departure, they had not revisited the subject.

The school was in the same street as her house, so she went by it every day and could see through the hallway into the yard, beyond which dozens of children played, their laughter reverberating off the walls around them. It did not look like a place where children were unhappy. She often saw the schoolmaster, and he waved to her cheerfully. He was handsome, with a clipped moustache and neat grey hair that suggested a regular visit to the barber. He always wore a three-piece suit and had a book in his hand, even when he was cycling home.

One day, she was passing the main door to the school as he emerged.

'Good afternoon, Kyria Vandis,' he said. 'When are you expecting your husband back?'

'Some time in the autumn,' she said. 'Still a way off.'

'If you need anything to read, Eirini and I have a good library, and you are welcome to borrow anything. Books are the essence of life. And there is nothing like a good story to pass the time.'

'You're so kind . . . I would love to do that.'

She had calculated that he must be well into his sixties, but he was still sprightly, and effortlessly mounted his bike before pedalling off.

A few days later, Antigoni sent a maid round with a note to the schoolmaster's house, asking if she could take him up on his offer to borrow some books. The days were dragging now that she had finished the priest's portrait. A time was set, and the following week she went to his home. The door was opened by Eirini.

They sat together on a settee, with Antigoni opposite them, to drink coffee. Eirini was a very beguiling woman in her early forties, delicate, with laughing eyes. She looked young for her years.

After an hour or so of conversation, and when she had selected some books, Antigoni plucked up the courage to ask if they would sit for a portrait together. They made a handsome couple, despite their obvious discrepancy in age. They were delighted and accepted immediately. Antigoni would return the following day at the same time to make a sketch.

When she returned home, the maid who had dropped in the note found an opportunity to tell her that there had been a scandal with the schoolmaster two decades earlier.

One of his former pupils had moved in with him. She was eighteen at the time, and he was already in his forties. They had never married. Many people wanted to get rid of him, but there was no one to replace him as teacher. The whole business was overlooked, though not forgotten.

It was pure pleasure for Antigoni to portray the pair's cheerful disposition and the love they had for each other. There was no judgement to be made as far as she was concerned, and the finished painting was her favourite so far.

One day in late April, it had rained all morning but the sky was bright, and the moon and the sun shone together. She walked along the sea to the harbour, noticing that the wooden door to the cave was firmly shut. No schoolboys were loitering that day.

Water always collected in pockets in the cobbles, and her leather soles absorbed the dampness in the road. Antigoni made her way towards a row of five or six fishing boats that were moored side by side. They all looked freshly washed, their yellow nets and blue-and-white hulls looked as good as new. She walked along, reading the names of the boats, though some of the plaques were worn and hard to decipher. *Maria, Sofia, Mihali, Ismini* . . . She thought fondly of her sister, who was now engaged to the son of a wealthy tobacco merchant. Antigoni was looking forward to her visit to Piraeus for the wedding in eight months' time.

The quayside was deserted. The bells of the dozen or so churches in the town began to chime six. The sun would soon be below the horizon. She had a strong desire to capture this moment – the strong shadows, the sharp colours, the geometric shapes: the moment before the sun went down when everything seemed to acquire a strength, a final flourish. Lining the edge of the water was a row of low metal bollards to which the boats were tethered. Using one as a stool, she sat down and took out a piece of fresh paper. It was a fine evening and she began quickly to sketch one of the boats, determined to use her colours while she sat there. She even drew the snake coil of chains that lay in a pile close by. It was a work of art in itself.

She was captivated by the detail of this small vessel. None of it was for decoration or vanity: it was a working craft, a useful thing, the opposite of her idle, empty house.

Suddenly, from inside the boat, she heard a cough.

A man emerged through the door. Behind him, she could see a narrow bed, with a grey woollen blanket twisted across it. She always noticed detail and she spotted that it had a hole.

'Are you looking for someone?'

Even the tone of voice was not the kind that she was used to hearing. It was rough and not remotely deferential.

'I was just doing a painting of your boat,' she said sheepishly.

The fisherman walked across the deck and began methodically to slice fish and bait his line. He continued, not looking up even for a moment. Knife, hook, knife, hook. It was hard to imagine how he avoided cutting or piercing his fingers. She watched, spellbound.

'I won't charge you for that,' he said, smiling.

His was a craggy, lined face. Constant exposure to the sun and wind had turned it the colour of ripe chestnuts. It was impossible to say whether he was closer to forty or seventy, but in any case he was handsome.

'You like painting then?' he asked, his eyes twinkling.

'Yes,' she replied.

She turned her sketchpad round to show him her watercolour.

'You can have this if you like.'

He laughed.

'And where would I put that then?' he asked, looking up at her. 'Not much space on my walls for art.'

She had not realised that the boat was also his home, and felt embarrassed.

'No, I suppose not.'

His friendliness emboldened her.

'Could I do a drawing of you as well? Maybe if I make it quite small you might find a space?'

'Why not? As long as I can carry on with my work. I have to take the boat out at sunset, and all the baiting needs to be finished.'

'I'll be done before then,' said Antigoni quickly.

The pair of them sat quietly for an hour or so. By the end of that time, she had done five drawings, one of which she gave to the fisherman.

Temperatures began to rise during June, so she was happy to work in the cool of the dining room (which she had turned into her studio). She was grateful for the high ceilings, the slats of the wooden shutters, which kept out the glare of the sunshine, and the tiled floor that cooled her feet. From time to time, one of the maids would bring her some fresh lemonade. They were silent, and never commented on the pictures.

She worked long hours to put the finishing touches to each portrait. They had become an obsession for her as she strove to capture the essence of her subjects. The four oil paintings leaned against the wall, each of them over a metre in width (the one of the couple measured even more). They looked incomplete. The local carpenter was summoned, and he happily created some heavy, moulded frames in a dark wood. The stiff ancestral portraits were replaced with her own work and the faces of those who had alleviated her loneliness in these past months now looked down from the walls.

More than a year after Christos had left, a cable arrived saying that his boat would be back in a week's time. Antigoni was happy at the prospect of seeing her husband, though she wondered how much of a stranger he would seem. The scent on his clothes had long ago dissipated. She stood under the portrait of him in the hallway and tried to reacquaint herself with this man. It was many months since she had looked at the painting.

The evening of her husband's return was the first time

that the dining room reverted to its original use. Antigoni had tidied away her easels, brushes and paints, and one of the maids had managed to remove some splashes from the floor.

She was at the door to welcome him, but there was a formality between them, just as she had expected. They had hardly known each other before Christos had left, and they needed to become acquainted all over again.

They walked together into the dining room, which was laid out ready for a formal dinner. Christos walked round the table and simply stood and stared.

At first he said nothing. He just looked, staring at the image of the 'wet witch' (whom Antigoni had painted semi-naked with strands of hair scarcely concealing her nipples, and a mermaid's tail), the maverick priest with his expressive hands, the couple (who looked even more like father and daughter than in real life) and the overtly sensual image of the rugged fisherman. Their eyes met his, and they all stared back at him with defiance. They were masterpieces, vivid, almost breathing. But Christos did not recognise the brilliance of her accomplishment. Not in the least.

Finally, he spoke. Almost inaudibly, he said:

'Where are the family portraits? What have you *done* with them?'

He was not looking at her, and his voice rose to a deafening roar.

'*Get these down – now!* NOW!'

As he stormed out of the room, she saw that his face had gone almost purple with rage.

Shaking with shock and fear, Antigoni went to the

kitchen, where she knew the housekeeper was preparing dinner. She and the two maids had heard Kyrie Vandis shouting and had not been surprised. They were smirking when she opened the kitchen door.

'Can you put the paintings back as they were,' she asked, with a tremor in her voice, 'and leave the others in the hallway?'

That night, the old, dusty portraits of three almost identical bearded men and one picture of a ship were replaced and the faded areas of wall paint were once again perfectly hidden.

On the following morning, at the breakfast table, Christos confronted his wife.

'Is that how you spent your time while I was away at sea? Is that what I expect from a wife? To go round the streets painting the prostitutes and the perverts? Who else did you paint?'

Antigoni struggled to reply, so he continued.

'How could you put them on the walls of this house? And replace my ancestors? What else did you get up to?'

'Some landscapes, too . . .' was all she managed to say.

'I gathered that,' he said. 'I found a portfolio under the bed. Come with me.'

She followed him out to the paved yard at the back of the house and saw her four portraits piled together on some kindling. On the very top was her leather portfolio. Antigoni realised that fire was already licking from below.

'You can't . . . !'

Christos grabbed her arm to stop her reaching out to save the paintings.

'Do what you're told,' he said. 'And show some respect.'

The man could not see past his rage, which wrapped around him, hotter than any flame.

As the portfolio began to melt and individual pictures curled upwards and floated out of the conflagration, she saw the one of Ismini. At the sight of her sister's burning image, she pulled away from her husband and ran through the house and out of the front door.

There was a ferry early the following day. She would gladly face every consequence of her actions. Soon she was knocking on the schoolmaster's door, and he willingly gave her money for the bus and for the ferry.

A few months afterwards, she sent him a painting as a thank-you. It was rich repayment indeed. A decade later, Antigoni had become a celebrated painter and the schoolmaster was able to sell the still life she had given him and finally retire.

Christos Vandis continued to spend long periods at sea, returning for short breaks to his dusty home. Antigoni never left Piraeus again. The Vandis mansion is now a guesthouse.

Like Antigoni, but without a paintbrush, I walked for hours every day using the old stone footpaths that criss-cross the island, but I was not alone. Angeliki took some days off from the museum to join me. It was a gentle landscape, not as challenging as Meteora, but perfect rambling country. These warm days were turning my skin dark brown and I was beginning to look like a gypsy. I felt as free as one. I am not sure that you would recognise me now, even if we met in the street.

I spent my last night in Andros with Angeliki. It was a casual thing for us both and we made no rash promises to meet again. It seemed time to leave and I had it in my mind to visit Ikaria. It was a short journey via the more touristic Mykonos (where I didn't want to stop off) to the port at Evdilos.

So much of what I had been told about Ikaria was negative. I heard that it was a windy island where little grows, with stormy seas, rocky terrain, numerous ravines and bare mountains. In the past, it was constantly attacked by pirates, a place from where men went to sea for years on end, leaving the women to survive without their protection. In the twentieth century, it became an 'open prison', where political exiles were sent. One person told me that now it was 'just old people there', a backwater which the young have left to find a better life. For years, it was out of sight and out of mind, as far as the Greek government was concerned. The list of deterrents was endless. One man in Tripoli said that it wasn't worth going there except for two things: to see the supposed birthplace of Dionysus and to drink the strong red Pramnios wine. The same person told me that the island was 'very Leftie', but I noticed he was reading the newspaper of the far-right party, Golden Dawn (and, incidentally, drinking ouzo with his morning coffee). I wasn't likely to take his advice on anything. Certainly not on where to travel.

By the end of my first afternoon exploring this remote and rugged island, I knew I was right to have followed my instincts in going there and had a feeling that I wouldn't be in a hurry to leave. I hardly saw another car, and the dramatic, rocky landscape was astonishing. I got out at one point and sat for several hours on a wide stretch of smooth, white rock that sloped down to the sea. The sun was on my back and I felt an extraordinary sense of peace. I can only attribute it to the light that seemed to saturate everything around me. Both sea and sky seemed luminously blue that day. Several times on my journey these joyous moments stole up on me and, that day especially, I had the feeling that time had stood still here for a thousand years.

I had not come to Ikaria just for nature and solitude. I was interested in the people, too. Behind the comment about the island being full of old people was something much more intriguing. Life expectancy on this out-of-the-way island is much, much higher than the average for anywhere else in Europe. Along with all the scientists who have come here to study this phenomenon, I wondered what the secret was.

Each day I was there I met energetic octogenarians and nonagenarians who were shopkeeping, running cafés and small hotels, fishing or mending boats. They have full heads of silver-white hair and the skin and physique of people half their age. Some say that their longevity is a result of a stress-free lifestyle. They get up late, open their shops at a leisurely time, do what they feel like when they feel like it and definitely don't go out of their way to encourage tourists. Or perhaps it has something to do with the radium-rich hot springs that emerge on the island and flow into the sea. Nobody quite knows the answer, but they say that one in three people lives into his or her nineties.

The most extraordinary person I met was a woman who called herself Ariadne. I gathered that opinions about her in the town of Agios Kirykos where she lived were mixed. Many said that she was a fantasist; others were less kind and told me she was mad. One thing that nobody could disprove was her claim to be the oldest person on the island, simply because there was no one who could prove themselves to be older. Her hair was as strong and silver as embroidery thread and her childlike skin was pale and smooth, like the inside of an eggshell. She could have been any age at all.

She was the island 'eccentric', a curiosity for the tourists, usually to be found in a café on the seafront, where she advertised her 'Icarus Tours'.

I joined one of these conducted walks. Ten of us stood on the quayside in Agios Kirykos, under a huge modern sculpture that represented a pair of wings. Sweeping her hand in a southerly direction, Ariadne announced that she was going to tell us about 'Two birds who came from Crete'.

When Ariadne began to speak, her audience was immediately enthralled. She talked in the present tense, as historians often do in order to bring a story alive, and the imagination of the group was stirred as she relived the events that she described.

As I listened, I was ready to believe not only that she was the most senior of all Ikarians but also that she had been born thousands of years before us all. Sometimes it is the storyteller, as much as the story itself, that makes a lasting impression.

WAITING IN THE WINGS

Sculpture by Nikos Ikaris
Ikaria

'I begin each day with an invigorating ice-cold shower. The water comes straight from a mountain stream. I hope the shock of its temperature will dispel all the dreams and thoughts that crowd my mind, fragments that never quite cohere and give me intense and frequent migraines. This is the penalty of a long life and having a million memories jostling for space inside my head.

'Then I make my way to the beach. Only the rhythm of the sea and its gentle beat on the sand can settle the racing pulse of my heart and the maelstrom of thoughts that swirl in my brain. I can slow my breath by watching the rising sun and, on a good day, its steadfast path might bring me a brief moment of peace.

'A French woman who runs a yoga retreat nearby sometimes brings her clients down to the beach. I watch as rows of skinny women in leggings face the sun, they are instructed to "live in the moment, live in the here and now, to be free of the past and the future". It sounds so simple, but tranquillity like that is hard for me to find. And of course, each day, I have another obligation. But I will

tell you more of that later. For now I must get on with the story. That's what you've all paid for. It begins a long time ago . . .

'It is a beautiful day, the skies are blue, the light is translucent. It is the middle of July and there is neither a cloud in the sky nor a breath of wind.

'My friend has spotted something in the sky from a long way off. On these islands, we are used to seeing enormous birds of prey, of course: eagles, falcons, all kinds of buzzard are a common sight. Only last night, as I was on my way home in the dark, a huge owl swooped past and watched me from a tree as I walked by. So we are used to sharing our island with these great creatures, and this is why we assume that what we are looking at is a mighty bird.

'But as this one gets closer, we begin to be afraid. It is a great deal bigger than anything we have ever seen. It's an impossibly large bird. Then we realise that there is a second one coming behind. It's a little smaller, but it's unmistakably another vast raptor.

'It is about mid-morning. The time of day when you stop for a break if you get up with the dawn. Word goes around the village very fast and we all gather on the rocks down by the sea to keep watch. As the moments go by, the fear in the air grows. No one is smiling or joking. Many of the men are away at sea, so we women are feeling vulnerable.

'This is a spectacle that we must all see, or a threat we must be prepared to face. Nobody is sure.

'We are all well used to pirates and vagabonds invading

from the sea. This happens often! And we have caves and other secret places to escape to. But an attack from the air! It's different.

'A few people are seized with panic. They pick up their children and run. But I am mesmerised. My eyes are quite good even now, but in those days I have razor-sharp vision. Scores of us line up on the rocks just over there. The birds that we are watching are graceful, their massive wings wave gently up and down, up and down.'

Ariadne moved her arms to imitate the bird, floating them slowly up and down, her elegant hands like the tip of the wing, always at a slight angle. As her arms went down, her hand pointed upwards and then, as her arms changed direction, her fingers flicked downwards. Up and down, up and down, up and down, her wrists soft.

'They are approaching, very steadily. The two dots in the sky that seemed so close together now have more distance between them. The one in front is about two hundred metres away and closing in on us. We are fearful.

'Suddenly, someone in the crowd cries out: "It's a *man*!"

'We have all reached the same conclusion, but we stare in disbelief. We can all see him clearly now. Yes. It is a man. A bird-man.

'How often do we dream of having wings so that we could simply take off and fly? It can't just be me who has those fantasies and thoughts? From childhood, we dream of it, don't we?

'His wingspan is immense, maybe four metres across, like a small, two-seater plane. By now there is quite an audience. We are looking out for more of these creatures, but it seems there are no more behind. Fascination takes the place of fear.

'More and more of us are gathering. A meteor shower, an eclipse of the sun – nothing has ever had a bigger audience. The first "bird" seems to pause. It is like seeing someone treading water, but up in the sky. His legs are paddling, his wings steadily moving up and down. He is waiting for the other one to catch up, but then the one behind stops, too.

'We can make him out more clearly now. He is slightly smaller, and the feathers are a lighter brown. It's as though he starts to show off. We don't know whether it is for our benefit, but we are cheering and clapping and whooping and calling to encourage him in this air display. He loops the loop, swoops and soars, and then flies higher and higher. The bigger "bird" is up to no such antics. He is still trying to maintain his position. The sun is high and burning hot in the sky now.

'Then the smaller one hovers for a moment, as birds do when they are about to dive for prey, but instead of plummeting downwards he starts to rise. His great wings beat steadily, and slowly he rises higher and higher and higher.

'He becomes a dot which is disappearing against the glare of the sun. We are all aghast. Instinctively, we know that something is not right. We can feel it.

'We hardly dare raise our eyes. The sun is directly overhead, and we cannot keep looking at him or we will be blinded by its strength. I feel the sweat pouring down my face. At this time of day we are usually in the shade, sheltering from the blistering heat.

'Someone dares to peek between his fingers.

'"He's gone."

'"What do you mean – he's gone?"

'"He's just a speck against the sun."

'Then the speck starts to get larger again. And we are all watching a winged creature plummeting, spiralling faster and faster. There is a cloud of feathers as he falls, whirling like a gyroscope, then whole pieces of wing start to detach, unable to stand the speed or the action of the fall.

'We can do nothing. The larger, darker bird is moving his wings up and down to try and maintain his position. He manoeuvres himself away, perhaps to avoid being hit. The small bird is coming down faster than a bullet.

'There is a gasp from us all as he crashes into the sea. For a moment we are frozen, and then there is pandemonium.

'"We have to get a boat out there!" says a woman.

'There are a few small boats still moored in the harbour but most of the bigger ones are out on fishing expeditions.

'I haven't taken my eyes off the bigger bird. He is now hovering over the place where the other one splashed into the sea. People are now hauling a boat off the nearby beach. They are mostly strong, teenaged boys and it takes the six of them less than five minutes to row out there.

'The bigger bird has landed on a rock but is still flapping his wings to stabilise himself. The whole construction looks unwieldy now he is on land, and a breeze has got up. He is struggling to maintain his balance. Two of the boys clamber up and help him remove his wings.

'On the shore, we can't hear anything, but the boys tell me later that the man kept repeating the same words. "My boy is down there. Help me find him. *Please* help me find him!"

'They do their best. For an hour or more they dive, come up for air, dive again, come up for air. They take it in turns. The old man admits that neither he nor his son is a strong swimmer.

'The rescue effort is hampered by the fact that the feathers and the wood have spread a shadow across the surface of the sea. Using the oars, the rescuers try to clear the layer of debris, and two of them jump in and dive as far down as their breath will allow them.

'"He's . . . over . . . there," one of them splutters as he comes up for air.

'Three of them swim to the point that he indicates.

'The wood used for the construction is light when it is dry, but has become saturated in the sea and weighs the body down. The boy is on the ocean floor.

'It takes all three of them to bring him up to the surface, and a supreme effort to get him in to the boat. The father is already sitting there. His sobs are audible to us, carried across the still sea to the rocks where we are waiting.

'Slowly, the boys row back. There is no hurry now. It is a funeral cortege.

'The body is carried to my house and we lay him out on the kitchen table. He is a beautiful youth, and I wash him lovingly, as if he were my own son. I put a wreath on his head, strew him with flowers, seal his mouth with a coin. All the while, his father sits in the corner of the room, his body convulsed with sobs. I believe nothing will console him.

'Then I call the young men to carry the body up the hill.

'We blend Ikarian and Minoan funeral rites and bury him with pots of food and drink and a small boat that his father has carved out of a piece of driftwood that morning. The man's lamentations are loud. He throws himself on to the grave and howls, not just for a few minutes but for several hours. The other mourners leave not long after the burial, but I sit under the shade of a tree. I don't feel that he should be entirely alone.

'Eventually, he is silent, and I lead him back to my stone-built house. He can stay as long as he likes. It's just me there. Each day for I don't know how long he walks to his son's grave and sits there for hours and hours until night falls, then he returns. For the first few days he eats nothing I put on the table. Then he lies, staring at the ceiling. Perhaps he sleeps, I don't know, but once or twice I am woken by his shouts. I think he is having nightmares. For several days afterwards, debris from the boy's wings is washed up on our beaches.

'On the sixth night he is ready to speak. Days have passed without us exchanging so much as a word but, once he starts talking, he talks and talks and talks and it's hard to stop him.

'He has been through so much, even before this terrible accident, and now it seems as though talking helps him with his grief. He starts to tell me his story.

'He is from an island a long way south of Ikaria, a place so big it is more like a country, with a king and a palace with hundreds of rooms. It sounds nothing like Ikaria, where there are no grand buildings and everyone is equal.

'His name is Daedalus, and he tells me everything. He is an inventor, something like a Leonardo da Vinci figure, creative, intellectual, innovative. If he were alive today, he would probably have invented the internet, or perhaps constructed the tallest building in the world. He is clearly very clever, which is why he is summoned by this king, Minos, to build a complex maze in order to imprison a monster (it's a monster given birth to by his wife). Men and women from Athens are sent into the labyrinth to be eaten by the monster, but one of them, Theseus, kills it and gets out. Ariadne (the king's daughter), advised by Daedalus, has given Theseus a means of escape. He elopes with Ariadne but subsequently abandons her.

'Minos is furious. First of all, his wife falls in love with an animal, then his daughter runs away. He imprisons Daedalus in a tower, along with his son, Icarus. For a man such as Daedalus, being locked up and away from the world is a terrible punishment, but someone as resourceful as he always finds a way round a problem.

'With nothing to do all day but watch the birds soaring, swooping, enjoying the pleasure of flight, Daedalus is full of envy at their freedom. He and his son are imprisoned very high up to minimise their chance of escape. It is an excellent place to birdwatch and over the weeks, he begins to understand all the complexities of aerodynamics.

'Being in this tower will drive him mad if he doesn't escape, and he suddenly realises how he can. Over the next few months, he makes traps for the birds and gathers dozens of them, large, medium and small (he wants feathers in all sizes). Nature kindly gives him the "glue" that he needs: bees are nesting in a corner of the ceiling, and he simply steals their wax.

'To start with, Icarus is upset to see all the dead birds but, when his father explains that this is their only hope, he happily plucks them and starts to arrange the feathers as his father wishes. His excitement begins to build. Flying! Who wouldn't want to give it a try?

'The day comes when two sets of wings are ready, and Daedalus knows that there will be no second chance. There is no test flight. It will be a question of standing on the window ledge and jumping.

'He issues his son with a set of brief but strict guidelines. If they fly too close to the sea and get their wings wet, the weight will pull them down. Equally disastrous will be to go too high, as the sun will melt the wax that holds the feathers together. They have a long journey ahead, so they must fly steadily and stick together. As his father fastens the binding on his son's wings, Icarus appears to be listening, but he is impatient to get going. People who sky dive tell me that when they did their first jump they were almost beside themselves with impatience to take that initial plunge. Daedalus can feel his son's excitement. He shares it.

'Of course, Daedalus will jump first. He tells his son that, if it is a disaster, he must abort the plan and stay where he is.

'The moment of truth comes. They are both ready, their wings magnificent. Daedalus has attended to aesthetics as well as to engineering.

'"Don't forget, my darling boy, be cautious and stay close."

'It is too late to hug his son. He wishes he had thought of doing so before the wings went on.

'Icarus gives his father a leg-up on to the window ledge. Daedalus leaps and Icarus sees his father drop for a moment (the boy's heart is in his mouth), then, as he is caught by the thermals, he rises again. He begins to move his wings. His father is flying. He is really flying! Daedalus circles the tower, then heads out north in a straight line.

'There is no time to waste. Icarus scrambles on to the ledge and launches himself off. Within a minute, he is laughing. Not just because he and his father are escaping but because the sheer joy of flight is beyond anything he could ever have imagined. No wonder there is a dawn chorus, he thinks: birds must be so happy to face a new day, much of which will be spent in flight.

'By the time anyone notices they have gone, father and son are far across the Aegean. For a few hundred kilometres they make steady progress, passing over a few small islands, where residents mistake them for rare eagles. Warm, dry air and a south wind make for perfect flying conditions.

'Then they near this island. By now, Icarus has become very confident. He is having a wonderful time. Daedalus is getting tired but they are well over half-way to Athens so he keeps going. Icarus isn't tired at all.

'Daedalus's voice cracks in the retelling, and suddenly I feel guilty. I realise that Icarus was probably showing off for us, his audience. When he saw us all looking up, watching him, spectating, I think that's when he decided to perform his tricks. To impress us. He did just what any teenaged boy would do.

'Icarus's pleasure in his freedom was intense and his love of the moment so overpowering that he abandoned moderation. I look at the weeping father, so wise, so clever, so accomplished, but in the end unable to control a son's natural instincts.

'Daedalus is overwhelmed by his loss, and of course he blames himself for his son's death and for having had the notion that the wings would be safe. This only adds to his grief. He is one of the most gifted men in the world, and yet this means nothing when you have lost everything you love.

'He stays on another week or so. Most of each day is still spent by his son's grave, but he starts to eat some of the food I make for him and soon he is sleeping better. The shadows around his eyes begin to disappear. We talk for hours each day and I sometimes accompany him to the graveside. One evening, we are eating together and I can tell that there is something on his mind. Eventually, he tells me what it is.

'He is in a state of grief but he has a problem. He is still on the run, and King Minos will be looking for him.

'I can see that he is torn between the desire to stay close to his son's grave, to observe the rituals that will take Icarus safely to the afterlife, and the need to keep travelling.

'Beautiful as it is, this island is no place for the ambitious. Daedalus has to complete his journey.

'"What about my son, though . . . ?"

He looks me straight in the eye as he asks this.

'"I will see to it that he continues on his way, so that you can continue on yours," I hear myself saying.

'I have spoken on the spur of the moment, without even thinking of the implications. But once I have made this promise there is no turning back. This will be my future, to remember Icarus and to offer libations at the graveside.

'The man is overwhelmed with gratitude. He weeps, but not in the same way as he wept on the day that Icarus was buried. He puts his arms around me, and I feel his tears fall on my shoulder.

'He leaves on a boat the following day. There are rumours that King Minos is on his trail. We all wish Daedalus well and a crowd gathers to wave him off.

'I heard that he reached Sicily. There was never any expectation that he would return, but he left me with this duty that I still perform today. Each time I see a butterfly, I wonder if this is the sign that Icarus's soul has flown. But I cannot be sure, so I continue. And I will do so for ever.

'This island, henceforth named after Icarus, has always been a place where people lived long lives. There have been plenty of theories about why this should be. In the days when Daedalus came, we ate little except fish, then we discovered the hot, radioactive springs, then everything we ate was organic, and nowadays people here keep their own idiosyncratic timetable and have very little stress. So who knows why other people live so long? But I know why I still live. Because I must.

'I keep the location a secret so that it doesn't get trampled by tourists, but I visit Icarus every day, just as I promised his father I would.

'As the years go by, real history, actual events, begin to be treated as legend. Listeners lose their belief in the reality. But this, the first plane crash, happened, right over there.

'And the exquisite feather you are now looking at is from Icarus's wings . . .'

Ariadne did not let go of her feather, it was far too precious to her, but everyone gathered around to touch it. I will never forget its silkiness under my fingertip. And I shall never forget this extraordinary woman. I am sure if I go back in another thirty years she will be there, waiting to retell her tale, her platinum hair still thick and strong and her skin like a girl's. The original Ariadne, daughter of King Minos, who was so cruelly dumped by Theseus, found new love on Naxos, where Bacchus fell in love with her and made her his queen. It's yet another Greek myth about the mending of a broken heart. Bacchus immortalised his beloved by throwing her crown into the sky, where it turned into a constellation, the Corona.

Immortality and mortality are ever-present themes in Greece, both ancient and modern. Death is everywhere you go in this country. There are death notices on the lamp posts, cemeteries on the edge of every small village and memorials by the roadside. I was more conscious of mortality during those months than ever before in my four and half decades. And yet, I saw that people challenged death, in the way they drank and danced and loved. In all the excess I witnessed, I detected defiance.

Ikaria is a huge rock in the middle of the sea, where people have survived great hardship from invaders and the elements themselves. It is not a place to feel sorry for yourself, and during a religious festival that took place while I was there I drank and feasted until late in the night.

This is where I learned to dance, where I found myself taken into a circle that moved clockwise, slowly and rhythmically. I towered above everyone else there, but they gave me warm smiles. The Ikariotikos soon sped up, but no one lost patience with me as I attempted to master the steps. I was part of a single entity, one organism with a hundred legs. I closed my eyes and went with the rhythm, and now I believe I could do this ancient dance in my sleep.

I stayed above an empty shop in Evdilos, swimming in a hot spring almost every day, talking to strangers. I went to find Ariadne again and we drank a coffee in the sunshine.

Without prompting, she looked at me and said:

'You've heard of Diphilus?'

I shook my head.

'He was a Greek playwright and is supposedly the person who said: "Time is a physician that heals every grief."'

'Do you think that was true for Daedalus?' I asked.

'Eventually,' she said. 'But more importantly, I think it is working for you.'

I cannot account for why she said it. I had never talked to her about myself. But perhaps when you have lived for thousands of years, you develop a sixth sense.

Ikaria is where I finally felt truly alive once more, where I found myself wanting to live into old age, rather than not wanting to live at all. I can no longer tell you that without you *these places are nothing. I have learned that the source of joy is not to be found in another person and we should not look for someone to complete ourselves.*

It is July now. I had been travelling for forty weeks (I had counted each one as it passed), but the road did not lose its fascination even once. I never had any idea what I would discover at the next place, or the next, or the next, and I know I haven't finished. For now, though, I am happy to be still. That's the reason I stopped sending postcards.

I am no longer travelling. I arrived back in Athens after Ikaria and decided to stay.

It is not an easy city to live in. At street level, life is difficult. The traffic is terrible, the paving stones are broken, many of the shops are boarded up and there is graffiti everywhere. Some of the time, life comes completely to a halt when there is a strike or a demonstration, and then it's often a bad idea to be too near the centre of the city. Things can get violent. People here are angry with the economic situation: the old people whose pensions have been cut and the young who have no jobs – and almost everyone in between whose earnings are taxed to the point that they end up with nothing. Added to all of this are the needs of the refugees who have arrived in Athens, many of them camping outside in the squares – people from war-torn countries with nothing but what they stand up in.

Fortunately, there is more to Athens than this unhappiness and discord. There are certain things that cannot be destroyed, such as the Greek habits of hospitality and storytelling.

Where I live, I have a beautiful roof terrace from which I can see the sea, the mountains and the Acropolis. I have a three-hundred-and-sixty-degree view. I can watch the sunset in one direction and the sunrise in the other. I can see the lights of the ferries making their way to the islands. I can see shooting stars and the wax and wane of the moon. When there is a storm and the sun breaks through from behind the clouds, I can see the whole arc of a rainbow. Its beginning and its end. Each time I see these things, I am reminded of the indestructible soul of this country.

The ancient Greeks worshipped the sun, the moon and the stars and made gods out of them, but we abandoned this way of thinking because a new religion told us that these gods were false and that there was only one God. I believe we lost so much by listening to this.

When I look up at the night sky I gain so much strength (a great deal more than I would by going to a church and being reminded of human frailty). On this sultry July evening on my terrace, feeling a warm south-easterly wind stroke my face, I realise that I am no longer waiting for you, or dreaming of you. I am in a place where I have found peace.

July 2016

September 2016

It was the last night of Ellie's holiday, and she was once again on her balcony. She closed the notebook and sat with it on her lap, looking up at the stars that Anthony loved so much. Only a moment later she saw one shoot across the sky. Over this past week she had learned it was rare for more than five minutes to go by before a star fell. She looked for Ariadne's Corona. The sea was so calm tonight that there was only the gentlest sound of water lapping on the sand. If she could make time stand still, this might be the moment she'd choose.

She found the envelope still folded in the side pocket of her handbag. Perhaps she had not tried hard enough to find S. Ibbotson. These stories were intended for her. The envelope had become very crumpled over the past weeks and, as she tried to put the book back inside, it tore right across. She noticed that there was an address written on the back.

Anthony Brown, 389 Aristophanous Street,
Athens 11281

She stared at it. She was flying back via Athens, but did she have the courage to go and find this man? This would mean telling him that S. Ibbotson had never received the postcards and that she, Ellie, had opened a package that was not addressed to her. She refolded the envelope, tucked it into her bag and put the notebook on top.

It was midnight now, and she got her suitcase from the wardrobe and began to pack. Everything bore the sweet smell of sun cream and was slightly crisp with salt and sand. Even the thought of unpacking at the other end of her journey, throwing these colourful clothes into her washing machine and eliminating the aroma of the past wonderful days, filled her with sadness. Perhaps she would not wash her sarongs but instead hang them up in her flat until the scents of sunshine and summer had naturally gone.

Even as she asked herself the question about the writer, she knew that there was only one answer. She was compelled to seek him out.

Ellie left her hotel in Tolon after breakfast the following morning, got a taxi to Nafplio and had one last coffee in the square. Then she walked to the bus station and soon found herself heading towards Athens once again. The motion of the coach sent her to sleep, and she woke up in the heat of day to find that she had reached her destination.

Disoriented and with a slight headache, she got out her metro map and worked out how to find Aristophanous Street. It was a long way to the nearest station and even then it would mean several changes, so she decided to take a taxi. Her flight was not until one the following morning, but her time was limited: she wanted to visit the Acropolis as well as deliver the notebook. It was already mid-afternoon. The temperature had not dropped below thirty degrees all day.

The taxi driver dropped her a long way from her destination in order to save himself time, but eventually she found the right street and number, and then, on a panel of several dozen bells, saw the name she was looking for.

She rang the bell and after a few moments heard a man's voice.

'Mr Brown,' she began nervously, 'I have a package for you.'

'Would you like to come up? I'm on the top floor.'

He must think she was a delivery service.

The bell on the outer door buzzed and she let herself in.

As the lift clanked slowly to the sixth floor, Ellie glanced at herself in the wall's mirrored surface. Her hair was dry and bleached from the sun, her nose burnt and she had beads of perspiration on her forehead. She wished she looked a bit smarter. T-shirt and shorts did not seem the right dress code for this smart apartment block.

The lift stopped and, as the door opened, she saw a man standing in front of her.

He had thick brown hair with a few wisps of grey and was very slim, wearing jeans and a grey T-shirt. He reminded her of an actor her mother liked.

Anthony immediately noticed what Ellie held in her hands. He had not even looked at her face, just at the battered blue notebook.

Ellie registered his shock and surprise.

'Where did you get that?' he asked, with as much self-control as he could muster.

Suddenly, Ellie felt like a thief. She had an urge to thrust it into his hands and run straight down six flights of stairs and out again into the sun-baked street. Only an instinct to defend herself from suspicion stopped her.

'You sent it to me,' she said, immediately realising that it must sound stupid.

'I sent it to *you*?'

Anthony looked really confused now.

'Sort of . . .'

They stood looking at each other in puzzlement. He was staring at Ellie, trying to work out if she might be the sister he had never met. He decided she was too young.

'You'd better come in,' he said. 'If you would like to, that is.'

Even if it was just for a glass of water, which she now desperately needed, Ellie couldn't see the harm. She felt she knew this man a little and was fairly certain that he was not the type to harm her in any way.

'Thanks,' she said.

'By the way,' he added, 'I'm Anthony. But you know that . . . And you're . . . ?'

'Ellie,' she replied. 'Ellie Thomas.'

Ellie followed Anthony into a large, light space, minimally furnished with low, modern furniture and book-lined walls. She glimpsed a small kitchen at the far end of the room. They went out on to a terrace, situated on the other side of sliding glass doors. There were some well-established olive trees in pots and an area shaded by a pergola where there was a table and chairs. Several large volumes were spread out on the table, next to a laptop.

'Let's sit here,' he suggested, indicating a comfortable cream sofa with a glass-topped table in front of it.

Ellie sat down.

'What would you like?' said her host. 'Coffee? Juice? Herbal tea?'

'Just water would be nice,' said Ellie.

Anthony disappeared to get a bottle of water and some glasses.

'It's strange seeing it again,' he said, sitting down opposite her and indicating the journal that sat on Ellie's lap. 'It was my companion . . .'

'Yes, mine, too, in a way,' said Ellie, putting it down on the table that divided them.

'I never imagined I would see it again,' he said, picking it up. 'But I'm glad it didn't disappear into the ether.'

For a moment or two he turned it over in his hands with exaggerated care. Then he started to slowly flick through its pages.

'Has something happened to Sarah?' he asked with great solemnity.

Ellie felt herself blush. Sarah. That must be S. Ibbotson. It was strange hearing the name.

'No,' she answered, taking a sip of water. 'Well, not as far as I know . . . But, to be honest, I have no idea. I don't know who she is . . .'

Anthony looked up for a moment, a look of surprise on his face.

Ellie continued.

'But it was delivered to my home, and so were the postcards, and I read them and kept them . . . and then the notebook arrived as I was leaving . . . And they somehow went together and I felt as if it was . . . as if . . . well, it seemed OK.'

She was aware that she was rambling.

Anthony was taking in everything she said.

'Delivered to *your* home?'

'S. Ibbotson . . . doesn't live at that address. So . . .'

Ellie could see that this came as news. There was a pregnant pause.

'That shouldn't really be such a shock,' he said with resignation. 'It was hardly her only lie.'

'Do you mind me asking who she was . . . is?'

'If you have read the journal, then you will know the most important things,' he said. 'I thought she was the love of my life.'

Ellie nodded.

'I met her in the bar at the Curzon in Mayfair,' Anthony began. 'The person she was meant to meet hadn't turned up, and I was sitting alone having a drink. I was killing time before going to a film by a Greek director called Lanthimos.'

Ellie tried to give the impression that she had heard of him. Anthony went on.

'I don't generally chat up strangers. In fact, when I think of it, she was the one who spoke to me first. Conversation got round to Greece. She had been there as a child on a yacht owned by friends of her parents, but just to a few islands."

'She doesn't sound like the kind of person who would have lived in my area at all,' interjected Ellie.

'Why?'

'It sounds like she comes from a posh background. It's a bit grungy where I live.'

Anthony gave a half-smile.

'Anyway, she was the kind of person who had been taught the art of conversation and always knew the right thing to say, the sort who couldn't be on her own for more than two minutes without starting to chatter.

'She was quick to catch on to my interest in Greece. She had read History of Art at university, so the conversation flowed, and her interest in my book on Cycladic sculpture seemed sincere. She remembered that one of the islands she had been to as a child was one of the Cyclades. Whether or not I was deluded, I fell deeply in love with her.'

Ellie nodded from time to time. She had met girls like Sarah, but they had never been her friends.

'I mistook the sparkle in her eyes for attraction, but I think the glistening was a mixture of enthusiasm for our conversation and the wateriness that people with contact lenses suffer. Probably it was nothing more.'

Occasionally, there was a crack in his voice. Whether it was from sadness or anger, Ellie found it hard to discern.

'So did she work?' asked Ellie, curious about this girl.

'She had a part-time job in a friend's gallery in Notting Hill, but nothing that stopped her making impromptu visits to exhibitions in the middle of the day. She sometimes came with me to the British Museum, where I was doing some of my research. When we stood in front of the Parthenon Marbles, she said that she wanted to see the rest, and to see where they had originally come from. It was a nice moment. It was her suggestion. "Yes, let's do it," I said. The new Acropolis Museum would be the finale, the apotheosis. We spent the next six months planning the trip.'

'She always came to stay at weekends with me. In the eighteen months we were together, she never invited me to her place – she said she lived with her sister and we wouldn't be alone.'

'She really doesn't sound like the sort of girl who would live in my place,' Ellie said. 'It's pretty dingy. A basement. Dark. With a kind of old-lady smell in the hallway.'

'That's definitely the address she gave me,' said Anthony. 'Perhaps she had once known someone there? In any case, I don't think she was the person she made herself out to be on any level. I persuaded myself that she was one thing and, actually, she was another.'

'Where did you live in London?' asked Ellie curiously.

'In a mansion block in Bloomsbury, close to the British Museum. It was nothing like this, but I had a clear view of those enormous pillars that seem to hold up the whole of the building. On a day when the sky was blue, I could even imagine myself in Athens.'

Ellie sat back and listened, sipping her water from time to time. Anthony clearly wanted to talk. She got the impression that he had kept most of this to himself.

They sat for a while, and then Anthony wanted to show her the various views from his terrace and to point out the landmarks.

'There's the Acropolis,' he said, pointing. 'And there is Lycabettus. And you can just see the Botanical Gardens. And there is the Parliament Building, the Vouli.'

'It's fantastic,' said Ellie simply. As they looked out over Athens, Anthony continued to talk. It seemed that there was more about Sarah that he wanted to get off his chest, as if, once said, he might never need to mention her again.

'For the short time she inhabited my world, Sarah *was* my world.'

Though he was old enough to be her father, Ellie felt that this man expected her to respond as a mentor or confidante.

'You thought this was *it*?' she asked.

'Well, it seemed like that to me, at least. My head was in the clouds. Everything I had read about love in classical myth, and about its power, now made sense to me. I felt connected with all the art that it had inspired: poetry, painting and sculpture of every period had new significance for me.

'Sarah willingly came to galleries with me, and bounced around them enthusiastically. She seemed to respond to things exactly as I did. I was completely seduced by her charm. By Love. By Erotas. It seemed a force that was bigger than myself.'

Anthony's thoughts came spilling out.

'In all my blissful musings on Eros and Psyche, I ignored the crimes that love leads people to perpetrate. I did not want to know about its darker side, the betrayals, the tragedies. I was never interested in the endings.'

Ellie did her best to understand and nod in the right places, though some of the references were new to her.

'There was a fifteen-year difference in our age, but in the end I think it was me who was the child. I held on to the ring I had bought for a while, but it's gone now. Only last week, I summoned the courage to return it. The money will cover my rent for a year, so it was almost worth the humiliation! And I am hoping that any new legislation will let me stay at least that long here.'

Anthony saw that the jug of water was empty.

'Are you sure you wouldn't like something else? I could do with a coffee.'

'Yes, that would be nice,' said Ellie.

Anthony noticed her glance at her watch. It was nearly six.

'Do you need to be somewhere else?' he asked, with concern.

'Not really,' she replied. 'I was hoping to visit the Acropolis before my flight. But it doesn't matter.'

'You have a plane to catch?' he asked, in surprise. 'What time?'

'It's not until one in the morning,' she said. 'It's hours away.'

When Anthony returned with the coffee, Ellie was browsing through the notebook. She felt more relaxed with him now.

'What happened . . .' she said, '. . . it must have been awful.'

'It's strange that you have read all of this,' said Anthony. 'On the other hand, it's nice to think that there is someone in the world who knows what I went through.'

Ellie blushed. The guilt of reading what was, effectively, a diary had not quite worn off.

'Even now, if I pass someone in the street in Athens who wears her perfume it almost overpowers me with memories. But how can I prevent this unless I never walk the streets?'

Ellie shook her head.

'You can't,' she said quietly, sympathetically.

The mountains were gradually turning rose pink. The sun was beginning to set.

To Ellie, Anthony seemed like a teenage boy with a broken heart.

'I had a pretty good arm when I played cricket but I couldn't throw that phone far enough,' he continued, with a wry smile.

Watching him reflecting on his infatuation made Ellie realise how gullible even intelligent adults could be. He was a highly educated and cultured man who had been struck with a temporary blindness.

'Unless all that had happened,' she said simply, 'perhaps you wouldn't be here now . . .'

'That's very true, Ellie. And it's not such a bad place to be.'

Both she and Anthony seemed comfortable with the occasional pause in conversation. It was never quite silent, in any case. Traffic noise came up from below, horns sounded with impatience and were answered with irritation and there was occasionally the noise of an aircraft.

The man she sat with on this rooftop was a total stranger and yet she felt as if she knew him.

'But we have done nothing but talk about me!' he laughed. 'You must think I am a total egotist! I haven't talked like that about myself for . . . perhaps for ever. I'm so sorry.'

Ellie laughed, too.

'Don't worry! You have been filling in the gaps for me!'

'Now you have to tell me about *you*. Please. I insist.'

Anthony looked at Ellie. She would not meet his eye.

'But my life is so uninteresting,' she said awkwardly, unused to being the focus of attention.

'Everyone's life is interesting,' he said encouragingly. 'I know where you live, that's all. What do you do?'

Ellie briefly sketched her life for Anthony: from Cardiff to London, and the unsatisfactory job in which she found herself. She found it impossible to conceal her dissatisfaction and boredom. He listened intently, just as he must have done when he heard the stories that people told him around Greece.

She described how her boss had reacted when she announced her decision to take ten days off.

'So what will you do now?' he asked.

Ellie shrugged her shoulders. She realised she could not give a definitive answer.

'I don't know,' she said, her eyes resting on the view of Athens. 'There's nothing particularly to go back for.'

She was not sure whether he was really interested in her life, so she changed the subject. In any case, she did not want to think about herself, as it would lead her to the thought of her plane and the moment when it would lift into the air and she would be gone. It was only a short time away now.

Ellie watched his hand on the notebook. She felt a sense of loss. Whose was it, after all? It had been sent to her address, a street name so deceptively and carelessly given, where S (as she still thought of her) had probably never lived.

'Did you really write down the stories for Sarah?'

It was the first time Ellie had spoken the name.

'Who does *anyone* write for?' he responded. 'I told myself that's who they were for but, in the end, I think we write everything for ourselves. My book on sculpture, for example. The world is not exactly on the edge of its seat waiting for it. I know that. Someone who reads it might be gently stirred to see how closely some of Picasso's or Henry Moore's work resembles a Cycladic sculpture, but they will just inwardly say: "Ah! That's interesting . . . That's nice." It won't change anyone's life. I have no illusions about that.

'It's not so unlike these stories. I had nowhere else to put them except on these pages, and there was nowhere for them to go except to your address. But I am very happy you brought them back. It seems like the very end of something – that she never lived there, that even this was a lie . . .'

They sat and continued chatting. He asked her about her holiday, where she had stayed, what she had done, and Ellie told him about Tolon and visiting Nafplio each day and how much she had enjoyed sitting in the square.

She looked at the beautiful stone sculptures on the roof terrace. They glowed in the dusk. Were they modern? Ancient? Were they original Picassos? Or Henry Moores? Or were they copies? Ellie had no idea and was not sure it mattered. They were graceful pieces of carved stone, timeless and elegant.

Anthony saw her looking at them.

'Wonderful, aren't they? They are the only things I had shipped over from London when I decided to stay here. They look much more at home here than in Bloomsbury.'

'They're . . . amazing.'

The word sounded banal.

'As well as all my books.'

When she had walked through the apartment to get to the terrace, Ellie had noticed that every wall was lined with huge art volumes.

'Greece is giving me so much,' he said. 'Without that experience, that . . . disappointment . . . whatever you want to call it, I wouldn't still be here.'

'And if . . . S. Ibbotson had been there to read the postcards or your stories, I wouldn't be here either,' Ellie added tentatively, unable to repeat the woman's name.

'Yes. All of those things have led to this moment. The two of us sitting in this place, on this night, with this moon, under these stars.'

The Acropolis was now illuminated and glowed golden in the distance. In spite of the troubles that persisted in the streets and squares beneath it, the Parthenon was unassailable, untouchable. It had survived the ravages of both time and vandalism.

Anthony's eyes were drawn to it, too.

'Perfect, isn't it?' he said. 'Only the Pyramids are as recognisable, but I always think of death when I see them. They're burial places, rather than somewhere to worship.'

'The Parthenon is definitely more beautiful,' commented Ellie.

Anthony turned to her.

'What are your plans? I feel a bit responsible that you might have lost your job.'

'I suppose I could blame you,' Ellie said, laughing. 'Your postcards, anyway!'

She told Anthony how she had pinned them up in her home, how much they had meant to her and how, when they had stopped coming, she had decided she had to come herself.

The reality was that she did not have any idea what

she was going to do next. The last time she had looked at the balance on her account, she saw that she was running low on funds. Though she had stayed in a cheap hotel, the holiday had cost most of her savings.

'It will be hard going back to London,' she said.

'Why don't you stay? You won't regret it,' said Anthony.

Ellie did not like to mention her lack of money, but she knew that he was right. Her journey to this moment had already enriched her life immeasurably.

In a lull in their conversation, Ellie heard the sound of a door shutting inside the apartment. A moment later, a young woman appeared on the terrace. She was small and gamine. For a reason she could not explain, she felt a pang of jealousy, especially when the new arrival strolled across to Anthony and kissed him on both cheeks.

'Athina. This is Ellie. Ellie. Athina.'

The two women shook hands.

'It must be time for a glass of wine,' said Anthony. 'The sun has practically gone down!'

'I'll bring some,' said Athina enthusiastically. 'Just give me a moment to change.'

'There's a lovely Cretan Assyrtiko chilling in the fridge. And would you mind bringing out some pistachios, too?'

There seemed an easy familiarity between them. Athina was clearly at home here.

'You read about Athina,' Anthony said to Ellie. 'Do you remember?'

'Delphi!' exclaimed Ellie. 'You met at Delphi!'

She was just as Anthony had described her.

'We're not a couple!' said Anthony, reading Ellie's mind.

'Athina has a girlfriend. You can imagine how that went down with her parents in Lamia.'

Athina had reappeared on the terrace with a bottle, and had overheard.

'They're still introducing me to the sons of their friends,' she laughed, twisting the opener into the cork. 'It's a whole other story.'

'Athens is liberal enough, though,' said Anthony. 'You'll meet Anna later.'

'Later?' said Ellie.

'Won't you stay and eat with us? I insist. It's just cold. Salads and some chicken, but . . .'

'I have a plane to catch!' protested Ellie feebly.

'I can give you a lift to the airport,' said Anthony kindly.

Somehow, despite everything, she had not expected this hospitality.

'I've picked up some good habits,' he said. 'Treating strangers as if they were friends. You meet more interesting people that way. But I'm not entirely a stranger to you, am I?'

Soon, Anna arrived, and there were more introductions. The three women discovered that they were more or less the same age. They briefly exchanged information on university careers and jobs. Anna was a lawyer. Ellie felt a twinge of shame over her job selling ad space.

Over supper, Ellie silently questioned whether life had anything better to offer than sitting on this roof terrace under the stars.

'Did you enjoy your time in Greece?' asked Anna.

Ellie smiled.

'More than I can begin to describe. I don't really want to go back to England.'

'What are you going back to?' asked Athina.

Ellie shrugged her shoulders.

'Not a lot, by the sound of it, said Anthony.

'Anthony's right,' admitted Ellie. 'I am not that contented with life in London.'

'If that's the case, you should change something,' interjected Athina. 'Life is too short just to drift.'

'She has a point,' said Anthony. 'I think you know my views better than anyone. Life should be full of possibilities. Not just promises.'

Ellie was slightly embarrassed at how much she knew about Anthony, and how personal the notebook was.

'Will you go travelling again? she asked Anthony, to deflect the conversation away from herself.

'Right now, no. I want to stay where I am. My mind is still so full. And I have my book to finish off.'

Suddenly, he seemed to have an idea.

'Can you type?' he asked.

'Type? Can't everyone type?'

'Some of us still write by hand,' he said sheepishly. 'We missed the computer age . . .'

'Why do you ask?'

'I need someone to type up my manuscript,' he said. 'The publisher can't read my handwriting.'

'Well, I know I can do that,' Ellie said, laughing. 'I had no problem with the stories.'

'Well, if you would like the job, then it's yours. And you can stay in my spare room if you have nowhere else.'

427

Ellie did not know what to say. It was a wonderful opportunity. Habit said that she should go back to London, as her family and friends would expect, but her heart told her to stay here.

Athina leaned across the table.

'Know yourself,' she said emphatically.

Ellie remembered the inscription. *Gnothi s'eafton.* Perhaps it was her turn now.

'Excuse me,' she said, getting up from the table. She needed some time to think and wandered over to the balcony railings to look at the view. One thing already on her mind was the next month's rent.

She reached into her pocket for her phone and called her landlady. It seemed an age before she picked up.

'It's Ellie Thomas.'

'Flat D?'

'Yes. I wanted to . . .'

'Flat D, you said? I already had a call today about flat D. An old tenant. Abbotson or something. Asking if there had been any post for her.'

Anthony had appeared by her side.

'Could you hold on a moment?' Ellie said, her heart thumping wildly. She put her hand over the mouthpiece, her palms damp with sweat.

'Anthony,' she whispered. 'Sarah has been asking about mail. What shall I say?'

'Just say "no",' he replied, drawing deeply on a cigarette. 'Please tell her there was nothing.'

Still shaking, Ellie resumed her conversation with the landlady, Anthony standing close by.

'I've just checked,' she said boldly. 'I'm afraid not . . . The reason I rang was to hand in my notice on the flat.'

A disgruntled voice on the other end muttered about deposits and guarantees. Ellie could sense that she was not going to be granted any favours.

'Yes,' said Ellie. 'But can I at least start my notice period from today?'

The discussion continued for a few minutes and eventually ended with a compromise. As she replaced her phone in her pocket, Ellie noticed that Anthony was still next to her, gazing at the rising moon, deep in thought. She did not want to disturb his contemplation.

A few moments went by before he glanced in her direction. His look seemed to pose a question.

Ellie smiled at him.

'It's all sorted out,' she said.

The two of them returned to the table. Athina and Anna stopped talking as they approached and looked at Ellie expectantly.

Ellie sat down again and Anthony refilled everyone's glass. There was a pause.

'I'm not leaving after all,' she announced to the two girls, with a new self-assurance. 'I'm going to stay.'

Of all the moments she had lived, this was the one in which Ellie felt most peaceful, but most alive.

Above them all, swallows ducked and dived on the evening air.

With thanks to:
Alexandros Kakolyris for his invaluable contribution to the
creation and development of Cartes Postales
Patrick Insole for his beautiful design
Emily Hislop for her creative rigour

PICTURE CREDITS

Victoria Hislop

Inspired by a visit to Spinalonga, the abandoned Greek leprosy colony, Victoria Hislop wrote *The Island* in 2005. It became an international bestseller and a 26-part Greek TV series. She was named Newcomer of the Year at the British Book Awards and is now an ambassador for Lepra. Her affection for the Mediterranean then took her to Spain, and in the number one bestseller *The Return* she wrote about the painful secrets of its civil war.

In *The Thread*, Victoria returned to Greece to tell the turbulent tale of Thessaloniki and its people across the twentieth century. Shortlisted for a British Book Award, it confirmed her reputation as an inspirational storyteller. It was followed by her much-admired Greece-set collection, *The Last Dance and Other Stories*. Her fourth novel, *The Sunrise*, was published to widespread acclaim, and was a *Sunday Times* number one bestseller.

Victoria divides her time between England and Greece.

To find out more, find Victoria on Facebook
f/OfficialVictoriaHislop,
follow her on Twitter ✖@VicHislop
or go to her website at www.victoriahislop.com.